Pimp of
Da Ratchetts II
Vegas

By Hitachi Choparazzi

Acknowledgements

I'd like to give all due praise to Allah. May my loved ones' souls rest in harmony. Unc Dale, Lil Bro, G-Pa Lawson and my day ones Teflon luv, too! May Allah's peace and blessing be upon G-Ma Lawson and all my real family in the middle of the map. My kids Kolany, Jr., Pierre Kydale, Kylan, and my daughter China. Daddy loves y'all unconditionally and uncontrollably! Words can't explain! Chop-A-Style Publishing. Self-Pub Independence.

ATTN:

This novel is a work of fiction. Any references to real people, events, establishments, or locales are intended only to give the fiction a sense of reality and authenticity. Other names, places, characters, online names, brands, companies, social media sites, and incidents occurring in the works are either the product of the author's imagination or are used fictitiously, as those fictionalized events and incidents that involve real persons and places.

Any character that happens to share the name of a person who is an acquaintance of the author past or present is purely coincidental and is in no way intended to be an actual account involving that person. It's purely a fiction work of art.

Contents

PROLOGUE

Soon as Twan stepped off of the Greyhound bus, hoes were at his toes! They recognized some real pimpin in Vegas alright. It was apparent skinny pimps were winning right now out here. He figured that all the P's from Baton Rouge—well, the boot shape of Louisiana, period—must have stuck a thumbprint in this fabulous high-fashion mobster and hooker town.

These hoes were bred to turn a trick and suck a few hard dicks— right off the famous strip! He was determined to get his issue by any means. Pimp or die!!

"Mama, take ya ass back to BR. I'm good from here! I got this fa-real. Keep ya lil money! And don't be worried about me. Nawh—just take care of yourself. I'll be sending you doe err year. Just don't smoke it up—Mama!" Twan said, cocky, dismissing her as he fixed his strings and popped his collar.

"Whatever, boy! Twan, don't come calling me later on when shit going all wrong, fool! Pssh...Please go home—unt-unhh!! Boy, I'm about to gamble and hit big on the slot machines. See if I can get LUCKY!! And I'll leave Vegas whenever the hell I please... Now move out of my way,

Twan!" Mama Lela replied slick, sucking her teeth with her jaw jacked and screwed to the side like a true crack fiend.

Twan waved her off nonchalantly with the flick of his hand and wrist simultaneously, then said, "Hhmm..." like Kat Williams off of *Friday After Next*. It was too funny. The yellow bitch he knocked at the terminal started snickering all goofy at him.

"Hold up—hoe! Bitch, get Daddy's bags!—Matter of fact, hoe, forget them bags, this Vegas. Go get Daddy cash and sell all that ass! I want all new shit and new fresh crispy Vegas tourist doe!" Twan said in a mellow pimp tone as he gave the hoe directions, realizing they only had one carry-on bag. That was all about to change that fast.

Things went from sugar to shit back in BR. Now it's starting to coat back to sugar, because it's too sweet in Vegas, baby! His first hoe came back with 15 stacks! You couldn't tell Twan nothing about his pimpin. Then he knocked 2 more fresh merch turnouts. Vegas was simple and overrated!

Pat-Pat!! "Twan—Twan! Boy, we here. Wake up, son! You sleep—" Mama Lela said, trying to awaken Twan.

"Welcome to Las Vegas, Nevada," the bus driver said over the loudspeaker, cutting Mama Lela off.

Twan woke up groggy, looking around. "Damn!"

- Chapter 1 -

"Da Terminal"

Twan saw all the bright flashing lights of the Las Vegas Strip as the bus pulled into the Greyhound terminal that sat off the strip. He saw the MGM casino/hotel as his eyes lit up. It was crowded and tourists everywhere. Even the bus terminal was helluva packed. He looked around and saw a few raggedy, broke, down-on-their-luck hoes. Then he realized he was visualizing Vegas off of them typical Vegas movie stereotypes. Why couldn't he hit it right off the bus, just like he dreamed?

People were complaining, trying to rush and get off the Greyhound, bunched all up in the crowded aisle. Mama Lela cursed some white lady smooth the hell out, being rude.

"Watch out, fool—MOVE, man!!" Mama Lela yelled at some guy who bumped her. Twan just shook his head, watching his Mama acting all ratchett. If this was how she was acting out already, he couldn't imagine her in Vegas turning tricks off the strips. She better not blow it for him. He knew she was cranky and moody dealing with the heavy concoction of the draining dreadful bus ride from BR and the constant crack withdrawals and cravings.

Twan just shook his head and told Mama Lela to come on as he grabbed her arm.

"Boy, get off me, Twan! Now we here, we gotta find a place to stay for the night," Mama Lela said, disoriented as she stepped off the bus.

"What?...Wait a minute, Mama! What you mean a place to stay? Don't you got money still? At least enuff for a hotel, right?" Twan said, short of breath, scratching his head, lost as the anxiety confided to his chest.

Mama Lela looked away and pretended not to hear Twan as she dragged her carry-on bag through the crowded terminal. She went to the locker section and began to dig through her carry-on bag for some change.

Twan followed behind her, watching her march off quickly to the lockers and dig through her raggedy bag. Damn, he instantly had a headache. Here he was in Las Vegas, Nevada, with his smoked-out mama, who only been sober for some days now. He should've known not to trust a crackhead, Mama or not! Especially Mama Lela without having a hit. She was liable to pull a straight stone cold junkie stunt any minute, Twan thought as he cursed himself, shaking his head.

"Mama, fuck dat shit. You came with me all the way from Baton Rouge broke? We don't got no money, food, or clothes? So we out cherr homeless right off the strip? I—"

"Shut up, Twan—Shit!! Damn it, I done told you—Boy, I already made enuff sacrifices for you. Now I got this! It's better than you sitting in a cold jail cell. You can ruff it out until we can get up some dollars for a motel room. It shouldn't take me long. Let me go to the bathroom and fix myself up to catch a big trick out here," Mama Lela said after cutting Twan off and slamming the locker shut.

Twan saw her taking the orange big locker key with the number 51 on it, then shove it in her flat smoked-out titties and adjust her sagging bra. Twan snapped!

"Bitch, come here! I'm gonna kill ya smoked-out ass. You got me out here riding on pure luck. I'm bout to break something!" Twan shouted as he snatched her wig out her hand and choked her up!

"S-Stopp...T-Twan, I can't breathe..." Mama Lela replied as she kicked, then scratched Twan's face up for dear life.

The terminal security came rushing Twan. They shocked Twan and threw him out of the terminal. He was shaking like bacon with a busted lip! He was bout to kill her. A groggy dismantled Twan stood up and secured the stable ground beneath him. He grabbed his swollen busted lip and said, "Shit!" He dusted himself off lightly, then he thought how he'd been in the same clothes since Baton Rouge. That was 2-and-a-half days ago.

It was 6 p.m. Vegas time. He had to make something shake by daybreak. He knew he was about to be out cherr all night. He hated pulling all-nighters because he felt like he was back in the projects curb-slanging. He knew he had at least one all-nighter in him, though.

If pimpin was easy, everybody would be doing it! Twan told himself to ease the pain. Dusk was approaching and more people started coming out down the strip. The crowd seemed to grow from tourists to freaks and tricks.

Twan was trying to chop and pop at all types of hoes. Big, fat, tall, small, old, young and all! Black, White, Mexican, it didn't matter. He needed to eat and get a roof over his head. Vegas was already a sweltering 108 degrees. He was dehydrated and been walking up and down the strip, trying to knock a bitch for a couple of hours now. They just weren't going or feeling Twan's Baton Rouge swamp Southern game.

Twan blamed his misfortune on his apparel. He was looking bummy, like a ratchett pimp. He needed a kit, a luxury whip, some jewels and strings.

He entered into the casino. He couldn't even shoot craps or play the slot machines. They had quarter machines, nickel machines, and penny machines. And he couldn't even afford to pull not one lever down. His pockets were beyond hurting. They were flatlined.

"Say, lil mah…Excuse me, how you doin', gurrl? You look lonely out here tonight and doing all the wrong things with ya money, blowing it on these slot machines. You need a manager in ya life, gurrl," Twan spit quick and slick.

"Oh, I'm good, honey! I see you're not from Vegas, huh? But yeah, I'm sorry, tho. Here, have this drink, cuz you definitely look thirsty, pimpin! Good luck on trying to knock a hoe in these casinos. They all in the hotels or escorting down the strip. ADIOS!" the Vegas girl said in a square tone as she handed Twan her drink and pulled the lever down on the quarter slot machine.

Twan took the double-shot drink gladly and gulped it down with one swig. He felt the warmness in his chest as the liquor burnt down his throat. He needed to get loose. Then he looked down at the square wavy-hair bitch.

"Ahh…Owwee, that's some yac right therr, baby! Hell yeah, now you need to get down with the get down, and let's get together and shock Vegas! We can make the whole Strip believe us, baby girl! So what you say we take on Vegas? I just need you to spot, so I don't drop, till I make it to the top! Digg dat, you just need correction and direction, not affection and caressing," Twan chopped and popped in a slick pimp tone.

"Pssh…Unt-unhh!" *Splat-splash!!* the Vegas girl, sitting down, sucked her teeth and uttered as she shook her head in awe, then doused Twan with her new drink, splashing it in his sweaty face.

"Ah-shittt… Bitch! Fuck! My eye!" Twan screamed as he tried to rub the burning alcohol out of his left bloodshot red eye. Then he lunged at the square bitch. She took off running and screaming through the casino. Twan gave chase, squinting out of his irritated stinging eye.

"Help—Help me! This guy is trying to kill me!!" she shouted aloud.

BOOM-Ching-Ching! Twan crashed right into one of the Harrah's casino waitress clerks, knocking trays, casino chips, and drinks everywhere, which caused the waitress to spill more drink on Twan as he fell on his ass. Damn it, Pimpin was sticky and exhausted, down on his ass! He wanted to just sit there to save all the embarrassment. Maybe Vegas was a bad-ass idea after all? He didn't have no luck! And each hour felt like it was getting worse by the minute.

"Hey, you right there! C'mon, man, you're out of here! You're done, buddy, and banned and barred. Your kind isn't welcome here harassing our clients—Man!" the casino security shouted as he tased Twan.

Twan immediately began sizzling like some bacon. It felt like his heart was jumping out of his chest. Then he blacked straight out.

Next thing Twan knew, he was sliding on his chin across the outside casino pavement. Then he heard car horns honking hard. Them damn casino security guards were more like some damn goons mob-style.

They tossed Pimpin on his shit in the middle of the street right outside of Harrah's.

Damn, they vicious out here, Twan thought as he tried to stand on his feet, holding his chin. He was drained and wobbly, trying to get the hell out of the middle of the street. Twan turned around and flicked his middle finger up high and grabbed his crotch up and down twice like Michael Jackson.

"Ohh...shit!!" Twan managed to say as he started shuffling down the strip. The Harrah's casino guards started chasing Twan down the strip. He knew they were trying to come fuck him up. Damn, he thought as he panicked in fear of being tased again. They were worse than the Ferguson P.D. Twan quickly got low in a pack of tourists with drinks in their hands, then darted into the casino hotel.

Twan came out the east entrance and ran across the street, finally juking them mobsters. Then he saw the Greyhound bus terminal. He was relieved and was ready to go! He felt like Vegas was overrated, and didn't see how not one pimp could even exist out here.

He was ready to go! Maybe Tennessee or Virginia, somewhere he could be successful. But Vegas was definitely out the question! He didn't care about imprinting his BR legacy. He was about to leave his Mama Lela ass out there. He was no longer mad at her for going out there on a long trip broke.

He would simply go to the terminal clerk and tell him how he was down on his luck and got struck, then to give him a bus pass anywhere down South besides Louisiana. He knew they all heard many unsuccessful heartbreak stories like that before. However, he'd promise them that he'd never, ever come back.

Twan pulled the door open to the terminal. It was a lot more quiet and slowed down. He noticed it wasn't the same employees there when he got kicked out earlier. He walked up to the ticket counter and saw it was deserted. He scratched his head and looked around. Then he noticed a small petite sister with dookey braids.

"Aye...Excuse me, Lil Mah?" Twan yelled real quick as he slapped on the counter twice. The clerk in the light-blue shirt looked at Twan and sucked her teeth. Twan instantly saw her attitude. Damn, did anybody want to really work in Vegas? he thought, knowing it was the wee hours of the morning.

"C'mon now...Damn—Aye...baby girl—Baby girl? Come from back there. I know you see me needing some help out here. I need a ticket! Don't do a pimp like that now, baby girl!" Twan shouted as he shook his head side to side.

"Boy—what do you want? Ain't no damn buses coming in until 7 a.m. and I'll be off so you can come back at 7 a.m.! Unless you can make it to Laughlin. They have a bus going eastbound from Los Angeles, tho?" the small-frame clerk stated as she rolled her eyes at Twan, folding her arms ratchett.

"Twan? Boy—there you go! I was worried. I'm so sorry, son! I thought I heard your voice. I was knocked out on that hard wired bench. Here, I got you a plate of food! It's a cold steak and potatoes. Take it, boy, and put something in your stomach. And I found somebody I want you to meet. She don't got no family and a nice little young lady. She over there on that bench asleep, too. She ain't working with much, tho. You gotta make something out of nothing, Twan. But be easy on her, she ain't no Neese, Twan. Now here, eat!" Mama said in a scratchy tone, looking wore out as she handed Twan a cold Styrofoam tray.

The little clerk emerged to the back. Twan looked over at the half-asleep bitch curled up like a puppy on the bench, peeking over at him. She was dark-skinned with a chicken head ratchett ponytail. She looked rough from a first impression. He already knew his Mama Lela done fished and hooked the little runaway hoe.

Twan smiled inside as he took a deep breath and sighed out heavily. Then he cracked open his cold plate. It was a nice juicy piece of well-done steak. He was going to need all the energy he could for his game plan with his fresh merch and turnout.

He and Mama Lela walked over to the bench and sat down. Twan saw the nervous little bitch batting her weary red eyes. He told her don't trip and to relax and get all the rest she needed for the night, because tomorrow, he had big plans.

She nodded her head in acknowledgement nervously. Twan noticed she was shy, but all of that was about to change. He'd break her of all bad habits. Long as she wasn't smoking crack and battling that damn pipe. Them hoes were the worst, because that dope was their powerful pimp! And Twan knew couldn't no pimp compete with that drug, no matter how much they chopped and popped their P's or how much of a strong dose they gave them hoes on some pimpin. It was game in vain.

Twan finished his cold steak as his mind stopped wandering. He looked down at the runaway broad, knowing she was sleeping uncomfortably. He took a mental note of that and stored it in his pimp pilot. Then he looked over at his Mama Lela snoring ass sleeping wild. She had a rough life, but seemed to be used to this type stuff. They were all stuck, stranded and homeless at the bus terminal. And she didn't seem to panic or have no worries like Lil Weezy. He was proud of his crazy ass Mama, despite their differences, the fact that she had been clean for a whole week now tomorrow. He said a silent pimp prayer. He prayed that his Mama didn't relapse and for God to forgive him for pimpin on his own Mama, because in the morning when they woke up, he was sending them both for sure! Twan rested his head back on the wired bench and stared up at the ceiling for a few minutes before closing his eyes and drifting off...

Twan's face was baking as the early morning Las Vegas sun rays beamed through the terminal windows on him. He wiped his beady forehead as he cracked his eyes open, blocking the sun rays with his left hand. He looked over at his Mama Lela and the runaway. They both were still sound asleep. Twan shut his eyes as he scooted out of the sun.

All of a sudden his heart jumped as he heard a roaring crowd of people entering the Vegas terminal from a Los Angeles bus.

Doom-doom!! "Mama, c'mon—y'all get up...chop-chop!" Twan said after he kicked the wired bench twice that Mama Lela and the runaway were crashed out on.

Twan saw the passengers crowding the terminal and rushing to the bathrooms. He jumped up on his feet and stretched out his arms as he yawned like a wild alley cat. He looked down at his Mama and told them to get up once again. Then he hurried up and dashed to the bathroom to wash his face and pull himself together.

He entered the bathroom and squeezed in between some older white man trying to take up all the sink. The white man wasn't intimidated by Twan, being from Los Angeles. Plus this was his third time in Vegas. He'd take a trip every year since he retired. The man noticed Twan rinsing his mouth out with warm water.

He offered Twan some toothpaste. Twan took the Crest whitening toothpaste and spread a big glob on his index finger. Then he began massaging his teeth and gums with his hand brush. The white man shook his head. He couldn't believe Twan was scrubbing his chops with his finger. He was shocked and just figured Twan was down on his luck and got struck out in Vegas.

Then he watched Twan dart back out the door before he could help him out any further. Twan saw Mama Lela and the runaway were gone. He looked around side to side and noticed Mama Lela at the lockers.

"Mama, I got a fresh trick. I know her young ass could crack him. You got too much ass for him! I hope you ready, Lil Mah, cuz it's a big trick in the bathroom. Just give him head in the stalls soon as I set it up real quick! Pull yaself together, and Mama, help her out!" Twan said to his Mama, then faced the runaway in a low tone. Then Twan took off back to the bathroom. He didn't even hear Mama Lela say the girl wasn't ready just yet. She never turned no tricks even though she was down. She knew Twan selfish ass simply didn't care and would send her regardless!

Twan damn near knocked the same older white man down as he was coming out. Twan grabbed him and turned him around.

"My man...check this out real quick. First off, I appreciate you and da toothpaste. However, me and my sister out cherr in Vegas stuck with no dough. So she wanted to just come and thank you real quick. Whatever you tip her is up to you, but remember what happens in Vegas stays in this bathroom. Now c'mon and hold down this last stall. I'll be right back. Let me go get my sister real quick!" Twan said, excited.

"H-Hold on! Wait a minute...umm-umhm, but my wife is out there. She is going to be waiting on me or looking for me!" the white man stated in a frantic tone.

"I got this. Don't be worried. This Vegas, baby! Now sit back and hold dis stall down, big man. Alright?" Twan replied as he nodded his head and winked his eye slick.

Twan shot out the terminal bathroom, running over to the mini lockers, looking for his Mama and the runaway. Nothing! Then he shuffled through the crowded terminal to the ladies room, yelling out for his Mama Lela and the girl to hurry up and come out.

Mama Lela heard Twan's ignorant ass doing all that damn yelling, scaring white folks and the little runaway. She was getting cold feet as it was. Mama Lela had to do a pep talk real quick to pump her head up. She told the runaway all she had to do was close her eyes and pretend like she was giving a million-dollar head job to the man of her dreams. And that all the white tricks cum too quick. She instructed her to talk to him dirty while she jerked him off, then put her warm-hot lips around his little dick. The older white tricks loved to get their fragile egos stroked while getting head from a black gal.

Mama Lela came out the bathroom, telling Twan to shut up with all that yelling. Twan was looking over his Mama's shoulders. He wasn't trying to hear that blah-blah shit!

"Man, where she at, Mama? Watch out, move—let me through! I'm bout to go get the bitch befo da trick dip!" Twan said as he pushed his thin Mama out his way.

"Ahh!! Hey!! This is the ladies room, sir!" some older white lady screamed and shouted.

"Twan boy, get out of here! You tripping, son. They gonna kick your dumb ass out the terminal again, then 86 your ass for good. This Vegas, boy!" Mama Lela yelled as she pulled him back out.

Twan told her okay fine, but she needed to go get the bitch before he go in and drag her out by the head! Then Twan saw the runaway girl emerge out the ladies room with her hair dooky-gelled back into that same ratchett ponytail. Her petite frame revealed her thin scaly ribs showing through her pink halter top. Twan could see her perky erect nipples.

"Damn—That's what I'm talking bout, baby girl! You look righteous and clean up helluva good. C'mon—let's go get this doe!" Twan said as he dragged the runaway to the men's room.

She was marching behind Twan nervously. Her heart was beating off rhythm as it skipped beats. Twan felt her clammy hands. He didn't have time to give her a motivation speech. He didn't care if she was too scared. He'd simply throw her in the men's room either way. She was his bread and meat. If he didn't pimp hard, he couldn't eat!

She tried to stop before entering the men's room. Twan felt the resistance and yanked on her arm, pulling her right on in. A few guys looked at Twan while washing and drying their hands like he was a lunatic. He told the runaway to go ahead, as he pointed to the last stall.

She took a deep breath and tried to go into character. Soon as she opened the stall door up she saw this pale 50-year-old white man with his pants down to his ankles, sitting bare ass on the nasty ass terminal toilet seat. She instantly went out of character. She turned around as she saw Twan shut the stall door and nod his head at the both of them.

The trick was playing with himself, trying to stand up at attention. She dropped down on her knees and began to stroke his little worm to life. It felt soft and cold as oatmeal. She was disgusted and wanted to just throw up. Then she felt his little worm begin to spring to life.

She closed her eyes and inserted his semi-soft penis into her warm mouth. He got a little more excited, but after 2 whole minutes he couldn't get off. He started running his hand up and down her skirt. She started to let out some sly pleasurable low moans, which instantly made the old trick rock hard.

"C'mon, sit on my lap, you sweet fine piece of brown sugar. I won't bite ya, now!" the old trick said excitedly as he pushed her head off his lap.

She just looked at him, lost. She didn't have no protection or ready to straddle him. However, she didn't want to upset Twan or Mama Lela and leave empty-handed. She turned around facing the stall, then grabbed his stiff shaft and guided it into her warm wet crevices. She rode him slowly reverse cowgirl. He loved her tight little ass going up and down. However, he still couldn't get off. It didn't do the trick. So he told her to get up. Then he bent her over the stall, spit on his hand and rubbed it between her legs. He mounted her by the waist and went to town with his old short strokes as they had little vigor to them.

Twan sat outside wondering what was taking the little bitch so damn long, and how much was the old trick gonna tip her? It felt like 10 minutes had went by already. She was slow as hell and needed a lot of work. She was in there making love to the trick or letting him have his way with her for a second go-around. He vowed to break her from all her bad habits. She was too damn green.

Then Twan noticed an older white lady, looking grouchy, approach the men's room yelling out for Jimmy!

Oh shit! His wife! Twan thought.

"Damn it, Jimmy! What the hell is taking you so damn long? Are you stuck? Get off the crapper! Well, I'm going into the casino. I'll be at the blackjack table. Make sure you check into the hotel!" the elder white lady shouted.

"Ohh...O-kay, Martha. I'm coming, honey. Here I come. Just finishing up!!" the trick yelled back to his impatient wife with casino fever just as he was cumming. For some peculiar reason hearing his wife's voice gave him a hidden guilty pleasure. His torso fell onto the runaway's back, which caused her to crash into the wall. Twan heard the loud thud, thinking the old trick had done fell out. He rushed into the bathroom.

"Hey, big man, are you alright in there? Y'all good?" Twan asked as he knocked on the locked stall door, as he was peeking through the small cracks.

She opened the stall smiling with a hundred-dollar bill and handed it straight to Twan. Twan quickly tucked the Franklin as he watched the trick buckling up his pants high and wiping the cold sweat off his forehead and gray hair.

The trick stepped forward and gave Twan his own Ben Franklin, then tapped him on the back, thanking him for a good time. He offered to buy Twan a drink at the casino, too. Twan gladly declined, though, then walked out the men's room with his new hoe.

"So not too bad...I see you finally got dem butterflies out of ya stomach, huh, girl? So what's ya name and story anyways?" Twan asked curiously.

"Ashley! Well, I was born in Seattle, Washington, but moved to Kentucky with my grandparents, who are all strict. They military, so you know I just had to go. I'm not that smart and the military wasn't for me. They were forcing me to join the Air Force. I just been rebelling because I wanted to know what's the deal with my real parents, and my real family in Seattle. So I went to Seattle to find out I was adopted and my mother died in a car accident and my dad died from unknown health problems. So I decided to start over somewhere. I bought a ticket to Vegas and I got stuck, then ran out of food and money. But I refuse to call my adopted grandparents and join the military," Ashley said, dramatic.

"And you don't have to enlist in no white man's army. Listen, Ashley, you're in good hands like Allstate, you dig? I got cha back like a spine. It's my job to keep you in line, all da time! I believe in you and us. Daddy just need you to spot, so I don't drop. Like Drake say, started from the bottom, now we here in each other's life. So let's go vic and stick Vegas! First we gotta get us a hotel room. Be prepared to catch more dates, tho. And listen to my crazy-ass Mama. Follow her lead," Twan said slick and quick.

As they approached Mama Lela Twan pulled out the big-face hundred and told her it's time to leave the terminal, so get all of her raggedy junk out of the mini lockers. She smiled as she snatched the hundred-dollar bill and told him she'd get the hotel. She saw how Twan was talking slick and quick all in Ashley's ear. She knew Ashley was too damn green like a thumb and needed helluva work. She was a good girl gone bad. Then to make matters worse, she fell into the hands of Twan crooked ass. Even though Twan was her son, he wasn't good for this square bitch. She'd be forever ruined after Twan done smashing hard on her. She shook her head.

She vowed to make it easier on Ashley and to guide her so Twan didn't have to keep his foot up her little ass. They all walked out the terminal and went straight into the casino for the breakfast buffet. Ashley skinny ass could eat. Twan didn't mind, though, because she needed some meat on her.

Twan looked at his Mama, praying she could still catch a big thousand-dollar trick. They went hotel searching but all of them were too expensive, so they settled for a cheap sleazy motel off the strip.

- Chapter 2 -

"Pimp Down"

Twan opened the rundown motel door. He saw the small room. It had 2 twin beds, a vanity mirror with one sink and a small bathroom right next to it. There was also a typical A/C and heater unit that had the knob from cold to hot with the high, medium, and low push buttons.

He let the ladies shower first so they could go get it. Then he showered off the stale smell of the bus terminal and handwashed his boxers out, then dried them on top of the heater as he put it on high.

Vegas heat was in the high triple digits. He stayed in the motel room mainly during the day. He had to wait to get fitted in some new strings first before he could knock some new game. Right now he was feeling like a straight bum.

Mama Lela would catch a few tricks. She'd get like $40 to $50 for turning tricks, because she looked too much like a crack whore. So they would throw her crack hoe prices, mainly for head only. Mama Lela didn't really know all the spots yet. Some of the tracks were blazing red zones with vice and LVMPD. Especially Las Vegas Blvd. They ran Mama Lela out of there twice in one night.

The runaway Ashley was catching a few dates but for some reason she wasn't bringing but a couple hundred a night back. Twan already cursed out Mama Lela, blaming her for not putting Ashley on game and showing her the ropes out there. He already laced her up. She was with the business all the way and down for Twan. She wanted to see him on top, and was proud of the new clothes and shoes Twan brought himself.

Twan would go up front and hustle the Arabian motel owner for free nights playing him in cards and siccing his Mama Lela on Abdul. Twan came back from up front when he heard the quarrelling from inside of the room.

He walked in to see his Mama and Ashley fighting and tangled up. Ashley was crying. Twan asked, "What happened now?" Mama Lela was shaking her head, saying it was her while looking hard at Ashley. Ashley pointed back at Mama Lela, crying and mumbling something inaudible.

"Twan, it's her ass! She can't even turn a trick right. I don't get what's so hard about sucking and fucking. Or she just rebelling, acting lazy. She ain't getting no callbacks, and I already had to go behind her like 3 to 4 times now!" Mama Lela shouted with her arms folded, leaning on one hip.

Twan looked over at the little duck bitch and scratched his chin lightly. He always knew they said the differences between a duck hoe and a snowbunny was a duck will make you pimp, and a snowbunny would let you pimp! Then he missed his old hoe Miley passive ass. He took a deep breath and sighed out harder, as he asked her, "Is this all true?"

"Daddy, I keep telling her I got this and move her old ass out my way. I can't do nothing right, according to her ass. Then she embarrassing me around all my tricks, running them off, scaring them. She isn't my Mama, so she need to stop acting like it. She is your Mama, Daddy, and I'm tired of her flocking all around me! Seriously!" Ashley screamed out loud, teary-eyed.

"Fuck dat, Tawn! Ask her to give you some head. Put her on the spot right now! Do it. I betcha—Watch!" Mama Lela stated, challenging Ashley.

Twan looked over at Ashley as she sucked her teeth and shook her head before looking away, which made Twan super furious. He snapped hard. He jumped off the twin bed and snatched Ashley up by her hair and wrapped a fistful of weave as he dragged her over to the bathroom sink. She was trying to free herself from Twan's knuckling grip. Twan threw her onto the floor, and told her to go ahead and give him some head.

She wiped her eyes and crawled up on her knees as she unfastened Twan's pants and proceeded to give Twan her best opening performance ever as she shut her eyes.

Twan popped her on the back of her head, telling her eye contact, always. Besides him not cumming in a while and Ashley's warm lips wrapped around his dick, that was the only reason while he was excited. He was semi-hard and she proved Mama Lela right. She was horrible!

Mama Lela could see the blank expression on Twan's face and knew she was right. Now she still knew that Ashley was their only hope right now to get on top real quick. So she went by Twan's side to watch and tell Ashley what she was doing wrong.

"Unt-uhh...Oh, hell nawh! Ashley gurrl, put some suction on it, slobber on it and suck the spit back off the dick!! And use ya damn hands, too. You got to be able to make them tricks cum fast and hard!" Mama Lela coached Ashley on as she hunched over low with her arms folded in disbelief.

Twan told her, yeah, to follow his Mama's orders and learn from the vet. The now sloppy head job got a little bit better. Especially since she was working his shaft, too.

Mama Lela looked up at Twan's face again. It was blank with no signs of satisfaction or pleasurable moans. He remained unfazed. Mama sucked her teeth and popped the shit out of Ashley on the back top part of her dome, then told her to blow on his dick like it's a million-dollar prize, and not to play explore the dick.

Ashley felt her head jerk forward and Twan's dick ram down her tonsils! She gagged and pulled her head back, then elbowed Mama Lela viciously in her side!

They started arguing again while Ashley still had Twan's shaft in her hand. Twan stood up against the sink, still shaking his head in silence. He knew long as she had 3 warm, wet holes she was a gold mine. However, this hoe's natural sexual instinct skills weren't there! She needed a boost drive and young Pimpin really didn't know where to start or if he could fix this broke-down hoe.

"Damn it! Ashley...You trifling ass lil hoe. Just watch real quick. This is how you hold it and work it!" Mama Lela said, annoyed as she pushed Ashley out the way and grabbed her own son's dick!

"H-Hold up now...c'mon, watch out! Just tell her how to do it. You can instruct her to do a proper hand job," Twan said stern as he pushed Mama Lela back and pulled back from her.

"Boy, Twan, shut up! I'm ya Mama, boy! And this damn dodo brain square head ain't bout to listen or catch on to shit!! You got 2 be hands on, PIMP! And STOP being shy. I'm ya Mama and used to change ya diapers!" Mama Lela replied, annoyed, as she grabbed Twan's shaft again.

Ashley looked at her like she was a damn crazy fool! She knew they were from Louisiana, but what type of ratchett time were they on? It was a little too close for comfort. Just too awkward!

She proceeded to watch as Mama Lela manipulated Twan's shaft with her right hand vigorously. Mama Lela turned to Ashley and asked her, did she see her hand motions and to twerk the dick just like that? Ashley just shook her head up and down in acknowledgement with a wide-eyed, puzzled face.

Then, out of nowhere, she witnessed Mama Lela take her own son's head into her mouth, as it disappeared quickly and Mama Lela proceeded to bob up and down viciously like for apples.

She saw Twan's eyes roll in the back of his head double time as her own mouth gaped wide open! It was less than 15 seconds and by the time she pulled Twan's slippery dick out, it had grown harder almost 2 more whole inches.

Twan just felt the warm and wetness of a womb as he heard smacking noises and slurping on spit noises. He couldn't believe how that felt in just those few sucks. A helluva difference from Ashley. It was more like Neese's infamous head jobs. She'd make it feel like he was in some wet bomb ass pussy. And now his own Mama made him feel like he was all in her womb. He had the instant urgency to cum now. He hadn't had that since Neese and was horny as a dog!

Mama Lela pulled back and quickly wiped the slobber from the cracks of her lips, then told Ashley to go ahead and use them same techniques.

Ashley was still so in awe she lost focus. She tried for the next 2 minutes until Twan told her to just stop! He would be there all damn day waiting to cum. He told her it was a little better, but she'd have to practice more and just flat back with her tricks for now.

As Ashley got up, embarrassed, with her head down and walked over to sit on the motel bed, Twan stood there with his rock-hard dick in his hand, stuck! His nerves were very bad. His dick ached hard with anticipation as it leaked pre-cum. His balls were tingling like they were dancing around with raging sperm.

Mama Lela couldn't see how her own son stared at her devilishly as she walked past him into the bathroom. She had to go relieve herself real fast. Twan saw her rush in and shut the door behind her.

He stood there stuck for like 30 seconds before he said fuck it and barged in the bathroom...

"Damn-damn...Boy, what the hell? I'm on the damn toilet, Twan. Get ya ass out of here and shut the fucking door, now!" Mama Lela shouted out at the top of her exhausted lungs, as the door hit her in her left knee of the small motel bathroom.

"Hold up now, Mama... Look, now I'm stuck. Don't leave me like this with blue balls and all. My dick all swollen! Like you said, stop being shy. You my Mama!" Twan said slick while trying to put his dick in her mouth.

"Boy, hell nawh—STOP IT, Twan. If you don't get ya lil dick out of my face and let me finish peeing!" Mama Lela replied, moving her head side to side to avoid Twan's manhood while trying to pull back up her panties.

They went back and forth for a brief second. Then there was an awkward silence throughout the motel. Ashley's stomach dropped down as her bowels shifted. She got off the bed slowly and crept to the bathroom to sneak a peep.

Mama Lela knew Twan was being persistent and wouldn't give up. She knew she was at fault in the first place. So she figured she might as well finish and make it quick. She closed her eyes and pictured she was sucking someone else's dick besides her son's. Then she just popped up with Twan's daddy picture. Because they both had them same signature curved penises. Down South they called them hook dicks or crooked dicks.

Twan just felt his own Mama take him into the warm wet depths of her throat. He threw his head back, closed his eyes and pictured Neese's Creole face, because it surely felt like her head game. Couldn't no young broad compete with her. He started feeling his knees buckle like they were about to kiss the floor. Then he quickly held his own Mama's head down there as he bucked like a wild horse and whole torso jerked in a frenzy.

Mama Lela felt Twan's dick lunge to the nape of her throat as he rammed her face into his stomach. Then her throat loaded with spurts of gooey warm cum. She felt like her son had her in the death lock choke, because she couldn't breathe and she was choking off all his little babies, which forced her to swallow fast as she could in gulps.

Ashley stood there bug-eyed with her arms folded. She was still fucked up! She just stood there in the bathroom doorway, no longer peeking anymore. She watched as Mama gulped down all of Twan's cum like it tasted sweet like candy. As Lela made a bunch of gulping and gasping noises, it sounded like she was chugging cups of water and having an asthma attack at the same damn time.

Mama Lela was trying to pull herself away from Twan's massive grip, but couldn't get her face out of his torso. She scratched and clawed in panic. But pain was pleasure to Twan at this time. His head was still leaned back as his chin faced the ceiling. He was in waves of ecstasy with a huge smirk on his devilish face. He said, "Ooo...Neese," as he loosened his grip.

"Boy—what the hell is the matter with you, Twan mutherfucka? Doin ya Mama like that. You disrespectful—"

"No, what's the matter with y'all 2 nasty mufu? Nawh—matter of fact I'll leave you 2 sicko lovebirds. I'm gone, Twan, you asshole!!" Ashley said as she cut Mama Lela off and then stormed out the motel, leaving the door wide open.

Twan felt like his whole body was floating from ecstasy. He quickly pulled his boxers up and shot straight out of the door. He saw Ashley just dart across the busy street and almost get smacked by an SUV! He gave chase barefooted with no shirt on with his spaghetti legs.

Twan chased her down half a block. He caught her and snatched her arm up, backhanded her like a vet PI. Then he dragged her in front of him.

"Umm-hmm...Yeah, come on hoe, what the fuck you thought this was, bitch? You didn't think I'll put my foot dead up on ya ass, hoe!? Huh?—Bitch!" Twan said while dragging her like a lifeless rag doll.

Ashley was crying and throwing a pure fit while she tried to claw Twan up. His arms were too long for her. He kept her at bay. She was just clawing up his arms.

"Fuck this, dig dat! You know what, hoe? Since you wanna throw a hoe tantrum—trying to be seen and shit! Hoe, take off dem slippers! Give'em to me. HOLD STILL, HOE!! Let you walk back to the motel and burn ya feet on this hot concrete. And it's gonna be a slow stroll home," Twan said sternly as he slid into her slippers to make her feel the burn and feet blister.

By the time Twan got back to the motel and threw Ashley back on the bed, Mama Lela was smearing her hoe make-up on her face and whore red lipstick on her cracked dick sucker.

"Well, Twan, looks like you got some dicking down to do, now. Especially after that lil episode earlier. You gotta conquer her body now, cuz you already fucked up her mind. Believe dat! I'm gonna get this doe, and Ashley, you should be coming shortly right behind me—ADIOS," Mama Lela said as she stuffed her titties and adjusted her maroon wig again. She made her ass sway walking past Ashley.

Ashley shook her head and pushed Twan off her. Twan already was creating friction between her legs pleasurably. She fought but couldn't resist the urge and comfort Twan made her feel between them.

Maybe she did want to feel affection, in any real way she could get it from Twan. Besides, in her mind she just looked at Twan as her boyfriend, not her pimp!

She let out soft small moans as she indirectly spread her legs open, letting her hormones get the better of her inner freak. Her hormones were now dancing with sexual anticipation. She pulled Twan down in between her legs.

Twan paused to get the Magnum off the nightstand and slapped it on. As he rolled it down his shaft, he hoped his Mama was right and giving her the "D" was the best solution to ever seeing the hoe again. Especially a runaway because they had priors and were known for running out on their problems. Pimpin didn't care. He told his hoes, Fuck their problems. Face the world and all the tricks in it.

Twan put the pussy in check quick and was slow-stroking her like a pimp. Pretty soon she couldn't resist the urge to climax. Then she seemed to forget whatever the hell she was mad at Twan for. All she knew was how much she loved his skinny ass right now.

Twan teased her, pulling his D in and out of her, making her gyrate and hunch up and down on it, until he finally beat it up like some Eastern Africa conga drums.

She immediately wanted to get up and cook or go to the store for her Daddy. But instead she got right up out of bed, straightened her wig up, freshened up and went down Vegas Blvd. to get lucky!

She had a classified ad on Craigslist back pages, SugarDaddys, and those DTF sites. She couldn't catch a decent trick in the first place. Then if she did, they wouldn't call her back. She needed to build her clientele base, where she didn't have to street walk in the desert 100-degree heat.

Twan had been stressing bad. For the past 24 hours he hadn't seen Ashley. Also for the past 72 hours he hadn't seen his Mama Lela's ass. And before that she had been drinking and came back to the motel pissy drunk, then passed out on the bathroom floor.

He figured their whole little awkward sexual mishap had been tearing between them and pushing them more apart. He knew she felt guilty, but he still was the one wrong. Damn, how shit happens in the spur of moment sometimes. Then he thought back to his Creole hoe Neese back in BR and shook his head, because it was his fault why she was gone in the first place either way.

He rolled up a swisher sweet blunt with some of that Class A Mexico weed from AZ. He could get a whole ounce for $60 and smoke all week and still get high. He was still down and looking like he was losing his Mama and lost his runaway bitch to a Vegas pimp.

He promised himself he'd get a phone with whoever or whatever money came in the telly door first. He was always using Ashley's or Mama Lela's phone.

He sipped the watermelon Four Loko, then sat it back down on the table. He surfed through the raggedy motel local Vegas channels, thinking of a new helluva game plan. He vowed to get him the new pineapple-flavored Cîroc. That Diddy juice, maybe it would give him some pimp juice, and a pimp boost!

Vegas was just too hard. Especially to start from the bottom with scratch. In Vegas it was either you were on or not. You had to come here with your bitches. The actual Vegas hoes were already turned all the way out or burnt out all the way so far. And the rest of the people in the bottom was from either drug addiction or gambling addicts. It was cold without no inbetween Twan was trying to be to pimp to the top, the real upper-class, but could he be successful? He felt like a fresh no-name actor from out of town straight trying to get into Hollywood.

Twan was experiencing what they call Pimp down! His pimpin was down so no hoes weren't around. He couldn't get no hoes to even come around, let alone stay down. He was in distress, knew Ashley was long gone on the Greyhound somewhere back east.

He couldn't sell the dope or have the plug in Vegas because he didn't know who he could trust or who were the Fedz.

"Pssh—haah...Shit!" Twan sucked his teeth and sighed out a deep exhausting breath as he cursed loud in a stressful tone.

Mama Lela walked through the motel door, smelling like a truck stop and cheap hooker perfume, just as Twan leant back in distress. She heard him say, "Shit!" agitated.

"Boy—Twan, get ya ass up, here go a stack shit!! I gotta keep me a few bills case I got to bond out. It's a new spot on Freemont Street. It's popping and a lot of young and old pimps and hoes! It's at the back up the strip. Right off of the back where Tupac got killed," Mama Lela said excited and threw the doe on the bed.

Twan sat up quickly. That money made him jump up real quick. Mama Lela snickered as she watched her son proudly count through the stack with his pinky held up in the air, like a vet P.

She told Twan it's bout time he ice both them motherfuckas up! Twan asked her was she drunk? And had she been drinking down on this new ho track Freemont she been talking about?

As she showed Twan off, Ashley came walking into the motel door. She had heavy dark circles around her eyes. Then she kept adjusting her nose and fixing her throat. Twan asked the bitch where she been and where was his doe at? Damn, the bitch had the sniffs. Something wasn't right.

"Un-huh…Yeah, bitch, you been off that blow, candying ya square nose," Mama Lela intervened.

"Shut up, woman! Daddy, I got into one of the lock-ins at the Planet Hollywood Casino Hotel. Here is 2500 plus the 500 before I got into the rich lock-in," Ashley said with a planted smile. Really she was worn out and asshole felt torn. Twan knew how the lock-ins worked and loved them.

- Chapter 3 -

"Freemont"

Twan had 4 racz. He was back! No doubt about that. He was about to act a straight donkey. Watch out, Vegas, here a young pimp come, bitch! That was all Twan could think about as he rolled another blunt of Reggie Bush. He sipped on the rest of his Four Loko before tossing the rest of the spit away, while staring at the table hard and eye-fucking the 4 racz. Uuggh...

"Uugghh...Uh-uugghhh..." Twan mumbled while nodding his head up and down, then grabbed Ashley's smartphone.

Mama Lela washed her funky ass up first, then Ashley took her dirty ass in there right after her. They fought over who goes first for a brief moment, but Ashley was too tired and Mama Lela was too damn burnt out, too.

Mama Lela crashed out on Twan's bed, while Ashley crashed out on the other twin bed by the door and A/C unit. Twan heard Ashley in the shower snorting and blowing water out of her nostrils. She sounded like a bunch of hungry wild grunting pigs. He knew she was washing down that nasty coke aftertaste, even though the back of her throat was numb.

"No Flex Zone—No Flex Zone!! They kno better—They kno better!! No Flex Zone—No Flex Zone!!" the new hit single blasted through the smartphone that Twan found on iTunes. He was viben and popping his shirt swiftly.

All he could think of while the girls were snoring in a quickly induced coma was, Freemont? Was the vice squad out trippin? Did they let the hoes catch tricks long as it wasn't on the main strip? Something sounded too good to be true. Mainly how was the P's doing it slick?

His curiosity got the best of him. He grabbed the motel card and Ashley's phone and went to get fitted. Then knock a tennis shoe pimp's ho. He could peel one of them sneaker pimp's hoes. They always had either amateur hoes or washed-up old vet hoes just like his Mama Lela.

"No Flex Zone—No Flex Zone!! They kno better...They kno better..." Twan sang along and swayed his head from side to side. He was feeling his nipples finally, again. He had almost forgotten how it felt to win! He knew Mama Lela and Ashley tired ass wouldn't be up until later on tonight around 10 o'clock-ish.

Twan caught a taxi cab to the Meadows Mall. He went to the T-Mobile stand and purchased a smartphone using his brother that got killed, Terrance, aka T-Nut's, info. He knew his brother's social by heart and really took it on as an alias when pulled over or in tight situations. He didn't care if he messed up his credit or had arrest warrants for failure to appear. A dead man didn't care either way. However, Twan knew one of these days his thumbprint and right index finger were going to match and catch up to him.

Twan went to buy him a few pimp strings, silk boxers, Stacy Adams and a few short brims. The Meadows Mall was flooded with hoes, so he decided to go get suited in his whole pimp attire in the dressing rooms. He would fake it till he made it. He found some inexpensive gold jewelry and earrings in the middle of the mall.

That's exactly where he ran into a curious snowbunny with platinum hair, sea-blue grayish eyes, with a funny L-shaped long nose.

"When you see a pimp! Pay a pimp? I see you reckless checkin, white gurrl?" Twan said quick and slick.

"OMG—So like are you supposed to be a pimp? That's so funny and UR cute and sexy. I'm from Idaho, well, originally from the Middle East, and my name is Jazabel. And I'm Arabic, not white. You ain't never seen a light-skinned Arabian girl before? I'm down here going to UNLV," she said with an Arabic accent.

Twan couldn't believe the soft-spoken Arabian bitch. He thought she was just a regular Vegas snowbunny. He wouldn't have come on too strong to run her off. He would've come different. The more he stared at her, the more he could see her foreign features. She was exotic or imported alright. Either way he had him one.

"Ha-ha-ahh...so are you going to just stand there checking me out or do you want to hook up sometime? Here, give me your phone and I'll leave my number," she said as she chuckled a little with the sexiest Middle Eastern voice ever, which made Twan's manhood jump.

"Ahh yeah...Um-uhh, excuse me, my name is Twan. It's nice to meet you. It's just your eyes are so foreign and hypnotic, damn! But yeah, I'd love to see you again. We'll talk about this pimp shit and I'll school you to what I'm talkin about. Here goes my phone. Do ya thang, gurrl," Twan replied in a slick tone.

"I dunno...hmm, can you come to one of my volleyball games on campus? We'll see how you act around the rest of them college girls and my family will be there, too. Just a fair warning. I'm very family-orientated. LOL!" she said in a flirty tone as she stored her name and number in Twan's smartphone.

Twan watched her walk away after she gave him a friendly hug. Damnit! He couldn't help but think about giving her some sausage. He wanted to put his sausage right between her slender frame and tight ass.

He knew he was in violation of pimp conduct. He couldn't tender dick or trick ever!! Nowadays a pimp would always admire seeing a good bitch that he couldn't break, but a main bitch, was he wrong? Neese had him torn from his high school young tender pimpin years. He just yearned for a main hoe, a bottom thorough bitch. And Ashley wasn't an alpha or beta ho. He shook the thoughts out his head and walked out the Meadows Mall into the cab, already dressed to impress and fandangle him a ho to sell that ass and get his cash!!

"Alright now, where to, buddy?" the overweight, sweaty, middle-aged cab driver stated while blinking his bad eyes through his raggedy spectacles. He appeared to be off something. Twan assumed speed or crack. There wasn't no telling in Sin City, tho.

"Freemont Street, the back end of the strip, baby!" Twan snapped.

"Freemont??—Freemont!" the cab driver replied.

"Aye...Hell yeah, Freemont—fool, you probably could get lucky and laid. It's all pimps and hoes paradise down there. You see a pimp in ya presence. You recognize a young pimp, pimp down and pimp up shine with leather and diamonds. Now let's go, fat ass. I bet if I pay you in crack it would be a wrap, huh?" Twan snapped hot, going hard on the older driver.

Twan couldn't believe this cab driver. He wanted to be seen in all his pimp apparel. Shit, he pimped hard for this fit and jewels. It was crazy. He sat back and thought back to all his pimp idols from since he was a little boy.

Santa Claus was a big pimp. He would always wear a red pimp suit with white fur. Even his hat dangled with a furry white ball. He was the coldest pimp ever all the way from the North Pole, LRPs (long range pimpin) he stayed poppin his P's and breaking hoes. He'd get bubbly and start laughing, saying ho-ho-ho!! Ha-ha-ha...Ho-Ho-Ho! Merry Christmas! Because he would make it rain and shower the whole world of kids with gifts as long as they be good and better than him. It was all in good faith but most of all out of a bitchhh!!

"Okay, we're here, pimp! Freemont," the tweeking cabbie said with emphasis on *Pimp*.

Twan snapped out of his pimp thoughts hearing the cabbie say something quick and slick. He hurried up and peeled him off a dub and told him to keep the small change. The cabbie told Twan, "Right on! Thanks!" Twan got out and slammed the door super hard, scaring the cabbie. He screeched off yelling, "Jackass!" Twan still thought Uncle Sam was the biggest pimp of them all. All the white pimps were the most vicious ones. Or was it just that they took their pimpin to another level? It was definitely a bigger scale. Some of them mixed vic'n and pimpin to form a cold concoction dose of pimpin.

Twan looked around and down Freemont. It seemed a bit quiet but it was just barely turning into dusk. He walked to the liquor store, then knew his next move was that strip club next to it. He smiled as he could taste hoes. He would knock a bitch or somebody else's. Pimps don't care long as the other cat played fair. If ya bitch wink, she'll fuck! If she fuck, she'll suck. If she suck, she'll get loose. If she get loose, she'll go!! If she go, then you already know...Bring Daddy his doe, ho!

Twan walked into the liquor store. The door bells jingled alarming the Hindus.

"When I leave the club, I bet ya boo gone. 2-Chainz but I got me a few on!! Aye y'all getting it in dis bitch cherr, Aye!" Twan said as he rapped the 2-Chainz verse, grooving side to side, doing his same little pimp 2-step from Baton Rouge.

The liquor store woman just stared at him funny and smirked. However, her husband didn't think it was funny or didn't even budge. He was on high alert easy. A liquor store in Vegas and on Freemont? It didn't mix; bad location, the profits weren't worth the headaches. He had to deal with dope fiends, robbers, prostitutes, shooters, and property damage. But most of all them damn pimps.

Every pimp on Freemont knew to stop-n-go. If Twan only knew himself. He strolled up to the counter, nodding his head to his favorite ratchett rapper 2-Chainz.

Twan heard the liquor store bells sounding off. He turned around as he put the $20 on the counter.

All of a sudden he saw 2 light-skinned pretty half-breed hoes. They both had on schoolgirl outfits. The uniforms were a half-tied white collar shirt with showing cleavage and a green pleated mini-skirt. Twan heard the click-clacking, then looked down and saw the 8-inch clear stilettos on their feet. They were giggling and all perky. One was thick with voluptuous curves. The other was more petite.

Twan instantly knew they're hooker hoes! He lit up inside and licked his lips. The hoes walked up directly behind him, singing the 2-Chainz blaring in the liquor store. Twan smelled alcohol and knew the hoes were tipsy, too.

"Butterscotch and Pink Toe, whatz Gucci, hoes? I'm pimpin Twan from Baton Rouge, Louisiana! Now choose or lose. And pay up and shut up!" Twan said, slick choppin and poppin.

"Pssh...Please—"

"Yeah...umm, who da hell is you supposed to be, nigga? You looking like a damn Mississippi cornhusker field pimp! Please, we ain't neva seen ya country ass on Freemont, and where's ya hoes at? Huh?" the thick half-breed butterscotch complexion ho intervened, cutting the younger one off.

"Yeah—and who you calling Pink Toe with ya black ass? Please, who's your hoes out here? I ain't never heard of you or a ho say nothing about some pimp named Twan. You ain't got no hoes on Freemont. And I'm half-black and Italian. Not a snowbunny or ya Pink Toe, fool. Vegas is home of exotic half-breeds you ain't know with ya country ass. I'll make ya ass speak English!" the young petite hooker snapped with her rosy pink complexion.

"We could tell you from St. Louis or wherever the hell you said you from, cuz we property of Fatz da Mac from North Vegas, baby!" Butterscotch replied in a out-of-pocket loud tone.

Twan shook his head and raised his back hand. "Man—y'all 2 out-of-pocket hoes. Y'all know the difference between a Mac and a Pimp, huh? I'll pimp-slap da shit out of both of y'all reckless eyeballing hoes and peel ya purse back or pull da stash out y'all pussy and y'all bra right in this liquor store, and then tell ya guy Fatz da Mac I did it, ho! Miss a pimp with all them damn country pimp jokes. Bitch, y'all bout 2 respect a swamp pimp from BR. I bet cha respect dis pimpin right cherr, ho!" Twan snapped, ready to snap his risk like Floch!

"Pssh...please, whatever, nig—"

POW! Twan slapped the words out of her mouth. Then he wrapped a fistful of curly hair on the other half-breed bitch.

"Ahhh...Ahhh, fuck! Let me go—let me go, dude! Okay, damn it!"

"Shut up, you out-of-pocket bitch. Now both of you hoes break y'all selves or I'ma break my foot so far in y'all ass, I swear y'all gonna be black blue, not light-skinned no more—"

"Hey—let girls go and get out before I call Vegas police! Take outside, now!" the Hindu liquor store owner said, pulling out a baseball bat and revealing a chrome .38 special in the nylon holster on his right hip.

Twan told him to fuck off and shut the hell up. He encouraged him to call the damn law. He wasn't scared of Vegas PD. Then he dragged both of them out-of-pocket hoes by their hair straight out the liquor store.

"STOP all dat damn screaming, ho, and both break y'all selves ASAP like Rocky, ho! Looking like two raunchy Catholic school STD-passing sluts!" Twan yelled as he went thru their bras one at a time, then kicked them square in the ass.

Twan peeled both them hoes back for damn near $600 apiece. They ran off crying down Freemont. Twan didn't give a fuck. He quickly went to grab his liquor and pack of blunts off the counter. The woman tried to kick him right back out but he wasn't going. He told Hadji to get his Hindu wife.

Twan tucked his Hennessy Fifth under his nuts to sneak in the strip joint next to the liquor store after he took 3 hard swigs.

He walked into the sleazy strip joint. It was 2 white bouncers and an old burnt-out-looking security guard with a Luger 9mm resting in its holster, too. Everyone appeared to be strapped up out here in Vegas. It was like the Wild Wild West style for real. Pimp Twan didn't want to touch or see another gun. Fuck that! It wasn't him. He already had to kill N.O. by force. All because he forced a pimp's hand. Pimpin was a game of finesse. A real non-contact sport. So he definitely couldn't be no damn gangsta.

2 ratchett hoes came rushing up to Twan, asking did he want a lap dance for $25 or 2 for $40. If not, to pick one of them.

Twan looked at both of the skinny meth-head-looking rough hoes with overdone titty jobs. He told them hell nawh and for both of them hoes to get their trailer-park trashy ass out a pimp's face. They both frowned, folded their arms, and smacked their lips as they turned around about-face style with their flat asses. Twan went to bleed the bar as usual and peep out the place. He saw 2 more snowbunnies and like 4 more duck bitches. There were 2 caramel hoes and 2 light-skinned bright hoes, too. So he knew he couldn't put Ashley black ass in the joint.

He saw a few tricks putting dollar bills in the G-strings of the ducks dancing on the big stage and corner stage, too. It was also a few little players and Macs in the spot playing cards, shooting pool, and throwing darts, all while talking big-boy bullshit. Twan knew they were all jiving turkeys.

The bartender was a cute Spanish mamacita. He instantly clicked with her. She instantly knew Twan was new to Freemont and wasn't a usual customer like all the other low-budget scummy bums and crack-sack pimps that controlled their hoes by dope! The crack and meth was their real pimp. She told him who was who and about the place, owner, and police. All the hot spots and nots on Freemont. Then she went into her own personal life, how she had a husband locked up for attempted murder and she was now a single mother of 3 badass kids. All girls at that. She seemed to be stressed out. All Twan did was nod in and out between what he needed to hear. Her name was Marissa. Twan paid for his first drink, a single shot on the rocks. Then 15 minutes later she started pouring Twan free double shots and started throwing some back on her own, then switched to Cîroc Pineapple.

Twan excused himself and went to the men's room. Of course there was a 2nd slot machine in there, too. There was one by the front next to the ATM machine. Twan just chuckled. Vegas had them in the McDonald's and everywhere you wouldn't expect.

Twan took a super-long piss as he was punishing the fifth of Henny he snuck in at the same damn time. The fat greasy-dirt white trick just peeked over at Twan all nonchalantly like he was drunk, too.

Twan knew the single Mami bartender was horny as a breeding billy goat and wanted some black sausage. He knew Mexicans were fertile and too possessive and attached. He would keep her right where she was valuable at, as a straight bartender, and just flirt with her and dangle her. Now it was time to blow this joint now that he had a hangout spot.

Marissa warned him, though, at night the place got ugly with dope dealers, pimps, robbers, hoes, and fiends. He smiled and told her it sounds like his type of party. Pimpin could taste it.

He had to go get his Mama Lela and Ashley up on Freemont before it got cracking and came to life. He didn't want to miss a beat. He remembered exactly what hotel Marissa the bartender told him to get, where the safety zones were. They all were trouble, truthfully, but some were hotter than others. He knew it was time to move it on up to the Telly off Freemont. Freemont was a pimp's paradise.

Twan yelled out, "Taxi!" like he was in New York City, then realized he was tipsy and tripping. He walked up to a parked taxi cab and caught the driver hitting a crack pipe. He jumped into the cab anyway and told the driver go-go-go!! like the police was behind him, freaking him out. Then Twan jumped, screaming out what the fuck, flinching.

Twan saw a small head and body pop out. It was a redhead cracked-out midget giving the taxi driver a head job.

"I got a gun, man—go!" Twan shouted frantically as the cab driver quickly shifted into drive, screeching down Freemont. The midget barely jumped out before Twan saw her little pint-size body doing the West Nile gator roll down Freemont.

* * *

"Bitch, I'm out front, ho!" Fatz said, menacing.

"Where you at, hello..." Butterscotch replied.

"What I just say, ho?"

"Fatz—Daddy, alright! Here we come."

Both of the half-breed Catholic-school-dressed hoes came out of the hotel, shuffling thru the parking lot. Fatz da Mac unlocked the black H3 truck. They sped off and pulled up at the liquor store, then parked and walked into the strip club next to it.

"Where dat Mississippi bandit? SIMP, dirty macking? North Vegas in this bitch, Fatz da Mac! Ho, point where this clown at?" Fatz da Mac said viciously while scanning the joint with his hybrid iron golf club on his shoulder. It was his weapon of choice. Him and his hoes went to the bar to wait for Twan to pop back up. It was jumping.

* * *

Twan told the cab driver he was just jiving him about having a gun, so the driver could stop driving so damn erratic. He threw him a hefty twenty-dollar bill and ordered him to the motel.

He texted Jazabel and told Miss UNLV for a sexy selfie. She sent a message back saying, *Awwhh...you miss me already, LOL?* Then she sent a regular selfie of her without no filter of her just waking up in the bed with her blonde hair sprawled out all over her pillow. She still looked exotic and like a billion-dollar ho.

Twan kept it short and asked her if he can meet up with her later on tonite? She replied saying nice try and how funny he was to her. She told him didn't he have a million other girls, pimp? Twan never replied back. He let her go at that point, talking bout his pimpin. And he wanted to let her mind wonder where he was from in BR. They dogged and dragged hoes, foreign hoes, too.

Twan entered the motel as the pissed-off taxi driver smashed off. He saw Mama Lela and Ashley sound asleep, snoring in their panties.

He knew they were both burnt out, but he didn't care. He went to the bathroom and filled the bucket up with cold water and ice.

Splash-splash. "Ahhh…ahhh!!"

"Whoa—shit, that's cold. Boy, Twan—"

"Shut up, both of y'all. This is the ice bucket challenge. Y'all got to pay a pimp charity…ha-ha-ha… Let's go, pack up! I hit big and got us a new spot. You was right, Mama—Freemont!" Twan said sternly, cutting them both off after he threw freezing ice water all over them.

The girls both jumped up, half-naked, screaming and sucking their teeth, getting on their feet. Mama Lela quickly grabbed her things. Ashley ran into the bathroom. Twan sparked a blunt and told them to be ready by the time he was done puffing on the medical marijuana.

He went down to Abdul's office up front to turn in his motel keys and find another cab. He stayed up front playing cards with the manager, Abdul, for 40 minutes until the taxi cab arrived. He texted Mama Lela to come on.

The trio pulled up to the low-budget hotel on Freemont, then tipped the driver. Twan told them to get ready after they check into the Telly to hit Freemont 100 miles running. They had to beat the rest of the renegade and crack hoes.

Twan was all gamed. After Ashley and Mama Lela got in their best ho attire, he took a selfie and put it straight on Instagram, stating that he was accepting all apps in Vegas. Just come to audition on Freemont. He would be right at the strip club next to the liquor store.

He told Ashley to follow Mama Lela's lead as he smacked her hard on her ass, telling her go get Daddy dem now-later gators. She smirked and felt special. However, if Twan could see the look on his Mama's face, trouble was brewing in a pimp's paradise.

Twan shot out the door and headed down Freemont. He manipulated his smartphone as he hit his blunt of medical mixed with that Hitachi spice.

"Take a couple of drinks with a nigga like me...ain't no love from a nigga like me...no love—no love! Don't come searching for love..." Twan sang the August Alsina "No Love" featuring Nicki Minaj download from iTunes, swaying his head and tilting his powder-white brim. He always supported his native Louisianan. August Alsina had some PI in his bones. Plus everyone from the N.O. go!!

Twan entered the strip joint, rolling his deuces up from side to side as he 2-stepped higher than a damn space satellite. Didn't nobody know who Twan was but Marissa the bartender. Everybody else could tell Twan was faded and feeling himself.

Slooushh!! Twan felt the wind break by his face as he shifted sides, then he heard a swift dart sound. He looked over his right shoulder just in time to see a chubby cat with a look of grimace on his face but it was now too late.

Sloushh!—CRACK! Doomp! Fatz da Mac swung harder, connecting his target, clubbing Twan on the crown of his head. He was knocked out cold standing up. Marissa watched his body hit the floor and yelled for security. She was tired of Fatz. "Welcome to Vegas, Pimpin!" Fatz yelled.

- Chapter 4 -

"Pimpin Silky"

Twan came to, blinking his eyes all fast to a familiar sound and hearing. He raised his aching head and looked down at Marissa sucking and slurping a sloppy wet head job. What the fuck? was all he thought. He couldn't complain much but he figured he might as well get one off and skeet his mini-babies all down her esophagus.

They were in a dim lit room. He could see Marissa's almond-shaped eyes as she made direct eye contact. She had silky thin black hair. She had a 36 double D with some vicious love handles. Just like Selena.

After he erupted like a Hawaiian volcano, he asked her what happened because he couldn't remember anything, not even how they got there. And he asked where they were at currently.

She explained to Twan the whole story and he grew more hostile as he rubbed his now throbbing head. Then he checked his pockets to see what all Fatz da Mac took.

"Fuck—cuh!! That fat bastard took my phone and hotel card!" Twan said, heated, scaring Marissa off his lap.

She told him to relax in Spanish, and that her kids and Nana were asleep in the other room. Twan thanked her and felt around for his strings, then fished for a fifty-dollar bill out of his sock, tipping her for saving his life. She offered to drive him back to Freemont. He preferred to call a taxi cab. He didn't want to risk Ashley seeing Marissa and getting jealous right now.

Soon as Twan made it back to his hotel on Freemont, his head ached even more as he banged on the door, trying to wake a drunken Mama Lela and Ashley up. Then he saw the next door open up.

"Damn—save all that banging and yelling, Pimpin. It's too early in the morning for that. They gonna call the law on you around here!" an older man said with a Bay accent.

Twan noticed he was medium-built with long shoulder-length hair. He seemed to be an old washed-up pimp with a black Kangol hat on.

Twan just looked at him. Then he told Twan to come in and have a drink. He knew Twan was new to Freemont and wanted to lace him up. Twan shrugged his shoulders like fuck it. He could use a drink and it may take away the headache. "Chuchh," he told the older P.

Twan entered the room as the washed-up pimp introduced himself as Pimpin Silky from Oakland. Twan let him know he was from out of Baton Rouge, LA.

Pimpin Silky took off his Kangol and had an eagle's nest. He was bald as a baby up there, with long silky shoulder-length hair. Silky was light-skinned and appeared to be in his mid-forties but the drugs made him look in his mid-fifties easy.

He watched as Pimpin Silky took out a gray aluminum platter with a bunch of white powder substance. As he proceeded to chop down the rocky chunks into nice neat singles, he sniffed 2 lines clean with a rolled-up dollar bill, then offered Twan a line. Twan gladly declined.

Silky then poured him a drink of cognac. It was something about Las Vegas that made you want to snort a line of that sweet soft powder—sugar bugger. Twan's nose itched just thinking about it as he shook the thought off.

"Peeling ain't stealing if she willing!! P—I said peeling ain't stealing if she willing! Man, young Pimpin, when I first came to Vegas like you, straight from the Bay area, they used to call me 'Banana Da Pimp,' real shit...cuz I use to peel these simps and vets hos all day every day, the Bay way, straight from East Oakland. Peeling ain't stealing if she willing, young Pimpin!!" Pimpin Silky recited as he sniffed 2 more chunky lines off the platter.

Twan stared at him like, damn-it, man! Either he was in beast mode, go mode, or just so burnt out. Maybe it could've been that cheap Mexican stuff that them Vegas D-boys Crip-walked all over it. He did know one thing, though, for sure: Pimpin Silky was a trip and funny to listen to and watch. He would pick his older useful brain and get put up on game. Maybe he could see how they pimp, mack, and slay in the Bay a major way.

Pimpin Silky snapped out of his initial high trance quickly and started poppin his P's, letting Twan know he was old-skool pimpin. Twan was soaking all the game and stories in, nodding his head and smiling at the same time.

Pimpin Silky knew that Twan was eager to learn and peeping game. At least he'd listen, which is so rare nowadays with a bunch of these new Millennium Pimps popping from the George W. Bush era. They don't last or listen.

Then he asked Twan about his 2 ratchett hos he had next door, telling him one looks too amateur for Vegas and Freemont Street, too. Because these pimps will either snatch her or peel her or she was gone. Then that vet ho looked smoked out, so she can't make no real ho money.

Twan told him that was his own Mama Lela and she was here temporary, helping him out till he knocked some fresh game and got on his toes. Then the other ho was some runaway bitch she knocked at the Greyhound terminal.

Pimpin Silky laughed as Twan shook his head, ashamed. He knew Twan was in bad shape. Even a washed-up snorted-out pimp still had coke hoes he was pimpin on, some young but mostly washed-up vet hoes that were strung out in one way or another. They would run over there for a place to crash and hide out from the law or trick they done robbed, usually for a couple days on out. Sometimes Pimpin Silky would have a full house to the Fire Marshal capacity, but would still break them hoes. He had been in that same room for 2 whole years now. Everybody knew and respected Pimpin Silky from the Bay.

Twan sat back, digging all of it. He decided to call Pimpin Silky "Peeling ain't Stealing" because he was always saying it and using it like a punchline, throwing his weight around.

They chopped it up until Twan was bubbly and headache free. He vowed to beat Fatz da Mac with a bat to a bloody pulp. Pimpin Silky said he knew of Fatz da Mac. He was a local out of Vegas but would rob, sell dope, and try to get ho money out of any stupid ho that was dumb enough to pay his fat greedy ass.

He explained to Twan why people brought their business to Vegas because there is no taxes in the State of Nevada. So how can they tax a pimp? Then Pimpin Silky laced Twan up about the infamous Bunny Ranch and Reno brothels. He told Twan if he gets a ho that's willing to sit her down in one of them and collect that doe lap style.

Twan nodded his head, saying, "Dig that, Peeling ain't Stealing." Then he heard Mama Lela chewing Ashley lazy ass out. She was telling her to get up and go hit the Freemont stroll to see if she can get lucky and catch a big trick.

Twan told Pimpin Silky he had some finessing to do and get him a new phone. He checked his bread from Ashley and Mama Lela, too. He snatched Ashley's phone and told her to hit Fremont and twerk something. She sucked her teeth as he pushed her out of the hotel door.

Twan noticed something appeared odd about Mama Lela. Then Mama Lela snapped on Twan in a drunken rant. She told him to stop trying to boss her around like one of his hoes and she only agreed to ho up to help him get on his toes. Also the fact that he was her only son left, and the only person she had, period. She told him then how he disrespected her from shoving his dick down her mouth in front of Ashley, embarrassing her, too. Twan wasn't trying to hear none of the above.

He waved her off and checked up on his FB status. It was a few friend requests of some fresh merch. Mainly all in the Midwest and down South. He also had 80 likes on his pics he posted from Meadows Mall. He grinned. It felt good just knowing that a pimp was trending. He needed to knock a virtual Vegas ho!

For 2 days now he had Ashley on Tinder. Tinder was a social site for locals to hook up for sex. He used the Tinder app in Ashley's phone to post more pics and catch more tricks. He needed to manipulate some dates to tell them they had to pay to play. Ashley wasn't ugly or all that but she still had sweet honey pot. He already set some dates up for Ashley later on. He went to get his neighbor Pimpin Silky, to take an old pimp out to the strip joint on Freemont. Mama Lela took a taxi somewhere. He didn't pay his crazy Mama no mind. She was 2 days away from Louisiana, because that's how long it'll take on the Greyhound to get back to BR.

Twan further manipulated Ashley's phone as he waited for Pimpin Silky to candy his nose and pick out a cranberry Kangol hat to cover his shiny bald spot. He had a hotel shelf full of them.

He swigged the rest of the Hennessy Black, trying to keep his head trauma pain down. He downloaded the Cuddler app to put Ashley on there, too. He always stayed sending and working ways for his hoes. The Cuddler was another social site for people who want to cuddle and spoon while posting pics. Of course Twan used that to his advantage to catch some dates for Ashley. He loved ho doe and tricks' money, because they were inflicted with the trick disease. Anyone who paid to get laid was sick and had mental issues. So Twan thought. Either way, he had passion for smashing and dragging a ho. He knew they weren't loyal, before Chris Brown.

"Man—P? Let's go!! See if we can peel some sucka's bitch. Hurry up, Peeling ain't Stealing! Don't tell me you gettin' too old and slippin on ya pimpin?" Twan said in a slick tone, heading out the room.

"P-Please...don't shit get old but clothes. Pimp don't get old or fold. It's always a new bitch and new doe. Most of all a new trick. I've really been pimpin since pimpin, since pimpin!! Shit, Young Twan, you really should be honored to be in a pimp's presence like me. A renowned Oakland finesse pimp! See how many P's and hoes know me than knowing you?? Lean back and learn something. Peep game and digg dat, you swampland Louisiana gator pimp!" Pimpin Silky replied slicker right back as he grinned with his eyes fully dilated, walking out the door right behind Twan. They strolled down Freemont, stalking the strip for prey and vics. It was already jumping and drug pumping. Hoes were out, pimps were out, and the dealers and fiends.

Twan saw a platinum Lexus come zipping by him, swerving side to side, and then hearing a light honk twice, the pimp way, the way of a pimp acknowledge pimps!!

He instantly noticed Jazabel, the Arab from Meadows Mall, then he saw Fatz da Mac with a cheesy shitface grin. Twan's eyes froze. His jaw stuck. Fuck! She done choose up! Orange is the new—pimp!! was all Twan thought. They were the only thoughts that sparked in his head. Instinctively he yelled the same thoughts and words Fatz da Mac ignited.

Pimpin Silky heard Twan and also knew Fatz da Mac dirty macking ass. Boy, he played it real dirty and had Scandinavian in his blood. Pimpin Silky saw Twan get crushed and face on stuck.

Twan tried to maintain his composure and keep it pimpin. But he felt his knees shaky, about to kiss the ground. Fucking around with Peeling ain't Stealing pimp got his lil Arab snatched. These hoes were out here on Freemont with nothing on. Twan could just smell the pussy in the October desert night cool air. And he wasn't about to be that big pussy that smells. It was nothing pussy about a pimp, besides the money he gets out of it. He couldn't show no emotional weakness. The whole Freemont was watching in one way or another. For those that the eye didn't catch, Freemont street talks.

They got across the street from the strip joint and saw Butterscotch and Pink Toe coming out of the liquor store. They both were wearing Hooter girl outfits except with orange mini-skirts. It had ass cheeks showcasing all out. These hoes in Vegas knew how to track attention! And not just a trick's attention, but police and thugs trying to train or take something.

Twan hit Pimpin Silky's chest twice, telling him those are Fatz hoes, as he darted across the street. The 2 hoes looked up as Twan came sprinting across Freemont with that look in his face. They dropped their Smirnoff bottles, busting them on the ground. They about-faced and grabbed each other's hands and ran frantically back inside the liquor store, screaming! Twan saw all pussycat, no thong or G-string. These hoes were really out here with no panties on. It made Twan slow his roll up and think. He would go in and snatch them up and break them, but this time put them on the squad. He saw they feared him and were already out of pocket, running and screaming. They had to choose now—choose a Southern BR pimp. He would give them a little time to come out before he went in and snatched them up. Plus he needed to wait for Peeling ain't Stealing to fully come across Freemont.

Two minutes later they entered into the liquor store and both of them chicken-shit hoes had escaped thru the back door. Damn it! Twan was heated and his head ached all over again. He copped some of that Freemont liquor store spice and a few grape blunt wraps.

Then they walked into the strip joint. He saw his lil Mamacita bartender Marissa working. Him and Pimpin Silky went to hug the bar. Marissa came from over the bar and hugged Twan as she sat on his lap. Then she handed him his lost phone that Fatz peeled. She didn't care who saw or if she got fired. Nor worrying about shit getting back to her baby dad in the Clark County Jail.

He had a bright smile sprinkled across his face, showing his 2 ratchett gold fangs. He was trying to stay in character in front of Pimpin Silky. He really wanted to tip the Mexican Mami. He asked her nonchalantly, how in the hell did she find his phone or get it back?

She went back behind the bar to service a few perverts and proceeded to tell Twan the story about how Fatz da Mac came in with some Arabian blonde hair and pewter-grayish eyes, bragging about how he macked and jacked a Mississippi pimp bitch! She automatically knew he was referring to Twan. Then somehow he dropped the phone under the bar stool right next to the pool table, where she found it at. Twan was amazed. He would continue to use Marissa and let her keep playing her position.

Then Twan started thinking of some getback on Fatz da Dirty Mac. And his head began to have a spiral effect. He couldn't help to stop thinking about Butterscotch and Pink Toe, Fatz's 2 out-of-pocket half-breed hoes. He had to put them in his pocket. Especially after hearing about all of Peeling ain't Stealing's infamous stories, too. He was turnt up!!

It was an art form to the luxury sport. He knew the power of the pussy concept that hoes like Butterscotch and Pink Toe abide by. They knew they had a gold mine between their legs and wanted to catch trick and vic a pimp. They wanted and needed protection. And they paid and used Fatz as a front man because he was more of a gorilla pimp, the type to knock a ho out to get her to go. He could see thru them 2 bum punk bitches. They were basically 2 renegade hoes in violation with a simp, a straight sucka impersonating Master Pimps. If these other P's knew the real deal, these hoes would be exiled from Freemont Street with a green light over their heads for any pimp to break and shake them hoes for everything on site.

Pimpin Silky introduced Twan to a few more of the older P's that made a career on Freemont and had hoes on both ends of the strip still. Twan was feeling Vegas and couldn't wait until he had his stable built back up, to set the strip on fire! He wanted to be seen and would make sure he was seen.

He took another free double shot on the rocks that Marissa hooked him and Peeling ain't Stealing up with. Twan was coaching Ashley thru the scene of this trick she found on Tinder. She caught a big fish. She already had been on one lock-in where the snowbunnies were peeling and stealing. They were robbing them rich white tricks coming to Vegas on those business trips away from their regions and wives to party and indulge drugs, alcohol, and kinky sex acts. Usually they didn't trip or complain when the girls ripped them off, nor call the police. They never wanted to expose their hands, especially with the "What happens in Vegas, stays in Vegas" mob mentality. Wouldn't no politician, professional athlete, or celebrity put themselves out there on blast.

He continued to coach Ashley thru his text messages, telling her to strip the penthouse suite wall to wall, jewelry and all. Normally he didn't allow his hoes to rob and peel tricks, but Vegas you had to, because they were playing with too much money. They would come from out of town on business ventures with $50-80k to play with and gamble off. Some hit big at the casinos and had them thousand-dollar chips lying around. Them purple chips and orange chips were the big-boy chips and eye-openers. All chips were accepted.

Ashley had been successful before with her little snowbunny. They went on a few missions together besides the lock-ins. However, Twan would let her go long as she came back successful and tear him off. Please don't sneeze or cough, ho, tear a pimp off!

Twan told Marissa thanks on behalf of him and Peeling ain't Stealing. They both were bubbly. Pimpin Silky had to snort a couple of lines to balance out the liquor. Twan watched him rush to the bathroom to candy his nose.

They walked down Freemont and posted up in the outside burger joint patio section when 3 goons in all black jumped out with navy-blue rags covering half of their faces.

"Cuz—Break y'all selves, pimps!! I ain't gonna tell you again, cuz… that's on 6-o Crip! I'll bust n leave you in the desert dust, stanky! Unt-uhh…Hell nawh, strip pimp. Shoes and socks off. Ya kno the drill!" the young gangbanger said in a menacing, vicious tone. His other goons checked their pockets and pelt them blind. Then they hemmed Twan up pinning him in the full Nelson lock while taking off his shoes and socks.

All Twan could think of, Damn, not now. And here we go again. At least it was dark and not broad daylight, like last time he got embarrassed and robbed back in a BR restaurant. They took him for everything. Pimpin Silky couldn't help to think that Twan was the blame of him getting robbed for the only $60 he had to his name.

The goons stripped them naked literally for all they had. Pimpin Silky was mad at young Twan and for being with him. Because everyone knew Pimpin Silky from Oakland on Freemont and they respected his pimpin.

"Peelin ain't Stealin—Aye, P! Aye, P, hold up. Shit, I got pelt, too. I took a bigger loss than you did. I seen them dubs. What's a couple of funky twenties? I—"

"Check game, you young ratchett Louisiana pimp!! I ain't goin out with you nowhere no more. They took my precious powder, too. You kno that's my main ho. I keep that white girl Hanna Montana. Now I can't even candy my nose. That's my pimp juice! Every pimp need sum juice to get they blood flowing and these bitches hoing. These lames and sucks ain't knowing. See y'all younger new era Millennium Lil Pimps just be off what y'all call that Diddy juice. Fuck sum damn Cîroc. Shit, I rather smoke some rocks, gott damn it, Twan! Fuckin with you," Pimpin Silky said, shaking his head after he cut Twan's ass off. He was heated and talking big boy shit to Twan the whole way back to the hotel room.

Twan didn't have nothing to do besides to wait to see how much Ashley twerked off of Tinder and whatever Mama Lela came back with. Either way he knew he wasn't totally on his ass. He'd be cashed out within hours. And he told Pimpin Silky he had him and would spot him a few dubs right back.

Pimpin Silky told Twan there wasn't no spot to it! He better have him, because it was his fault they got robbed in the first place. He warned Twan already that Vegas is a gun-friendly state and like the Wild Wild West. Them rolling 60's Crips is straight from LA and all they do is shoot up, kill up, and hold up stuff. All gas, no brakes. And that ol Crips saying is true they don't die, they multiply. Vegas PD will kill 2 of them during a bank robbery and high-speed chase and then 20 more will pop up straight from LA off the expressway. They usually gave Pimpin Silky a pass on Freemont. Truthfully they knew and could see he was just a washed-up, smoked-out older pimp. Pimpin Silky had a knock at the door.

- Chapter 5 -

"Las Vegas Blvd."

Jazabel had just come out of the Golden Nugget casino. She had been texting back and forth with Twan and kept sending him selfies. For some reason he seemed too excited and turnt up.

She was now walking down Las Vegas Blvd., the strip. She was waiting for Twan. He told her it would be a surprise and to be on the lookout for a platinum Lexus with clear windows. Also, he was about to take her out to a spot on Donna Street. And that to give him a few because he was on the I-15 coming from North Vegas.

Jazabel wasn't the average college girl or Middle Eastern. She was more American Westernized. She had grown up out here and being from Idaho, she already was hip and knew what time it was. She also knew Twan was more of a nonchalant type of guy. So he had to be either tipsy or off some type of drugs right now. She would only give him a few more minutes and then she was ghost. She hated the strip and all them damn dumb tourists. Vegas wasn't nothing new or special to her or any of the locals. She just took an interest to Twan for some peculiar reason. Maybe it was his 2 gold fangs. Nawh...She couldn't quite put a finger on it? Her mind was drifting in stars. She was in a daze as the desert sun beamed on her forehead. She flipped her Chanel frames down, shading her pewter-gray eyes, as she sighed out. She was out there and started heading back up Las Vegas Blvd. The strip was jam-packed like Times Square on New Year's Eve.

Where u at?

Leaving!!

Hold up!

Hold up what?

I'm pullin up da strip now.

I C U sexy.

They texted back and forth. 40 seconds later Jazabel saw the platinum Lexus with see-through windows pull up and stop in front of her. The passenger's door opened as he reached over opening it for her.

"Jazabel, get in, sexy. C'mon. I'm taking you to see Twan. It's a surprise," Fatz da Mac said in a convincing tone.

"Well, where is Twan at now? Let me text him and check with him first?" Jazabel replied, looking skeptical at Fatz. Then she picked up her phone and texted Twan real fast. Fatz da Mac went for Twan's smartphone and shot her a text real fast at the same time, too, while she had her head down. Soon as she sent the message she already had one coming in from Twan...

He's Gucci, sexy, Jazabel read the text while still looking up and down at Fatz big ratchett-looking ass. Maybe Twan was drunk after all and sent for her. He was a little too turnt up on his texts. So she sighed out a deep one, shrugged her shoulders against her better judgment, and sat in the passenger's side with a stranger.

Fatz da Mac had a shitface grin as he pelt off, burning rubber down the strip. He turned off Las Vegas Blvd. and headed to Freemont. Jazabel already felt uncomfortable. She asked Fatz could he please slow down and stop driving like a blind bat out of hell!! Then she sent Twan a text asking him about his out-of-control driver. This time he didn't text her right back. She assumed he didn't like the text or getting ready to surprise her. She snapped her safety belt on and reclined the seat back as she put the visor down to block the sun rays reflecting thru the front windshield. Fatz da Mack saw her buckling up and leaning her seat back. He hurried up and put Twan's smartphone on silent mode, so she wouldn't hear the texts coming through and figure him out. He didn't want to blow his cover and have her panic before he accomplished his mission.

They pulled up at the strip joint next to the liquor store on Freemont. Jazabel looked around and asked him, what the hell were they doing at a strip joint? She wasn't game to go in. She texted Twan, pissed off, asking WTF? Still no reply. Fatz yelled at the ho to get out the damn car and bring her ass into the joint. He told her stop acting all Spongebob Squarepants. Jazabel poked her lip out like a little kid and folded her arms as she stormed into the strip joint.

Jazabel stood there looking around for Twan with her arms folded. She had a stanky look on her face with her nostrils flared up from the smell of raunchy sweaty pussy and stale cigarettes mixed with blunts of Reggie Bush. She watched Fatz walk over to the bar and then signal for her to come over and join him. She stormed over to the bar and asked Fatz for the last time, "Where is Twan at?" Fatz da Mac told her to shut the hell up and sit her ass down on the bar stool. He demanded for Marissa the bartender to pour her a double shot on the rocks.

Marissa sat there and listened to all his stories he was showboating to the rest of the movers and shakers up in the joint. She knew Fatz was stunting and fronting, no doubt. Then she overheard Fatz talking to another pimp about how he snatched up Twan's Arabian ho. Then she noticed he kept receiving text messages and would just ignore them, until he just put the phone on the empty stool.

Jazabel was pissed, texting Twan with hate texts. She didn't know what type of time was he on or games he was playing but she wasn't playing no more or about to sit there and find out. She got up, grabbed her cell, and headed for the exit.

Fatz da Mac saw her trying to take off and gave the Mac he was talking to the pimp handshake and went chasing after her.

Marissa saw Fatz had left a smartphone on the stool and then quickly grabbed it and put it behind the bar. She had a feeling it probably was Twan's phone. If not, she would still give it to him and tell him to go down Freemont to get it flashed at the Hindu cellphone shop.

Fatz da Mac told Jazabel, his bad! And could he at least drop her back off because Twan was on some bullshit? Jazabel stopped in her tracks in the mention of Twan's name. She turned around, folded her arms, and sighed out, pissed off. She had enough and didn't want to mention Twan's name ever again. He had paid someone to pick her up and embarrassed her with a total stranger, then chose to ignore all her texts and calls. She had enough and was done with Twan, period.

She told Fatz to take her back to Las Vegas Blvd. to pick up her car. Her car was in the casino hotel parking lot right off the strip. So as they pulled off down Freemont, she felt the whole car swerve from left to right as Fatz tapped the horn twice. She looked up and saw Twan with some older man that looked like an alcoholic. Twan stared at her in a state of shock. He had a puzzled look on his face. Something didn't seem right at that point. She immediately told Fatz to stop! She needed to talk to him right now. She started swinging on Fatz and screaming for him to let her out!!

He swatted her off and bent the corner wildly just as Vegas PD pulled out of the QT parking lot. They instantly hit their cherries and gave chase. Fatz wouldn't stop. He was nervous because he was a felon with a Glock 26 handgun in the glove box. He told Jazabel to say the gun was hers and to put it inside of her purse. Jazabel shook her head like, hell no! She saw additional units joining the pursuit.

She was shook and told Fats, okay, she would say the gun is hers and to just stop, please. Fatz didn't seem too sold on it and killed the rest of his drink in his red cup. He heard the Vegas police sirens blaring and chirping as he swerved in and out through busy traffic going 60 mph. Half a minute later he heard the police chopper above. He was headed for the I-15 in attempts to go into the deep parts of North.

"Okay—O-kay!! I'll put the gun into my bag. Just give it to me and pull over before you kill somebody or both of us," Jazabel shouted frantically.

As Fatz somehow believed her and reached for the glove box, he got rammed on the left rear corner panel by the squad car, causing him to do a maneuver and swerve out of control right into a white mini-van, sideswiping it. It was full of casino acts.

Jazabel screamed, then the tire blew out as she heard a loud *BOOM!!* then a vicious smack sound as they crashed into the pole. There was glass everywhere and all in her hair.

The Las Vegas PD drew down their service weapons on both of them and rushed the car, demanding their hands up. Fatz was dazed still from the impact. Jazabel had her hands high out the window, screaming she had been kidnapped from Las Vegas Blvd. and didn't know Fatz. Also he had a gun in the glove department.

They snatched Fatz out of the platinum Lexus thru the driver window. He was tussling with the Vegas PD until they tazed his fat ass like some bacon. They arrested him and seized the gun. He was headed to Clark County Jail. Jazabel was still in tears being questioned. She couldn't believe it.

* * *

Twan entered into the hotel room, exhausted. He had just left Pimpin Silky's room after their long night and loss. The room was pitch black but he knew something was out of place. It was different! A different smell? He smelt warm sweet pussy with a Beyoncé fragrance, too. He didn't hear the usual snoring of Ashley and Mama Lela from a super long and rough night.

He was curious to see what was new to his ho. He stepped quietly over some bags to the vanity mirror to cut on the bathroom lights.

Click! "Damn it, Twan! We just got in and out the shower. Boy, cut that damn light back off!" Mama Lela shouted, half asleep.

However, Twan cheesed ear to ear from the lovely silhouette of the duo on his bed. It definitely wasn't Ashley. The half-breed bitch was squinting as she shielded her baggy eyes from the bathroom light.

"Unt-uhh…hell nawh—Lela, I told you we don't do no pimps. And I thought you didn't have a pimp. Now you trying to get us in trouble?" the half-breed bitch said, awaking and startling her bestie.

"I don't have no damn pimp! I told y'all about my son? Twan? He be trying to pimp. Y'all all good," Mama Lela said nonchalant.

Twan smirked at her. He instantly knew who they both were, and they recognized him. It was Fatz's hoes. They both were butt naked with clean shaved bald pussy.

They both got up and scrambled to their feet for their clothes and heels while trying to run away from Twan. Twan pushed both of them hoes back down on the bed as they covered up with the scrunched-up pieces of clothes over their exposed parts. Twan then ran over and blocked the door. He told them they were out of pocket and to call Fatz da Mac.

They were scared and looking over at Mama Lela to bail them out and save them. She told Twan to leave them girls alone and that they were her new little friends. Twan told his Mama, Bullshit. They had him set up, jacked and pistol-whipped. Then he kicked her out the room, telling her to go over to Pimpin Silky's room for a hot minute. He at least needed an hour with these bitches. Mama Lela saw he was serious about getting to the bottom of it. However, Twan had something else in mind. These hoes weren't leaving or taking the easy route out. They were about to break themselves once again and respect his pimpin.

Soon as Mama stormed out the door, Twan got right on both of the naked shaking hoes. They were both hugging each other, scared as hell. They thought Twan was about to kill them. Twan told them to text Fatz da Mac and tell him he needed $1500 apiece for each ho's bail. So 3 racz total.

Ten whole minutes went by without no answer or reply. Twan rolled up a blunt and poured both the girls drinks.

"See, I told y'all that fat-ass bastard ain't bout shit or a real pimp! He ain't trying to pay y'all bond. Or maybe you 2 hoes together is lazy and not worth shit? Especially 3 racz? We started off on the wrong feet. Y'all in my bed sleeping butt naked and using my shower. Why don't y'all got y'all own room? It's plenty of tricks down Freemont. I got an ugly duckling bitch on Tinder and up and down Freemont. Y'all been out of pocket. Now y'all out of bounds. Stop crying, bitch! It's time to pay the pimp piper. Now choose up, ho up, or blow up," Twan stated firmly.

Butterscotch wiped her teary eyes dry and scooted forward on the bed. Pink Toe spread-eagled, busting it open for Twan, showing off her pretty pink pussy and the glistening pearly pink insides. Twan's dick jumped in anticipation. It was crazy it was a thought of Neese that flashed thru his head. It was something bout Pink Toe. He tried to shake the thought of Neese off. He couldn't be tender-dicking and pimpin.

Butterscotch cat-crawled slowly, then grabbed her iPhone 6. She played Nicki Minaj's "Anaconda." She started pulling him toward the bed and unbuckling his Versace belt and pulling down his silk Versace boxers.

Twan sat down on the bed as Butterscotch slobbered all over his dick slick and began to massage his shaft, sucking hearts around his dick. Her popping and smacking noises were enough to drive a sane man ape shit!!

Then Pink Toe got up, touching her toes, spreading both her ass cheeks from the back, showing off some more of her sweet pink wet crevices. She wanted Twan to see all of it. Then she started making her booty roll as she squatted with both hands on her knees, sleazy. Then she placed her hand on the ground and flipped up against the hotel wall on a handstand and started to twerk her ass slowly and softly.

Twan just stared at her soft Jello ass making small subtle waves like the 7 seas. He knew this dynamic duo did this before and was probably one of their several routines that they performed. He knew they were trying to make him lose his mind or blow his mind. Not just to please him but to keep him wanting more. It was something about Pink Toe, though? Or maybe just about the way or just petite frame and phatty. She had an apple bottom with a small 19-inch waist which made her shaped like a bee. Uugghh...

He had to keep it pimpin no matter what. Pink Toe got up and ran over to her Coach handbag and fished out her Mollys. She gave him a capsule with powder substance in it. She opened hers up, sprinkled it on Butterscotch's extended tongue, and the rest on his hard dick.

She licked it off Twan's head and flicked her tongue around in figure-8 circles. Then she licked the rest off Butterscotch's tongue, French-kissing her as they both French-kissed Twan's dick and began to fight with their tongue and mouth over it, until they started taking turns. Twan hurried up and popped the Molly, dry-swallowing it. Fuck it, he thought. It was going down for sure. This would probably be the best threesome yet. Because these 2 hoes knew tricks he never seen.

Butterscotch's head game was way better than Pink Toe. It was phenomenon and killing Pink Toe's head game. Pink Toe could see Twan's toes curling up every time it was Butterscotch's turn on the D.

So she grabbed Twan's shaft, jealous, and mounted herself raw right on top of him. She sat right down slowly on Twan's dick. She began to ride Twan wildly up and down and swerving side to side on the D! Just like a Brazilian porn star. Twan couldn't believe how her petite ass could take dick oh so well. He was letting out some manly moans as she played with and massaged his balls rapidly. She reversed cowgirl and bent all the way forward, sucking Twan's toes while still riding him. He saw all phat ass cheeks only.

Butterscotch climbed on the bed and began to lick his balls, flickering her tongue ring all around them. She got a taste of Pink Toe's sweet pussy juices and went ham!! She began to eat her asshole out and spreading her ass cheeks wide apart, which caused Pink's pace to decrease.

Pink Toe's body started to tremble as her pussy began to contract. Twan felt her getting wetter and pussy walls collapsing down around his dick. She definitely at the point of no return. She was cumming and Butterscotch was freaking her to the max, no doubt. He watched as Butterscotch spit and slobbered all on her asshole, then worked her thumb in and out of her ass.

Pink Toe's legs shook like she was having a seizure. Then Twan felt a hard gush of wetness come rushing down all over his lap and legs. It felt like someone busted a water balloon down on his lap. Pink Toe screamed in ecstasy and began to whimper as she panted out of breath.

Butterscotch took Twan's dick out of Pink Toe hot creamy pussy and inserted it slowly in her asshole. Pink Toe moaned and began to throw it back, slowly working Twan's dick to that Nicki Minaj mixtape iTune.

Next thing Twan noticed Butterscotch took it out and put it in her mouth! She was bopping up and down on it while making direct eye contact with Twan. She took it out her mouth and stuffed it slowly right back into Pink Toe's ass. She did that a few more times until Twan couldn't take no more and exploded.

Pink Toe felt Twan's shaft throbbing in her ass. Knowing he was about to bust, she quickly turned around and gobbled down on Twan's dick, catching all of Twan's salty little babies. Butterscotch wanted to get some. She needed a taste. Twan only had a squirt left. She wanted to swallow some babies and blow his mind, too. That bitch Pink Toe always trying to outshine her and compete with her. She was pulling them same stunts trying to impress Fatz, too. Fuck that, though. She was about to get Twan back up and running. He was off that Molly, too. It was her time to ride his country ass even if her pussy wasn't as tight and sweet as Pink Toe's was. She went to work rubbing his balls and flicking both her tongue rings around his dickhead.

"What the fuck?? Oh hell nawh! Twan? Daddy, what the fuck? Who is these bitches? I got $1800 for you sucking and fucking, but I can't get absolutely no dope dick from you!! Now I find you freaking these 2 light-skinned Vegas hoes who I can't stand in my bed? Muthafucka, you better be drunk, Twan. They gotta go else I'm gone. Well, Twan, say something," Ashley said, whining.

The 2 half-breed hoes continued to really put on a show while giving Ashely 2 devilish grins. Twan just looked at her on stuck mode. That Molly had Twan. He was rolling hard and on Pluto. He was gone and couldn't talk or move if he wanted to.

Ashley busted out in a full-fledged cry, then threw the stack of funky money at Twan's head and ran out the hotel room barefooted, crying and shouting, "Fuck you, Twan!!"

Twan couldn't be mad; lose one ho and gain two more hoes. It was the name of it. Besides, he knew Ashley would come running back. Mama Lela popped up next, hearing all the commotion. She couldn't believe her son. Twan and them 2 scandalous ass hoes were having a damn orgy. She started cursing Twan out and telling his hoes to get out now.

He couldn't quite put his finger on it but something was out of place with his Mama Lela. He saw her angry like this before back in Baton Rouge. He knew she was emotional because Ashley was like a daughter to her now. Mama Lela slammed the hotel door after she threw some drink on the trio. She splashed them with the red cup, but they all still didn't stop! She went back to Pimpin Silky's room.

Ashley was gone for the next whole day. Twan done seen her disappearing act before. She wasn't cold at pulling stunts, though. He got the 2 half-breeds some $750 Greek goddess lingerie outfits.

Twan heard the news all on Freemont about Fatz da Dirty Mac getting booked. He caught a frivolous case, the dumb dummy. Fuck him and Jazabel faggot ass, was the way Twan really felt. That's why he had both Fatz's half-breed hoes. And he was sending them for sure and smashing on them for real. They were getting his doe. He set them down on the real strip, Las Vegas Blvd. They would work in and out of the casinos and hotels on the strip. They looked like locals and call girls. They were in and out quick on their toes despite being in 6inch clear stilettos. They brought stealthiness to the strip. That Freemont mentality. Twan called it that shake-shake like a pitt shit! He would tell them both shake-shake and twist his body or torso side to side while standing in place. He looked just like a pimp doing a touchdown dance. But it wasn't the dirty birdy victory dance. It was more of the bitch-go-get-them dance.

He named them officials what he called them when he first crossed their path at the Hindu liquor store that first night after the crazy ménage-à-trois. Them hoes went the extra mile and brought back damn near $2800 apiece.

Twan was standing in front of the Flamingo casino when he saw a tall, 6 ft. Japanese ho in stilettos come click-clacking past him and jump into a Bentley. Twan looked in the Bentley coupe and saw a super-young nigga with a blonde mohawk looking like Roscoe Dash. He stared back at Twan, smirked, and flashed his deuces brief like a pimp! Twan recognized it and greeted him back with a head nod. Then the Bentley smashed out.

He sat there looking at the young nigga stunting on the strip. He was clowning hard. Twan checked some bread from Pink Toe. She had been trying to be closest to him. She thought she was slick by saying she was scared to hold too much doe on her because how little she was and the fact she could get robbed on the strip or by a trick. Twan wasn't worried about no damn tricks because they were too busy worrying about paying to play. Them perverted sickos needed their fantasy fulfilled. Most of them tourists came to Vegas to trick off or fuck off their money. Either way it was to party and play. Viva Las Vegas is all Twan thought.

Awwhh...Man—it felt good to be a pimp in Vegas and winning. Twan knew pimps were trending. He took a selfie of his doe. He had 10 racz on his lap with a Gucci link and some red-bottom boots. He posted it straight to his Instagram account. He wanted to flex on them suckas and try to catch a bitch. He also hit his FB app and posted an identical selfie on his wall. Except this time he held his left icy pinky ring finger up, showing his chunky rocks bling-blinging.

He took the taxi cab to Berkley Square, 10 miles from the strip, to buy some of that Blue Dream kush. This whiteboy had a medical dispensary out of Cali and Arizona. Butterscotch turned him on to dude. That's where Fatz would get all his kush from, too.

Utt-ooo...His FB page was jumping. He already had 12 messages in his inbox by the time he came out of the connection spot. He loved new merch! It was fresh game and all these hoes had to pay a pimp!!! In his eyes everybody was a vic, he was trying to vic the whole world just like Kendrick Lamar says.

He caught a taxi from Berkley Square back to the strip. Butterscotch texted him to pick her up from a trick spot on Donna Street. He had the cab detour.

Butterscotch jumped in with gold glitter all over her body. She smelt like old whiskey and Cuban cigars. Twan cracked the window. She broke him off with $800. The money was sweaty and moist. He didn't want know where it came from, even though he saw her pull it from her titties.

Twan looked at his tweets pouring. Twitter was going berserk. T.I. had stole on Floyd Money Mayweather and it was a brawl at the burger joint around the corner from them right now. He couldn't believe it. He promised himself he'd go to Mayweather Boxing Gym and personally meet Mayweather and shake a million knockout artist's hand. He knew Money's team ran Vegas. Now he was 44-1. T.I. crazy ass broke his flawless record. All over his wife, Tiny. Twan wasn't mad at TIP cuz he knew how that feeling was. He murked N.O. for Neese and shooting his baby mama, Diamond Cutz.

Soon as Twan and Butterscotch got back on Las Vegas Blvd., he saw that same youngin in that Bentley coupe shining. This time some tall snowbunny with platinum-blonde hair and red fishnet bodysuit came running out the Mandalay Bay casino.

Twan saluted him and the youngin acknowledged each other and he smashed off again. Then Butterscotch began to give him the rundown.

"Daddy, that's young J Pimp. He from out of Portland, Oregon, and only 17 years old. He used to be on Freemont a couple months back at the strip joint, trying to buy bitches from Fatz's ass—"

"Okay, bitch, did I ask you for the rundown? Get out of pocket even further and watch me embarrass your yellow ass even more out here in front of the whole strip! How you kno I ain't trying to sic you on him, huh? Now shut ya ass up, bitch, and get in the casino, bitch!" Twan snapped back as he cut Butterscotch off.

Butterscotch was half-Asian and black. Her mother was Asian, originally from Vietnam, and her dad was from California. He was in the service and they moved out to Vegas when she was 10 years old. Her dad moved back to Cali after his term in the service was up. Shortly after he filed for divorce, leaving her Mama for a white lady. He didn't want too much to do with Butterscotch or her Mama, either.

She met Pink Toe in middle school and they'd been besties ever since. They would ditch school together, go to parties, drink, and sneak into casino clubs together. They even both lost their virginity at the same time.

Pink Toe was half-white and black. Her mama was an exVegas showgirl who now was an old washed-up drunk. Both of the girls wouldn't listen to nor honor a word they say. Pink Toe had been pregnant twice and

Butterscotch had 4 different abortions since high school. They couldn't afford to bear responsibilities to a child. They were too busy ripping and running up and down the strip, chasing dope. They got turned out on coke and started snorting a mile a minute, which led to them turning their first tricks themselves.

Twan didn't know much of their stories, but knew they both go, though. He was anticipating sending Butterscotch to the Penthouse strip joint club back in New Orleans, right in the French Quarter. She could do private shows and still dance. It wasn't too much about the money, because she could make that right here in Vegas. It was more about splitting the double duo up. He figured he could push Pink Toe to a whole new level. He could pimp harder on her without jealous-ass Butterscotch in her ear. It was clear that Butterscotch was the more dominant alpha female. He knew it was time to break them up.

Twan was lost in his thoughts. He always thought pimp, though. When he received a text from Ashley astray ass, she asked him, where was he at? And if he still had them 2 light-skinned dirty hoes around that she caught him making love to. After he chose to ignore the text message and look away, it sent Ashley in a further downward spiral. She texted him again, telling him she had $500 from today and $800 from the other night.

Twan quickly replied, telling her he was at the hotel on the strip and to just meet him inside the Mandalay casino. He had to catch the elevator downstairs. He had on his Gucci loafs with an open chest Versace gold shirt. Twan didn't care if he mixed-match designers. He was styling and profiling while keeping it pimpin. You couldn't tell him he was ratchett. Twan wasn't just pimp of the ratchetts, he was king of the ratchetts.

He had to shake Butterscotch at the hotel room. He told her to get back to work. It was a big international convention in Vegas right now. It was tricks from London, Germany, Spain, Brazil, Japan, and the islands. His hoes were making good lucci right now just off the land, working the casinos and busy hotels. It was tricks checking in by the hundreds. Las Vegas Blvd. was alive and a breeding ground. The crazy part was it wasn't even dark yet and going bananas. He knew soon as dusk hit, them strip lights definitely would glow in the dark, signaling tricks for partytime booze and hookers—escorts. That would be the time when all international business meetings would come to an end and all the big Microsoft executives ready to spin.

Twan waited around the casino, trying his luck at the craps table. He would down shot after shot. He was bubbly and losing money. Straight fucking money off. He could throw dice right now. All of sudden Ashley texted him, *I'm here.* He texted her back, *Come to the craps table in the rear of the casino.*

Ashley popped up with her eyes all bugged out, looking in all directions for them 2 light-skinned skanks. She wasn't going to build up enough strength to call Twan on it and fight for her man! Twan was all she knew. She didn't care that he called himself a pimp! He was her pimp only. Then she noticed Twan's slow dragged movements. He was definitely bubbly. He smelt like heavy liquor all on his pours.

She handed him a fistful of cash. Twan snatched it and half stuffed it in his pocket effortlessly, either like he didn't care or it wasn't nothing. She took it as it didn't matter like he was sick and disgusted with her. She flipped out and started cursing him out and swatting all the chips out his hand. They immediately called casino security, escorted them both out front.

Twan snapped right out of his drunken slumber and snatched Ashley black ass up. He roughhoused her around the tourist-packed front walk. Then he threw her frail ass to the ground. Twan saw the same Bentley in the corner of his eye. Then Butterscotch came running down the strip. She just turned a big trick. She gave some old guy from France head for $500 proudly. It took her all of 10 minutes max. She couldn't wait to sock it to Twan's pocket. She knew Pink Toe was his favorite ho. Before she could maneuver fully thru the tourist-packed strip, she saw the same girl from Freemont, the one that busted in the hotel on them, freaking Twan.

Then she saw the black girl wrap her arms around him and Twan push her back off of him. She hurried up and took her heels off. She pulled her long silky hair back and quickly wrapped it in bun. It was on and popping like Chris Brown sang. She was going in! She was about to put on a show for Twan and make him into a believer.

J Pimp was sitting in his Bentley coupe, listening to Future Honest CD.

"Pimps up—Pimps up…Hoes down!! Gotta lot guns but u ain't popped nothing!!" Future rapped thru the speakers as J Pimp fixed his $1800 Louis Vuitton frames, looking in the rearview mirror. He had his black leather skinnys on with $2500 red-bottom soles. He looked around for his Asian ho. What was taking this bitch so long? He scanned thru the crowd for his silly long-leg Asian ho, with her goofy ass. This was her second time being late today.

All of a sudden J Pimp seen a stiletto flying wildly and 2 hoes locked up cat-fighting on the strip. The stiletto got bloody real quick. The light-skinned girl was cracking it upside the dark-skinned skinny girl's head and face as she held a fierce grip of her hair. All he heard was, "Help!!! Helppp!!" over the Future playing in the coupe. Then he saw that same Mississippi-looking pimp moving all slow. Security rushed out of the casino and sirens could be heard blaring down the strip.

J Pimp was shaking his head, texting his Asian ho. These dumb duck hoes knew better, not on the strip. It would attract heat. Everybody knew what's going on up and down the strip and it's not just gambling. Security was breaking up the fight and Twan was trying to make a run for it, but them double shots of Pineapple Cîroc had him moving chopped and screwed. Just as the goofy Asian propped open the door and sat in, Twan pushed her out of the way and jumped in the back seat.

Twan just didn't know J Pimp would bust that thang in a millisecond. He had his Sig .40 cal under his left leg on his seat. But J Pimp knew the bizz and that Twan wasn't from Vegas or the West Coast. Niggas had heat out here. Even the pimps kept missiles.

"Aye...P—I need cha right now, young pimpin. I need some aid and assist real quick to get me up out of here before one of my hoes tell and have me in one of these Vegas jails," Twan said, exhausted, panting like a German Shepherd off of a *Cops* episode.

"Man—don't trip, pimpin. Stay low. I got cha! I'm J Pimp from Portland. Bitch, shut up all that scream fore I put you out this Bentley. Ya dumb Chinese ass had me out here waiting for the second time today, ho. I'm putting ya Chinese ass on a tofu or cat food diet, ho! Pimpin, she might like da chow-mein shit! Man, P, I see you got trouble in paradise fucking with them duck bitches! I'm bout to show you all the ropes and back routes of Vegas. I only been out here 3 months and I'm 17, P! You can rent these Bentleys and Maybachs off the strip or hit for over 100 racz on the casino black card. I'll put you up on G!" J Pimp said boastfully. Him and Twan rolled around all night chopping.

- Chapter 6 -

"Ratchettness"

Mama Lela dropped the towel from around her waist. She still had helluva ass and it still had its rounded shape. She was still dripping wet fresh out of the shower. She had just finished up a long night on Freemont. She had lowered her standards now for some reason. She was turning tricks at crackhead prices, $20 and $30. She had given head for $20 4 times that night.

She had been staying over at Pimpin Silky's room, right next door from their room. Ever since that night Twan told her to go over to Peelin ain't Stealin's spot, kicking her out to turn out the 2 half-breed hoes. However, Pimpin Silky turned her back out by candying powder up her nose.

Pimpin Silky would give her line after line. After awhile she couldn't take it. It was more like a tease to her. She would go rock it up over the lighter and with a spoon and tab of baking soda. She would freebase it, too. Pimpin Silky didn't know no better and Twan didn't want his Mama back on that shit. Especially how smoked out she'd get and start clucking off everything, including all his shit. Then Vegas was out of her element. At least back at Baton Rouge she knew her environment. Pimpin Silky would offer anybody a line. This was Vegas and coke was a social drug out here, just like weed was everywhere else. He even offered Twan a few lines several times before.

Once Mama Lela realized both of Pimpin Silky's white hoes were gone, she got down on her knees after dropping her towel. She tooted her ass up and wiggled it from side to side as she proceeded to give Pimpin Silky a vicious blow job.

He couldn't believe how ridiculous her head game was. The smacking and popping noises were the cherry on top. She was doing the most! Then she took out her crack pipe, loaded it, and sparked it to life.

She knew Pimpin Silky was more of a sack pimp and controlled all the local dope fiends that turned tricks to go cop some dope from him. Silky just couldn't let go or get out of the game. He was no longer in his prime, but you couldn't tell him that shit. He slapped his furry white Kangol hat on to cover up his bald spot and started smacking her ass super hard, telling her to get it—get it!! She started twisting her neck sideways and yanking hard on it. It was all neck and wrist action. He threw his head and hands back.

"My mama ain't raised no ho—My mama ain't raise no ho!! These niggas ain't got no ho—These niggas kicking down doors!!" The Future blasted thru the Bentley coupe. Twan was bubbly. He had been riding up, down, and around the strip with J Pimp for a couple of hours now. They both were bubbly. Twan thought at first J Pimp had him around so he could buy his underage ass liquor, but his hoes were all of age. He still had the tall, lanky Chinese ho riding shotgun. Twan didn't mind, he didn't have to shine or be seen. It was J Pimp's time to shine. He didn't want to steal it. He just picked J Pimp's brain and sipped the Pineapple Cîroc all night.

"Roof-roof!! Arrrr..." the pint-size teacup Yorkshire Terrier barked at Twan's feet. Twan jumped, spilling his Cîroc all over his lap. The Chinese ho started laughing and calling out for the Yorkie pup.

"Aye, P, that's my fault, that's my Yorkie pup. I call him Tea, pimp. My Chinese ho bought it for me, but for some reason he scared of her ass, thinking she might eat him, my guess. But we pulling up at the hotel, P! Twan, you got the iPhone number. Shoot me a text when you want to chop and pop at some fresh game and new merch. Chuchh..." J Pimp said.

"Chuch—P!" Twan replied and they did the pimp shake. No fingerprints, no evidence.

Twan texted Pink Toe. She told him that Butterscotch was in Clark County Jail and she needed $1500, 10 percent of $15,000, to post her bond. And that Ashley was in the hospital getting her face and head stitched up. Twan texted her back telling her, So what?! And he don't got it and to bring her ass back to the Freemont spot.

He went to Pimpin Silky's room and knocked on the door. He heard Peelin ain't Stealing say come in!

Pimpin Silky normally didn't leave his room door unlocked, but how sudden Mama Lela put it on him, he said, fuck it. And even if LVPD ran up in his room, they would only get a couple of grams anyway. He thought it was one of his goofy white hoes coming to spend with him again.

Twan opened the door and walked in on his Mama Lela hitting the crack pipe and blowing crack smoke out all over Pimpin Silky's dick! She just kept going at it in her crack trance, high as hell, zoned out! Twan wigged out! They had priors since Twan was back home in middle school. He had been to jail a couple times before for domestic violence, but Mama Lela never showed up for trial.

"Oh hell nawh…Bitch, you back smoking dat shit, huh? C'mon here—"

"Ahhh…Boy—Twan, stop, s-stop it! Get off me!!" Mama Lela yelled, cutting her son off and trying to release his monster grip of her hair.

"Shut-up, you crackhead bitch! I should've known better. Mama or not! You still a dope fiend and I can't trust you—now go pack up all ya lil shit and take ya ass back to BR with that cluckhead shit!" Twan shouted, turnt up as he smacked his Mama Lela around the face hard while pushing her out of Silky's room butt-ass naked.

"Fuck you, Twan—I'm grown! I hate ya selfish ass! Ppeww!" Mama Lela screamed and spit Pimpin Silky's pre-cum in Twan's face!

Twan wiped his face, turned around, and rushed Pimpin Silky viciously.

Bing-Pow! Pow-Bing! He caught Silky with a jab right, a hook, and then another left hook, then a stiff straight right hand, dropping Silky. Silky was sprawled out on the bed leaking. He spit out blood and his front tooth. He was telling young Twan, "What the fuck?" and, "Hold up—hold up!!"

"Shut up, nigga! You giving Mama dope, turning her back on to dat monkey on her back so she can turn tricks for ya ol washed-up ass! I thought we was Gucci. But I kno dis Vegas," *Bing-Pow-Pow!* Twan said in a menacing tone as he fed Pimpin Silky with another 3 piece combo.

"Aawwhh…Shit, okay! O-okay, Pimp, you killing me, man. Okay, young P. My bad—my bad, man!!" he screamed for his life. He couldn't take it no longer. Twan was all on top of his head, stinging him like some damn killer bees.

Mama Lela ran in butt naked, screaming for Twan to stop and leave him alone as she jumped on his back, scratching and hitting him with the side of her fist wildly.

Pink Toe jumped out the taxi and saw Pimpin Silky's door all open up wide and heard the big commotion. She heard Mama Lela yelling and Silky screaming like a little girl. Then she saw all 3 of them rolling around scuffling on the hotel floor, then noticed Mama Lela was butt naked in a full-out brawl. WTF, she thought with her mouth wide open. She knew this was some awkward shit. However, out in Vegas this family domestic shit didn't fly. The LVMPD would take the whole house to jail around here.

"D-Daddy—Hey!! Twan! Daddy, y'all got to stop before the cops come. Y'all not in Louisiana no more, this is Vegas. Twannn, STOP! Let's go. He ain't worth going to Clark County for. Trust me, I been there, Daddy!" Pink Toe pleaded for a brief moment but she thought it fell on deaf ears because Twan was still tussling with Silky and Mama Lela. Everybody was all entwined, doing the gator roll. She shook her head and ran to get the cold bucket of ice and filled it up quick. She was about to give them a cold dose of the ice bucket challenge. *Splash-Splash!!*

Everybody lost their breath and Mama Lela naked ass was the first one to let go and get up. Then Twan jumped up and looked down at his shirt and chased Pink Toe around the parking lot. He was fired up. She ran into their room and soon as Twan ran in, she slammed the door. Mama Lela went back over to Pimpin Silky's room just as the Vegas cops pulled into the parking lot. Twan didn't care where she went but she couldn't come back here or around Freemont. She better get back on that Greyhound bus. Really she went to hit that pipe again. Her and Silky played possum as Vegas PD flashed their spotlight on their room, looking around. They knocked on the door to do a health and welfare check. They stayed there for an additional 15 minutes, knowing Silky was playing possum. He wasn't asleep and had priors at the same spot. They received a call and peeled out to the strip.

Pink Toe was pleading with Twan after she calmed his ass down. She knew he was faded and she smelt the Cîroc all over him. It was on his breath and steaming thru his pores, too. She gave him the $700 she made for the rest of the day and told him, can they please get her bestie Butterscotch out of jail? He told her, hell no! And she can stay her dumb ass right there to think about what she did. She took money out his pockets in both ways and injured one of his hoes, then almost took him down in the middle of it. She waited till Twan passed his bubbly ass out and went to find a bail bondsman who she could do some sexual favors for on call to get her bestie Butterscotch out anyways. Twan was just going to be mad, but she will take a slapping around or being kicked square up her ass to get her bestie out that ho cage full of all them other stanky-skanky cracked-out hoes. You couldn't cage no ho and lock her down. It goes with the old saying, you can't turn a ho into a housewife because she needs to spread her legs and play to pay.

Ashley got released from the Northeast Vegas Hospital at 5 a.m. She was groggy and stitched all up like the Zipperman himself. She was walking away from the hospital with her pumps in her hand, barefooted. The Vegas sun was barely peeking so she didn't have to worry about the hot desert concrete punishing her feet again.

By the time she arrived back at the hotel on Freemont, to her surprise a snoring Twan was passed out solo. Where were his 2 light-bright hoes?

One went to booking but where was her hooker in crime—Pink Toe? She didn't notice any signs of Mama Lela, either. She sent her a quick text, asking her where she at this early. She texted back quickly saying, Leaving! And she was staying with Pimpin Silky next door until she got her train ticket back to BR. Ashley was lost. She cleaned up around the room, washed up, and crashed out next to Twan butt naked. She needed to hug him and feel affection even if it was coming from her giving it out in false hopes to quench her thirsty desire of affection.

J Pimp got a text from ol Pimpin Silky, one of his old pimp partners from Freemont. He laced J Pimp's gator Air Force Ones up a couple months when he was new to Vegas, too. He told J Pimp that he was just a mere sneaker pimp—a tennis shoe pimp! He told J Pimp even though he was young, he was still in Las Vegas, Nevada, and these people and places will eat his ass alive. The strip was brutal and it was more to it than the bright flashing lights. After the long talk and a few nights of some rundowns, he broke J Pimp of all his young mind millennium-thinking flaws. He woke J Pimp up. Now he was alert and saw what was this pimpin really about. And thanks to Silky, he stepped his game all the way up and started smashing extra hard on his hoes non-stop. All gas, no brakes!!

He knew he owed Silky one so he would keep in contact and swing thru the old strip joint to check on him. He sat in the jacuzzi on the 15th floor of the Palms hotel luxury suite like he was Scarface with his snowbunny and Chinese ho washing him up like he was a little baby. They were holding his arms and scrubbing between them hard and roughly.

"Damn—Gentle, ho! I'm a pimp! What's the matter with this Chinese ho?? My bad, Pimpin! Silky, whatz Gucci? You straight, P?" J Pimp asked with a squeaky voice. Pimpin Silky could hear the cracks in his voice as his manly voice was starting to mature.

"Hey—young blood! Yeah, I'm good, P! I just needed you to talk to that ratchett ass pimp Twan ass from Baton Rouge. He just don't get it. Meet me at the spot or pull up on me later tonight at the strip joint, pimp? And remember it's all on a ho—Chuchhh..." Pimpin Silky said in a raspy tone. He seemed burned out.

"Chuchh!!" J Pimp replied in a high-pitched squeaky tone.

Later that day Twan got a message from J Pimp after he met up with Silky. Silky laced J Pimp up about his Mama Lela, the ass-whooping, and the dope-smoking. J Pimp was all in and was about to keep it pimpin. Pimps didn't fight or shoot unless it was very necessary. Pimps hated jail and couldn't stand police confrontations at all.

Twan jumped in the Bentley coupe. J Pimp still didn't turn it in yet. It better not be hot and stolen, was all Twan thought as J Pimp smashed off down the strip. This time Twan rode shotgun. He never saw a pimp with a Mohawk, and a blonde one at that, or a pimp in skinny jeans. The boy had on practically tights, some Wiz Khalifa pants. He doubted they were real Versace because he never saw them in the Vegas Versace store. Unless he got them literally out of the woman's section? He just shook his head and sipped on the bottle of Diddy Juice, his pimp juice. He passed it to young ass J Pimp and warned him not to wreck the Bentley coupe.

"So whatz really Gucci, young J Pimp?" Twan asked, puzzled.

"Man—P! I-I mean it ain't shit...I just wanted to lace ya up with some game and FYI. I already know you well seasoned in and out, but P, it don't work out here like it do in ya city or back home. Just like Eugene,

Oregon, and Portland don't operate the same. Shit dat fly here don't fly anywhere else in the States, ya digg? I'm trying to tell you fuck them lil duck bitches you have. Lose them ratchett hoes and really get paid, my nucca, get paid, P! Them hoes is trouble and going to be ya downfall. It's many great pimps that had full potential that fell short of his pimp dreams. Them penitentiaries and graves is packed with them, knocking them out of a career and right in their prime. A black ho is problems, P! A dark ho bring a dark cloud. Trust and know that. P, I love my black woman cuz my moms and GMa is black queens, but only thing I want black is the tires on my car, pimp! Look at me, I'm getting from 2 to 10 racz apiece out of both my bitches every night. I'm smashing and getting it all out of their funky smell cotts! Now Pimpin Silky told me what happened, and he laced my shoes up and looked out for a young nucca when I first stepped out here, going hard on hoes and trying to pimp on strong. And it's none of my bizz, but P, don't lose it over ya smoked-out ass Mama. It's too late for her. Let her do her! I would leave her alone, and so what if she chose Silky. She just there cuz he her dope plug and she can come and go as she pleases. Silky just can't get out of that life, and even tho he don't have no young tender hoes that they call them flower between 20 and 25 years old, he still thinks he got it, P! And really gonna pimp or die literally until he dies. Silky gonna be in a wheelchair with a furry Kangol hat cocked, having hoes push him around, feed him, and change his pissy diapers, by sack or his old slick mouthpiece. He'll game one of his caregivers long as he still pimpin in some form. And I'm trying to be in one of his many stories. He a legendary pimp and been to players balls and all. Won Pimp of the Year award 2 years in a row. Then they invented a Peelin award just from Silky peelin every pimp and mac bitch. He started telling all them peeling ain't stealing if she willing—it all depends what you dealing and what she feeling. And P, I remember cuz it sticks in my head. I don't want to be the average P or just one with the same game as the next pimp. I kno every P pimp different, but I just want to elevate my game and expand my pimpin worldwide, P..." J Pimp said in a serious low tone.

"Hell yeah...Chuchh! I feel ya, J Pimp. I can digg it. Thanks for the game, and building wit me. Sometimes we don't move forward if we standing still, ya digg? Ain't nothing wrong with growing, tho. I just hate them snowbunnies, too. They tell too damn much, but I do know the difference. They let you pimp whereas the ducks make you pimp and stay with ya foot square up their ass, ya digg?" Twan replied slick in a matching low tone.

They both sat quiet for a while, spinning around the Vegas strip, enjoying the desert nightlife. Twan was deep into his thoughts and still sipping on the Pineapple Cîroc. He still hadn't heard from Pink Toe all day. Ashley was on the injured reserve list. She was soliciting tricks off Tinder.com to come thru on Freemont. He also thought about going back over to Silky's to apologize, but he tried to get at him and his Mama Lela early today, and Pimpin Silky was scared to let him in. He knew Pimpin Silky lied and his Mama Lela was still in town and right in there smoking dope. He told J Pimp to drop him back off. J Pimp swung him around to see the back area where the Vegas showgirls took their smoke breaks at from the casinos. Twan saw all their long pretty legs and all their glittery shiny outfits with old-school feathers draping like a peacock. All Twan saw was dollar signs. He knew it was every businessman's fantasy to get laid by a Vegas showgirl for one drunken wild night.

Twan got back to his room to find Pink Toe ass laid out naked, snoring. He kicked the bed super hard to awake the sleeping bitch. He quizzed her and told her to break herself once again. She complied and cashed him out with $450 even. He slapped the bitch for playing with his pimpin and asked her, was she stealing from him now or smoking some type of new dope? She shook her head both ways, crying. She broke down and told him the truth about going down to bond out Butterscotch. She went on to tell him how she was up in Butterscotch's room hoing with her. They had gone to a special private party to seek arrangements with a lot of rich sugar daddies where she made $500. Butterscotch went to some swingers mansion party to get cashed out.

Twan was pissed the hell off. He kicked Pink Toe square in her butt-naked ass. That was becoming his signature move. He kicked her right on the floor and told the ho to lay there for pulling that bogus stunt. Nobody didn't tell her to go bond Butterscotch trifling ass out. She was trouble from the jump. He was disgusted with Pink Toe dumb ass and her so-called loyalty to her BFF. He knew that on the low Butterscotch was hating and growing jealous of Pink Toe. She was waiting to get rid of Pink Toe. Twan looked down at Pink Toe holding her ribs like her insides were burning up. He didn't feel shit or have no sympathy for her out-of-pocket punk ass.

His smartphone went off, the Young Thug played. Twan couldn't understand half the time what the hell Young Thug was saying but he knew it was hot! And that rich gang lifestyle went hard.

He read the text. It was from Pimpin Silky next door. He read it and replied. Pimpin Silky told him he heard all the ruckus over there and he wanted to chop it up with him and invite him over. He gave Twan his word that his Mama Lela been gone for awhile now. Twan said, what the hell, he'd go smoke a blunt and holler at Peelin ain't Stealin. After all, he was wrong and just into his feelings about his crackhead Mama

Lela. He just didn't want to accept the fact she was back to smoking and couldn't ever change or clean up for too long. He guessed the saying was true, once a crackhead always a crackhead, clucker.

"What's Gucci, P? My fault, P...I was out of character, but you Gucci, tho?" Twan asked in a shameful tone.

"Awwhh...P, don't trip! It's all good. I'm good, young blood—I just want to lace you up tight and right. It's my job to give you and J Pimp good game. Young Twan, I would've done the same thing for my Mama. God bless the dead, too. Let's sip this Diddy Juice you luv and relax. We gonna chop it up but I want you to be easy and comfortable so you can take all this game in, ya digg? Consider this a sit-down. Twan, you like a son to me and remind me of myself. You full of promise and potential in this game. This ain't fo errbody or no suckers, ya digg? And if I didn't care or have no love for you, I wouldn't take time out to tell you or waste my breath, ya digg?" Pimpin Silky said in a stern fatherly tone. Twan just shook his head up and down in acknowledgement. He now was curious that Pimpin Silky piqued his interest.

Thirty-five minutes elapsed and they were both chilling and choppin-n-poppin, laughing like when they first met and would do inside the strip joint on Freemont. Then the conversation switched up; it shifted into a more serious conversation. Pimpin Silky began to talk in a stern tone with a father-son demeanor. Twan knew Pimpin Silky was about to pour it all on him. However, he looked at Silky as his pimp mentor.

Pimpin Silky went on to tell Twan how his ratchett hoes were his downfall and he needed more classy fashion sophisticated-looking snowbunnies. That will attract high-end tricks with big revenue. That it wasn't just his duck hoes that were his downfall and holding him back...really it was him!! He was the ratchett one, he was a ratchett pimp truthfully. He was pimp of the ratchetts.

Twan was just nodding his head up and down, as much as it hurt him to hear, though. He felt silly and shameful like he was a clown pimp. How could anybody respect his pimpin if he was ratchett with some damn ratchett hoes, and duck hoes at that. Not bunnies.

Twan's head started spinning as he soaked up everything like a soft sponge. He finally woke up and peeked game. He could see clear and took it all in. It was definitely constructive criticism good and bad, but it was time for him to step up his game. He had to upgrader his pimpin. He was just a Southern-raised boy. Nobody in Louisiana saw nothing wrong with it. Pimpin was pimpin where he was from, long as you had hoes that were willing to go!

Plus the older P's were either old-school pimpin or too ratchett and country themselves, mainly having ratchett hoes, too. They were Twan's influences. Now he was on the main stage—Hollywood. He had to go mainstream, not a local ratchett joker. Vegas was the main spot, it would be his breakout spot. He had to conquer Vegas first and knock some bad showgirls/call girls. It was on a broader scale now.

Pimpin Silky watched Twan go into a trance, he was zoned out deep into his thoughts. But Silky could tell he was really hurt and his ego had been crushed and his pride rubbed the wrong way. Twan had a shell-shocked look to him. He was stung. Silky kept it raw!

"Say—Say...Young Pimpin, see it's been a black-and-white thing. Since the slave days, these snowbunnies been flocking to strong black men. It's the power and strong mind that we have. They love the authority we hold over them and the presents we demand. We look at them all as dirty white bitches and they know it and love us for it. They see we recognize the ho in them and the nasty dirty side, like licking assholes and sucking on toes type shit. But their husbands and fathers look at them as innocent and pure. A superior dominant woman. However, they love our masculine dominance, tho. White woman knows her man is weak-minded and lacking in areas and slacking in that department. She knows that the black man has true dominance over her white man and will overpower him and outdo him anytime, any day, anyhow. And they can't compete with that, P! These snowbunnies is bred to pay a nigga. It's in their genes, P! They get pleasure into sucking a million dicks and turning tricks to cash you out and make you rich. It's in them naturally and them crackers know it. That's why they'll give a pimp a million years for smashing on a white bitch. It's a law called white slavery that carries a mandatory life sentence for taking hoes state-to-state cross-country. It's ugly and now a raw game cuz they starting to charge pimps with a sex crime for pimpin and pandering to throw salt in the game and make you register as a sex offender and charge ya hoes with soliciting and give her 6 months in the County Jail if she don't tell on her pimp! Damn, P—now I'm mad cuz these crackers always hatin on some pimpin when this one of the oldest trades known to mankind... they can't stop these bitches from hoing, going or showing. They are tricks themselves, all the politicians, lawyers, judges, law enforcement and government agencies. So, Young Twan, pimp on...and take game in that I'm dishing out. It can't stop, won't stop! I'm done preaching now but hope my ism is good to peel ya eye back. Chuchh!" Pimpin Silky said quick and slick in a drunken tone.

"Chuchh—P!! Yeah, I dig dat, Silky, and I appreciate the ism. It was Gucci. Tomorrow I'll start fresh plan, plot and pimp!" Twan said anxiously in a low drunken tone off the pineapple Diddy Juice. He was definitely bubbly as he shook his head up and down with a devilish grin. His eyes glowed bloodshot red, tight. He knew Pimpin Silky was spot on and that a snowbunny's ho money was limitless. And she was priceless, especially if he had knocked one of them long-legged Amazon snowbunnies with the blonde hair, blue eyes. It was something about a blonde pubic hair landing strip that them tricks went berserk over. It boosted their feature price.

Twan had it and knew enough was enough. He went to his room to see a naked Pink Toe laid up with Butterscotch like they just got thru bumping pussies on the lo-low. They were both cuddled up. Then he saw the cash displayed all neatly in sequence on the nightstand. It was Butterscotch's tilt. It appeared to be a couple bands.

- Chapter 7 -

"Showgirls"

Twan woke up groggy with cotton mouth. He looked around. Both of his hoes were gone. It was almost 4 p.m. Vegas time. Damn, he had overslept. He got up, jumped into the cold shower to wake him up and shake the Cîroc off his pores. He had to hurry up and put his plan into effect. He plotted in the cold shower, then got out and rolled a green crack kush blunt he had gotten from his buddy from AZ with a dispensary shop.

He blew out the kush smoke thru his nostrils like an O.G. He picked up his smartphone and scrolled down it to find his Arabic ho Jazabel. He thought she chose up, but knew Fatz da Mac pulled a cold stunt. And he was still in the Clark County Jail fighting a pistol charge.

He texted her twice and called her once. She texted back a few minutes later asking, *Who dis?* He told her Twan, and he apologized for all the bullshit that went down and he gave her time to heal and get over the change of events that occurred. She told him, yeah right, and to lose her number or else she would change it and get a restraining order out on him. Also she didn't know what type of sick games he was playing. Then Twan replied, telling her the whole story how Fatz was his enemy and played it raw and got down foul by stealing his phone and attempting to hijack her, too. She texted back saying, Awwh how cute, and goodbye, Twan, have a nice life without her in it!

Twan shook his head and texted J Pimp to come thru. Then he texted Ashley. Still nothing but bullshit drag. He knew she was slipping from his pimp grip. Twan had a cold plan for Jazabel. He needed to step his G up and she was a perfect piece of the puzzle for it. J Pimp pulled up to the hotel off Freemont and told Twan he needed to start by getting out this ratchett hotel. Twan smirked and told him, "Let's go knock some showgirls and snowbunnies!"

Ashley and Mama Lela had been staying with an old 69-year-old Italian trick in northwest Vegas, both hiding out from Twan. They had become like mama and daughter, except Mama Lela was turning Ashley out to dope. She had her and the 69-year trick smoking crack heavy like the '80s epidemic.

Ashley and Mama Lela had both been on PlentyOfFish.com soliciting tricks, where they found the old Italian trick. Ashley still had been ripping off them mini-mansions for cash and jewelry. She had been slow paying Twan ever since Butterscotch clocked her with that stiletto and she got introduced to that pipe.

Twan was hot and had been hunting for Mama Lela after he found out she was hiding Ashley out and she turned her out on that shit, too. She was definitely in a flagrant violation. Twan really wanted to bust her head open when he caught her! Mama or not!

Ashley went to turn a trick she caught on Tinder.com at a fabulous mansion in the Mountains Ridge. It was a college student from USC visiting his parents for the weekend. She had seen him also on Cuddler. com trying to hook-up so she figured she'd vic him and break him for everything, then have Mama Lela rob the mansion for all of its precious assets. They went strictly off the play action like Peyton Manning, Omaha-Omaha-Hike!!

Ashley was busy packing lube down her asshole while the USC undergrad masturbated to her manipulating it. Soon as Mama Lela heard Ashley screaming and letting out erotic moans from the white boy penetrating her viciously, punishing her, she acted on it and began scouting thru the mansion, taking trip after trip to the car. She took jewelry, vases, frames, and any miscellaneous thing with face value.

The trick busted little squirts as he came over her ass crack. Ashley's screams and moans were silenced as he jerked his shaft up and down. She was ready to smoke some crack after that excruciating butt fuck. She felt her anus was ripped.

All of a sudden he heard the chandeliers chiming. He was startled as he jumped off the back of his king-size bed. He grabbed his 9mm Berretta, cocked it, and ran to the foyer of the mansion, knowing his parents were in Dubai. He rushed down the double-spiral carpet stairwell. He saw someone with a blonde wig on. He caught the backside of her, realizing it was a black lady. She saw him and ran, dropping the hefty pillowcase of the belongings. She dashed out the mansion!

Bloch-B-Bloch! Bloch! Bloch!

The 9mm Berretta sparked multiple times! A body smacked hard on the ground. Ashley curled up in a fetal position, screaming, then she heard a loud crashing sound followed by a thud like a bowling ball thumping down the gutter lane. She knew whatever Mama Lela was carrying, her greedy ass dropped it. She should've been gone, it had been at least 45 minutes the white boy had been butt-fucking her with them short rabbit strokes. She had the 69-year-old trick's truck. Damn it, she cursed Mama Lela under her breath, shaking her head, praying she wasn't seriously hurt or shot up. But all the silence throughout the mansion begged to differ. She quickly texted Twan 911 and told him call her ASAP, please. The white boy came running into the room on his iPhone, holding Ashley at gunpoint, telling her to get dressed slowly, that the Vegas PD was coming and she was going to jail. He already got her friend!

Twan saw his smartphone going off like crazy, it was Ashley's out-of-pocket black ass. She texted 911 emergency. Twan called her back but she never picked up, then he called his Mama Lela real quick to go check on Ashley's crazy ass. He knew ever since she was smoking that shit, she been tripping and never was the same. Her other text mentioned Mama Lela and help like she needed her to go pick her up. He didn't know or care for Ashley's little games or melodrama crack problems. She was late for 3 days in a row now. He passed the spice/kush mixed blunt to J Pimp and cut back up the volume in the rented Bentley coupe.

"Get da fuck out my face...You get da fuck out my face... Get him the fuck out my face!!" Young Thug sang the hook featuring Rich Homie mixtape as Twan reclined back in the front passenger seat. Something didn't seem right and it wasn't just the King Kong spice. J Pimp asked him, was he Gucci? He nodded his head up and down slow. J Pimp knew Twan wasn't used to smoking spice or none of that synthetic imported from China shit, especially down there in Baton Rouge, Louisiana. He was the one who introduced him into the synthetic world that boosted his high times ten.

J Pimp pulled up to the Vegas Stop-N-Go to buy a pack of blunt wraps that he loved. The grape flavor was the best. J Pimp stood up and tucked his .40 cal in his hip as he walked into the Stop-N-Go. He looked back to see Twan still on stuck mode off the spice. Twan looked like a damn zombie. He didn't even blink as he stared into oblivion. J Pimp checked for his fake driver's license out of California. In Las Vegas you could get anything you could think of black market—passports, birth certificates, socials, you name it. It was all a hustle in a mafia-style town that bet it all big or get hit trying!

Pat-Pat-Pat!! Twan jumped out of his spiced concoction daze. He looked over at the panhandler tapping on the window.

"Say, Pimpin...Aye, Pimp, I got them cards for ya hoes. You can put ya hoes on an escort service card, Pimpin. I make it look legit... sometimes you got to fake it til you make it and compete with the big-time competition, Pimpin!" the local hustler said in a white tee, fast-talking Twan. Twan couldn't reply. He was still on stuck mode.

"Back up off the Bentley, nigga!" *Click clack!!* J Pimp shouted as he racked the compact .40 cal.

Twan snapped out of his trance as he saw the hustler with the hands-up, don't-shoot style as he stepped back up off of the Bentley slowly. Twan let the window down and told J Pimp it's all Gucci, to be easy. J Pimp reminded him of a younger version of his big homie Choppa Face back home. They were quick to spark something up!

He told dude he was all gravy, baby, and sorry for the inconvenience, too. Dude handed Twan his little printed-out homemade business card. It was just in case he changed his mind. He also told him he had the plug on fake ID's for his hoes or the best call girls hotel services available. Twan told him good looking out for a pimp and stored his number into his smartphone under Picture Man. J Pimp was still mean mugging him like he was crazy and trying to pull a stunt and jack them for the rented Bentley coupe. He was naturally paranoid and didn't trust nobody, especially somebody he didn't know.

He shook his head side to side and decocked his .40 cal pistol, then jumped in the driver seat and smashed the luxury whip off. He told Twan to hit the cognac and shake that spice off him. He was about to taking him to knock some snowbunnies Vegas showgirls. It was lights, camera, action! Show and go!! Ho and show! Either way it was all ho business.

Twan texted Marissa the bartender from the strip joint on Freemont. She was excited and asked Twan if she could see him and buy him a few rounds on her to just come thru the spot. Twan declined, knowing she was just trying to get drunk and trick him out his dick and rob him for his youth.

He told her, was she ready to solicit tricks for him from the bar with her Mexican fine ass. She texted back LOL! Damn! And told him that ratchett black hoes wasn't doing the trick. Huh, LMBO! She told Twan she couldn't risk getting her son taken by CPS, plus her husband in jail would put a hit on her because he was running with some prison political gang. So even if she did want to ho up and solicit tricks from the bar on the down low, once the cat got out the bag, she was a dead duck in water, and she let it be known.

Twan heard the Bentley come to a halt. He tucked his smartphone and followed young J Pimp into the Mandalay Bay casino back entrance. It was a break area where the showgirls would take their smoke breaks and guys pick them up. It was snowbunnies with pretty white feathers sprawled all out in skimpy sparkly thongs with tails. It reminded Twan of some Victoria's Secret angels with wings. He loved it and he was around some real love.

Two showgirls eyeballed Twan and J Pimp as they stepped out the Bentley coupe and walked into the back entrance. Twan felt good because they were winning and trending. J Pimp's stallion Chinese ho approached, hugging J Pimp. She had a beautiful snowbunny with her. Twan didn't know J Pimp's Chinese ho was a showgirl or really worked at the casino, too. He just thought they worked hotels turning tricks out, like he did.

"Who dis?—Damn!" Twan said anxiously.

"Oohh...Daddy, this is my friend Kelly. She is new here... she from Seattle or Sea-Town!" the Chinese stallion informed them.

"Hi—Hi...I am Kelly! Nice to meet you two. He-He-He..." the showgirl stated, goofy.

J Pimp told Twan to go ahead and chop-n-pop! That's all you, pimpin!

"Yeah...P, I'm just trying to figure out whatz so damn funny? Miss Kelly, huh?" Twan said slick in a curious tone.

"Ummh...He-he-he...Nawh, it's just that you look like Rich Homie Quan and he looks just like Young Thug from Rich Gang. I'm sorry... He-he-he," she said in a charming manner. Twan smirked and was intrigued.

"Oh...how cute, Miss Kelly, that's all Gucci, it just means we winning and trending. You want to see what it means and how it feels to be what a real nucca with a franchise winning team? Can you be a winner and hit big for a P named Twan from out of BR one time? Stop messin round with these clowns and get down for ya crown—gurrl!" Twan said quick and slick in ya suave tone.

"Okay...Damn! All you had to say is you want me or come on?" Miss Kelly the showgirl stated nonchalantly.

"Well, come on den, bitchhh!! You trynna be funny??" Twan replied seriously.

As they walked back out of the Mandalay Bay casino, Floyd Money Mayweather and TMT Money team came thru the back, Twan's Vegas idol. He knew Floyd had pimpin in his Michigan blood. He ran Vegas. "Oh shit..." Twan mumbled.

"Pimpin Moneyweather! Can me and my new snowbunny take a selfie wit cha, Pimpin Floyd?" Twan said on a good one like Money Mayweather was his bestie pimp partner. Shit, he even had Money May fooled, too. Floyd thought he already met and knew young Twan from Baton Rouge.

"Awwh...Pimpin, it's all good...I see you out here 10 toes 2 da ground. Come on, doe!" Mayweather replied in cool-ass tone.

Twan put up a clenched fist next to Mayweather and told his snowbunny, squat down in her still white feather showgirl attire, glittering like a billion-dollar ho! Right then was when he started calling her Oprah! A snowbunny called Oprah, the billion-dollar ho!

Twan snapped one more selfie with Money Mayweather, J Pimp and the 2 hoes dropping off the side of both pimps, catching half-face split-screen shot with Money Mayweather center.

"Good lookin out—Pimpin Floyd. Be easy, champ…And keep Hitaching them vics!!" Twan thanked Mayweather for his cooperation and did the pimp no fingerprints, no evidence finger tinkle shake.

He saw his snowbunny Oprah get up and noticed her soft Georgia peach shape ass cheeks swaying. Damn! He sparked his eyes like a Bic lighter! Damn it, Pimpin was really winning and trending. It wasn't luck of Vegas draw or the showgirls that surrounded him, it was all skills, no luck! This wasn't a coincidence! This was in him rooted and booted firmly! This was good game but most of all good pimpin at its finest.

Twan screenshot his pics and posted his Mayweather selfie on his Instagram flexing with the champ. Then he posted it on his Facebook wall, too. The FB timeline was all about him and Floyd.

Oprah the Seattle snowbunny looked at Twan. She captured the essence of Twan. She dug his swag, his pimp juice. She instantly chose and fell in line. She got stuck on Twan on the spot. It was something about him that demanded money. And she was about to get a thrill bringing it to him. Really she knew Twan was a hood nigga. And she loved bad rebellious boys, OMG!

Twan truly knew it was an art form to this and them pimp bones was in him, not on him! He had already had IG going berserk with the hashtag #TwanMoneyTeam and with over a few hundred likes and counting on FB. He had the book jumping and all types of messages in his inbox and friend requests. His followers on Twitter had him #TwanMoneyTeam trending topic in Cali and Vegas right now!

Twan told J Pimp to take him to a top-notch hotel with the Jacuzzi in the middle of the room on the 15th floor above the night desert lit-up floor. Flashing bright lights and fast luxury foreign cars, party buses and stretch private limos. J Pimp told him he gonna take Twan and Oprah to a $10,000-a-night penthouse.

- Chapter 8 -

"Viva Vegas"

Vic'n was a form of pimpin. Vic'n had a pimp trait. It was the son of swindle. Twan knew J Pimp young crazy ass knew how to Vic-n-Stick. He also knew the difference between vic'n and pimpin.

J Pimp took Twan to Palms Penthouse suites. It had a 2-lane bowling alley, small court, loft, vanity double bathroom, patio view, theater and surround sound. It was dope penthouse but for 10 bands a night it better had come with a cater service and room tailor service and free expensive edition sparkling champagne. That bubbly!

Twan got stripped down to his black silk boxers by his new showgirl while she unclamped her big white feathers. She stepped down into the Jacuzzi first as Twan led her hand up, stepping behind her. J Pimp handed him the other bottle of bubbly. The both shook them up and said, "Chuchh!!" as they popped the cork, spraying both their hoes. They were hosing them down from their hair to their titties. Then he saw Oprah's big ol booty protruding out the bubbling hot water as she turned sideways, flinching from Twan spraying her relentlessly. They were celebrating for knocking fresh merch and for a new ho to add to the well-groomed stable. He had a real 10 pink toes down now. He just needed to chop some more ho toes off! Then really have a superior super fierce stable. It would probably be imitated but never emulated. He was already knowing long as these snowbunnies were going and obedient. But he already knew they were loyal to the soil and will obey swell, from his first snowbunny Miley twerking frail ass from BR.

His smartphone was going off. He was getting tweets, texts, and FB messages. He hit his FB mobile app. He saw a message from Neese play Creole cousin from South High School back in Baton Rouge. Twan got burnt by that nasty bad bitch twice. She gave him that Ebola. She made him sick. He almost died and had to get a shot of antibiotics in his left ass cheek. She disgusted him so much but somehow he was always so attracted to her. Probably because she reminded him of his bitch Neese and he had a thing for those Creole cockpit mixed girls. They had an exotic look.

She commented on the Mayweather selfies and the posted video on Instagram. She told him she was on her way to Vegas for a job interview and she may move out there so she needed Twan to show her around for a few nights and take her out once or twice, especially since he was tweeting so damn much about Vegas and how it's supposed to be his second home.

Twan told her to bet dat and he looked over at J Pimp, not knowing that he recorded a video during the whole Money Mayweather encounter and posted Instagram video. They were trending topics for the moment and Twan just felt like Ace off of *Paid in Full* movie mixed with Scarface when he was smoking that big ol Cuban cigar in the middle of the Jacuzzi with that "The world is mine" mentality. You could tell him nothing but somehow he couldn't even grin. Something didn't feel right. Things weren't seeming right and it wasn't from his joy with his Oprah snowbunny.

He got a text message that read, *Son, call this number 702344-4155 ASAP! 911.* He never saw his Mama Lela text all proper or sound like this. Something wasn't definitely out of whack, but he couldn't quite place his finger on it.

So he texted her back and asked, *Whatz Gucci?* curiously. She texted back and told Twan to pick up the phone. It was very important. An emergency! He replied in another text message asking what happened now and just to tell him, ignoring the incoming call from Mama Lela.

Once she didn't text back ASAP Twan grew impatient. He didn't have time for all her crack fiend tantrums. He pressed Mama Lela's number on his touchscreen. He was about to curse her ass smooth out the southside BR style.

"Hello, this is Clark County Homicide Detective Stanley Sims. I want to inform you that a woman with this phone has been involved in a homicide. And she had your number stored in her phone under 'Son' in her contacts. We believe we have a Louisiana State ID on her as Lela M. Burdette? Sir, I send my condolences if this is your mother true indeed, but however I need you to meet me down at the Clark County Morgue, please. I need to ask you a few questions for the record and for you to identify the victim and claim her body. You have to sign and witness the death certificate, sir. Well, I'll just call you Mr. Burdette. I'll give you an hour to pull yourself together and grieve and get down here. This is Vegas, baby! I'm a busy guy. Remember, Detective Sims," the homicide detective stated effortless like it was no biggie and the normal day-to-day routine he did all day long. Fuck that, Twan thought and fuck him. That was his Mama he was talking about. Not no damn Vegas transit squatter.

Click! Twan cut off the homicide detective. He already didn't like him and needed to watch his tone because he was being disrespectful. Especially being the bearer of bad news like that.

Twan seemed unfazed. He wasn't really trying to take it all in that he heard. He put his smartphone down as his whole mood changed dramatically. He didn't want to repeat the bad news, still in denial and really praying it was somebody else that had his Mama Lela's phone. It wasn't wishful thinking to him, though.

He texted Ashley back-to-back, then called her twice. He could tell that her cell was turned off! He hoped that Ashley didn't kill his own Mama else she was dead sitting duck, literally! He knew something definitely went wrong and remembered how Ashley called him and texted him 911 ASAP earlier before he bumped the Oprah showgirl and brushed shoulders with Money Mayweather Team. Money Mayweather had pimpin Twan trending and him and young J Pimp on fire. But he'd give it all up and take it back for his Mama Lela to be here to see it all and pimp on strong. Finally show his Mama Lela he made it and mastered these snowbunny hoes to be a renowned pimp straight out of the boot shape of Louisiana. Baton Rouge, to be exact.

Viva Vegas! It was Viva Go! To live...not die. He stood up and told J Pimp to get dried off and dressed. He had to go to the Clark County Morgue ASAP!! J Pimp instantly thought it was one of Twan's ratchett ass duck hoes either got killed because the strip is dirty and will leave a ho in the desert dust stinky. You can become a victim of the Vegas strip, too. It wasn't always promising. Shit, J Pimp lost one himself and saw another one go right across the street from him when he was on Freemont. Or Twan's hoes could've killed each other with all that cutting and fight them little ratchett hoes did. J Pimp knew how they got down true indeed, especially coming out the hood part of Oregon.

J Pimp told Twan, "Fuck that, come on, let's just smash...fuck drying off, get dressed." They put on their pants, wet drawers and all. They told the hoes to grab some towels so they wouldn't get the Bentley rental seats all soaked wet and to hurry up and come on, as the foursome rushed out the luxury penthouse, spoiling their big boy plans for the night.

J Pimp was whipping the Bentley like it was his fuck stolen. He had handles and whippers like he grew up in New Jersey drive, taking the jake on a chase. Nobody didn't dare to say nothing to Twan. He seemed possessed. He had a demonic ill look to him. It was a look that nobody in Vegas knew or saw yet. It was that same look his Mama Lela saw in Twan when Neese got Hitachi'd back home by that hatin ass nigga N.O. Rest in peace! That's what started this whole West Coast Vegas shit. Twan killed N.O. for choppin up his bottom ho that he was gonna really run away with one day when his pimp days were long behind him out his prime. They were promised a long career, but nothing was guaranteed with these hoes. However, Neese's was really personal. That was his bitch and the only ho he came close to having feelings for. That pimp was sinister like that sometimes. They say it may not always be right but it was always fair if you be fair to it!

Twan still sat with that same exact look as he stared into that same spot in the front windshield. J Pimp saw him in a zone, zoning the fuck out. He liked Twan on his ill hood ish. He seen that Twan wasn't no punk and would go, right then and there! Ugghh...J Pimp knew Twan was plotting ill intent and he was going to toss him the .40 cal or the choppa, whichever one he preferred if it's all that serious times 10.

The 2 showgirl hoes were cramped in the back of the Bentley coupe, lost. They saw Twan also was in a plotting trance, but remained silent. Twan appreciated their code of silence. Only thing that could be heard throughout the Bentley sound system was Future's "Honest" playing.

"My Mama ain't raise no—ho!! My Mama ain't raise no—ho! These niggas ain't got no hoes—they running and kickin these doors...Fuck dat bitch—Fuck dat bitch—We don't give a fuck about a bitch. I just went and got me a better bitch. I just went and brought another bitch!" Future's lyrics hit home to him and struck his heart, which signaled his brain and aching anxiety pain.

J Pimp pulled into the Clark County Morgue in 20 mins flat. He was smashing thru all red lights after he got off the I-15 freeway. He didn't care or have regard for no damn law, especially at this time of night in Vegas. They better respect his mind or check it for all he cared. His pimp partner was hurt so he was hurting as well. Besides, J Pimp knew most cops in Vegas respected high-end price ticket whips. It could be someone important that know people that knew people that could possibly take their jobs and snatch their badge straight away from them, leaving them unemployed. So they extra careful who they pull over and piss off. Soon as J Pimp pulled into a parking spot, Twan was out before the car stopped!

He was the first one out. Everybody else followed shortly after. He had to be buzzed in but the morgue clerk came out front to let them in the secured entrance. He led them downstairs into the bottom floor of the morgue to meet with Detective Sims and the medical examiner to identify these women's bodies and possibly his own Mama Lela's tired body.

The smell of decomposing flesh and rotten spoiled coagulated blood concoction with embalming fluid had Twan and the girls' stomachs doing the somersault. The girls were both holding their noses and clinching their stomachs, coughing frantically. J Pimp, on the other hand, didn't have a weak stomach like the others.

At the entrance of the double swinging doors that kept the morgue's bodies on ice, everyone came to a halt as the clerk went to get Detective Sims and alert him to the party there awaiting on him. Then the clerk came back out, saying the detective will be out with them momentarily as he walked back up the morgue steps.

The detective came out with white medical/cleaning mask. They all placed one on their faces. He asked, who was Mr. Burdette that he spoke to over the phone shortly ago? Twan raised his hands. Then the detective could see the resemblance between him and the woman corpse that laid stiff on the steel examiner's slab.

He was surprised at the support for the frail woman. She looked like she had a rough life, judging by how aged she looked and rough scarred-up her body was. She appeared to be strung out on something. That's the only reason the homicide detective was so surprised. Usually people that come in as a strung-out corpse or homeless corpse, their loved ones don't care to miss them. He was lead detective and told Twan to follow him but warned him it was graphic and the victim, possibly his Mama Lela, had been shot a few times running.

They went to the end row towards the office window. It was other bodies covered in sheets. Twan even saw a little boy's body that got hit by a truck hit and run. They knew it was a little boy because his shoe was falling down as his broken leg dangled off the slab that the sheet half covered. It was sad but reality.

The girls were clingy to each other, all scared and clinging onto J Pimp's long arms. They were all more nervous than Twan as the detective asked Mr. Burdette, was he ready? before he pulled the dark blood-stained sheet back.

Twan couldn't shake the heavy stench dancing around his nose hairs in his nostrils. He smelt death. He told Detective Sims, could he hold up a sec, and did a silent prayer over the body as he bowed his head.

Then he blessed the body and asked for God to have mercy on his Mama Lela's soul, and lastly not for him to take the only woman he knew, loved, and had. He asked God if he could spare his Mama this one last time and don't let this woman be his crazy ass Mama Lela.

He nodded at the detective after he pulled himself together to face the slow music that seemed to be on pause. The detective pulled back the sheet. Twan closed his eyes, took a deep breath, exhaled, then opened his eyes!

"Hell nawh! Not my Mama Lela? That ain't my Mama—Hell nawh!" Twan yelled, turned-up!

J Pimp jumped. Twan's words sent a deep chill surge throughout his whole body, it was bone deep! He had goosebumps all over. He was confused, too.

The detective asked, how did he think this lady got his Mama Lela's phone and did he know this woman here? Then he asked, what about Ashley, that was a prostitute who solicits sex ads online and solicits off of Tinder and Cuddler.com?

Twan shook his head side-to-side and told the detective she is his Mama Lela as he looked back down.

* * *

Mama Lela saw a half-naked white boy creeping out. He startled the mess out of her. She was caught red-handed being too greedy. Right then and there she knew she was just high, but after she saw him raise that black pistol at shoulder height, she ran for her life. However, she couldn't run 60 yards per second faster than that 9mm bullet. She attempted to run for the old trick's truck.

The first bullet struck her in the upper shoulder and exited out her inner elbow. She never heard the second fatal shot. The slug caught her on the left side above her jaw, instantly ripping viciously through her cheek, knocking her unconscious. It went through her mouth and burnt a dime-sized hole thru her cerebral cortex, short-circuiting all her brain and body functions and taking the life right out of her. It sounded like she got sucker-punched in her stomach as the air constricted at once out her lungs. She was dead in mid-air before smacking the foyer marble floor and stolen goods crashing erratically with her.

The white boy stepped into the other half of the extended foyer with his 9mm Berretta still raised. He knew she was wounded but not dead? He walked up to her twitching body as he heard the most eerie whining disturbing sound like the body was trying to still breathe in on its own. It was a suckling cracking noise which got drowned out by blood clogging her windpipe. It was awful and instantly sent a cold chill down the white boy's spine and made the hairs on the nape of his neck to rise up like a wild scared wolf. He saw her head tilted sideways from the fall. She died with her eyes open. He was scared to touch her as he stood looking at her lifeless body as pools of dark blood stained the Italian marble tile. He phoned the police as he stared at the oozing wound in her cheek.

* * *

Twan saw the abrasion above his Mama's right eye as she smacked the ground and swelled up her left eye shut. Then he stared at the fatal shot to her cheek. It indented deep like a dimple, similar to the same spot 50 Cent got shot at. It gave Mama Lela like a half-smirk effect like a dimple upon death. It was gut-wrenching, which sent Twan on a spiral effect and caused him to lose it terribly. He dropped down to the floor as his knees weakened and kissed the morgue floor. J Pimp hurried to his side to aid his mourning pimp partner.

Twan tried to get his feet back under him and started getting real irate and hostile. He was scaring the hoes next to him. They never experienced nothing like this as real in their square lives.

"Hell nawh, cuh! Hell nawh, not my Mama, J Pimp. We was all we got, P! She couldn't be here to see me really do it right at the top of my pimpin career, P! Man—Fuck dat shit. Where Ashley at, you Porky Pig donut-eating cracker? Huh? She had my Mama killed? Where is she?? Man!! Come here, pussy—"

"Awhhaa!" the girls screamed as Twan jolted towards Detective Sims. He clearly didn't care it was a homicide detective he was plunging at. He had lost his rabid mind.

J Pimp tall ass snatched Twan up, trying to keep him from getting booked into Clark County Jail, too.

"Hey, don't try me, buddy—not tonight! I've helluva paperwork and I don't got time to fill out no more. So take ya best friend's advice and relax. It's not going to bring her back. It's tragic, yes, but it's life. Now try to go home and get you some rest. I'll call you tomorrow when I wrap up the investigation. Don't worry, I'ma charge Ashley's ass, too. This Las Vegas—Viva Vegas brings a lot of homicides too around this desert heat and alcohol with fast money. This is the real Sin City, kiddo!" Detective Sims stated agitated in a defensive tone.

Twan had tears of pain flowing drastically down his cheeks. It was a long quiet walk back to the Bentley. The girls still were in so much shock. They both felt bad for Twan. But Oprah just wanted to be there for him and comfort him no matter what! His Mama's death seemed to already have brought them closer. It was the first day she had met her, when she was dead. Her actual last day alive. She felt like Twan's new protector and loving angel. She massaged Twan's neck and shoulders as he sat back, speechless.

Twan sat there with that Southside Baton Rouge other side of the tracks mean mug face. He had that bottom boy killa look. That look was worse than he had for N.O. when he chopped up his Neese. It was more sinister! Right there Twan wasn't never the same. His heart twisted and turned black as coal and cold as Alaska.

Twan was really lost deep in his own thoughts. He couldn't leave his Mama Lela out here, not bury her in this Vegas. She had to leave with him. But could he finish what he started and conquer Las Vegas? He was skeptical but knew his mission all right. He decided right then to get Mama Lela cremated and her remains in a purple urn. Purple somehow symbolized his Mama, power and the struggle that she represented. It also was honor for a wounded soldier, too. So why not give his Mama's ashes a purple surrounding?

"Aye, J Pimp, download that Lil Boosie 'Super Bad' classic from iTunes. I need to hear some of dat real BR Southside music. Dat 'No Mercy'—'Clips and Choppers'—'Mind of a Maniac.' And hand me that Diddy Juice and kush, P," Twan said in a scratchy low tone. You could tell he'd been bawling inside and out.

J Pimp nodded his head and complied, being there for his dude. Twan was his nucca! They all went back to the penthouse. Twan laid up in the luxury bed, staring at the ceiling while Oprah tried to please, giving him head all night long. She had Twan's whole pubic area smelling like her Michael Kors fragrance.

That next morning Detective Sims called and explained all the concluded final details from the burglary, to Ashley and the guy who killed his Mama in the mansion. They charged Ashley with felony murder for being in a commission of a crime and aiding Lela. She still denied knowing Mama Lela or what was going on. Twan had scheduled Mama Lela to be cremated and to hold a little service for her. He was hurt.

Twan could barely sleep. He didn't shut his eyes. He saw his whole life and childhood flash before his eyes with his Mama Lela and his Pops. He needed to feel some pain to substitute the real pain.

J Pimp took him to a nice old-school tattoo shop that sat off the strip. Them Mexicans could tatt their ass off and freestyle just about anything. Twan got a pic out of his Mama tatted from his smartphone that he screenshot from one of his girl cousin's Facebook page. He got it straight off her wall.

His long-distance family kept texting him and hitting him up on social media. He had to text his Pops in Angola Louisiana State Prison. His Pops kept a cellphone like the boss he was out here and in there.

Then he sent his cousin Jill and old ho a message on Instagram along with his portrait tatted of his Mama Lela on his right side rib cage. It said, My Queen Piece, with her face on the Queen chess piece in front of the King on the checkered board. It was hot! Jill told Twan she was sorry about Mama Lela and she would love for him to come back to BR to visit her. Twan still didn't trust her or buy it. It just sounded like a setup, she's the Feds.

Twan also tatted #RIP_MAMA_LELA on his face above his right eyebrow that followed along the natural shape and curve of his eyebrow. He wanted his hoes to see the hashtag tatted and know to—GO!!

He also put the #RIPMAMALELA on Luv1s.com. He posted her pic with some family pics of him, his big bro TNut, Mama Lela, and his kingpin Pops. Luv1s.com was the latest social media site. It was the first ever social media dedication-only site. It was used as a way for you to post your love, condolences, thank-yous, and congrats to your loved ones in front of the world. The white folks used it for world tragic events, but the hood used it for their family, lovers, and friends to let it be known. He had her hashtag on her loved ones page going bananas. He had mixed some of her ashes in with the ink tatted. He had her in a purple marble stained urn.

- Chapter 9 -

"LVMPD"

Oprah sat there in the passenger seat of the lime-green Lambo that J Pimp's long-legged Chinese ho rented for him off the strip. She looked over at the fresh tatted hashtag of his Mama above his eyebrow. She felt him and didn't want to let go. He had just picked her up from the casino working. She would forever shake and sell her ass for cash to give to him. Pimpin Silky was right. Snowbunnies let you pimp, duck hoes made you pimp!

She sat rubbing on Twan's leg as he zipped down Las Vegas Blvd., weaving in and out of the lanes, being a hot boy stunting and fronting, acting a pure donkey! He had been drinking on Hennessy heavy lately and started snorting powder! It felt like it brought him closer to his Mama Lela. It was something about Vegas that got to him. It was the same effect it had on pimps! The rush!

After he met up with Silky after he left the tatt shop, they both sniffed and cried their hearts out. He had been binging. He guessed them white girls and white lines were besties. He had both the white girl and that white gurrl.

Twan saw LVMPD thru the rearview and downshifted, popping the 6-speed clutch and hitting on the brakes. He saw lights flashing as the LVMPD hit his cherries. Twan couldn't believe he disrespected the Lambo like that. He smashed thru the middle turning lane and accelerated thru the red light swiftly as cars hit their screeching brakes and blaring their horns. He busted a hot ass right, then darted to the I-15. He had to use the HOV lane so no LVMPD chopper would get on him. He had a place to be, called UNLV. He couldn't wait, it was time to pay a bitch a visit!

Twenty minutes later Twan pulled up to UNLV campus and whipped thru the student parking lot. He spotted her car with her specialized Idaho license plate and smirked devilishly. Oprah the snowbunny knew he was up to something. She prayed it wasn't nothing to do with his 2 other light-skinned hoes that she hated. Twan parked and told her to stay there and watch his rented Lambo.

Twan walked onto campus and headed straight for the gymnasium stadium where the girls played volleyball at. Soon as he walked into the semi-filled stadium, he noticed their opponents ASU in maroon and goldish-yellow color.

He walked around and noticed his tall Arabic ho Jazabel. He spotted her funny-shaped Arabic nose and saw her sparkling bright gray-greenish eyes. Her long legs were so milky with a creamy tone. She rested her hands down on her knees as her teammate served in the second set.

Twan saw her wet spots from her beady sweaty head to all her moist spots under her armpits, her midsection, and the back of her ass. Damn sweaty pussy! It turned Twan on and reminded him when he used to bust Neese right on down when she came straight home from work. He just shook his head.

Soon as Jazabel saw Twan, she started messing up. He had her game all fucked up. She was super nervous. He still had some type of effect on her and he noticed that, too.

After they lost to ASU for the second year in a row, she blamed Twan for the bad luck. She went straight up to him.

"Uughh...You're bad luck all the way around the board, huh? Well, I see you don't give up, and I like that, but Twan, I'm sorry, you know, after that high-speed chase and police encounter with your frienemy...I'm done, Twan, sorry!!" Jazabel said in a skeptical manner. She was so stuck on Twan still for some reason.

"Ain't no skills in luck? So I can't be bad or good luck! I'm all skills. Misses Idaho, the Arabian Queen, are you gonna forgive your king, and allow me to really take you? You kno I'ma keep it pimpin..." Twan replied in a sincere sweet tone that had her melting and feeling some type of way. She didn't understand how Twan had that effect on her and she really wanted him to take her back in the locker room and make her scream orgasms as he gave it to her from the back, her favorite sexual position. She had to snap out of her lustful trance. He had her horny wett.

"Oh...And I'm so sorry about your mom, too. I seen all of the love on Facebook so I felt it wasn't my place to send you a message on that personal note. Especially after I said some mean things to you, too. And I seen you, Mr. Pimpin, with Money Mayweather at the casino on Instagram. You trending and winning as you tweeted, huh?" Jazabel commented in an envious tone. Twan could tell she was jealous and still digging him for some reason.

"So you been following me on Twitter, liking me on Facebook, and stalking me on Instagram! Why you just didn't text me or send me a message on social media to send ya love and let me kno and feel the love? Yeah, she's gone, so are you gonna be that one to take over, huh?" Twan popped at her.

She sat there in awe, staring into Twan's grill. She noticed he got his peeling ratchett gold fangs fixed. But on his left front tooth he had a new gold tooth. It was 14 karat gold that was his Mama Lela's ring that his Daddy gave her. Twan had a Las Vegas dentist office melt the ring down and slug the front tooth up with the 3 crushed diamonds on it, making it look like glittering diamonds in the sand. Now he had that bright-yellow Louisiana gold mixed with that 14k gold. She loved it and loved Twan's realness. He was so hood.

"Okay, Twan, let me take a shower and get dressed. I'll let you take me out for lunch, so wait out in the parking lot for me. Of course I still have your number, too. And Twan, don't blow this first and last chance!" she said seriously.

Twan pulled her tall, sweaty ass in close to make her feel his power and said, "No, don't you blow this," and gave her a kiss around all of her teammates being nosy, which fucked her head up and made her want him even more. Then the slap on her ass made her want to cum all over herself.

Jazabel hurried up and rushed into the girls' locker room all sweaty and hot and bothered. She had to pee real quick before she jumped into the shower. Most of all the UNLV volleyball teammates were already in and out.

She closed the last stall door, peed real quick, and soon as she wiped herself, she couldn't help herself and let out a sly moan. She couldn't believe herself and how naughty she was acting! She was so wet and her clit so swollen, her whole vagina was throbbing in anticipation of a highly needed orgasm.

She rubbed her clit pleasurably with her middle finger as her index and ring finger busted her soft vagina outer lips open. She was moaning as she raised her legs up and rested them on the stall doors. She was moaning indirectly, thinking it was just her endorphins dancing in ecstasy in her head alone, not knowing just how Twan had her pussy so excited. She needed to cum now!! She felt her body shaking and swollen clit tingling. The pulsating pressure buildup was about to cream.

The UNLV team captain saw Jazabel when she shuffled by her like she had to pee bad. However, she had been in the stall still after she got out of the shower. Then she heard her clear as day. Wow!

"OMG—OMG, Jaz...like I can't believe your horny ass is really doing that in there right now. OMG, get over yourself...and you need help! Get laid! BYE—I'll leave you to yourself by yourself!" the volleyball captain said in a shocked tone!

"Oooo...Ohhh...Oooo...Damn it!! Oooo...O-O-O...Shit!" Jazabel shouted as she climaxed. The girl startled her and snapped her out of her zone. She jumped back, letting her feet hit the ground as she squirted fast and hard like a cat pissing all in the toilet. It gushed. She rubbed her now sensitive clit as she felt the convulsion and juices flowing at a rapid water speed. She couldn't believe how reckless she was and smirked.

Twan sat low-key in the lime-green Lambo like Jay-Z and leaned back. Oprah sat with her pink flamingo feathers on, restless. She was hot and Vegas was super hot 24/7, even with the chilled A/C flowing high. It didn't stop the Mojave Desert sun rays beaming through the Lambo windshield. She kept sucking her teeth. Twan popped the snowbunny for being funny. Pop!

"Oouchh...Twan, what was that for? Geeezz..." Oprah cried.

"Shut up—Ho! That's for being funny and all that slick teeth sucking, bitch!! So stay in ya lane and know your place," Twan replied, not seeing Jazabel at his window with her arms folded, leaning on one hip jealously.

She had that "Who the fuck is she?" look on her face as she glared hard at Oprah. Oprah noticed her low dreamy sex eyes like she just got through fucking or either was up all night and day.

Jazabel told Twan she good on the lunch and she saw he had company, noticing it was the same girl from FB and IG she saw with him and Money Mayweather.

Twan told her to get off that young-minded bullshit and they all were adults and didn't have to hide shit, then scooped low and used his Mama Lela as leverage.

"Man—Y'all both know I just lost my Mama so I need to be around some love. Y'all both can love and be here for Daddy. Now are we going to fight and be silly? Or be civilized? It's 2015 and this Vegas, so Jazabel, get in ya car, my Arabian princess, and follow me. If not, then—BYE!! I don't got time for this blasphemy!" Twan stated coldly with an even colder stare at her. He meant business and didn't have time to play, sit, and babysit. He wasn't about to hold this bitch or no bitch hand! He was smashing on all hoes hard! Especially now his Mama Lela was resting in harmony. He had a zero-tolerance for a ho or any bullshit.

Jazabel looked at Twan and saw he was dead serious, and once he put his Mama Lela into the category, she knew he really was serious and hurting. She just wanted to support him, even though it went against all her Islamic beliefs. Her family were Muslims and a lot of the American ways were forbidden. She didn't kiss until she really was 18 years old, or have a boyfriend. She hated competition, but she was a competitor. She would show this local Vegas showgirl up. So she thought as she told Twan okay! And ran to her car to follow Twan that already pushed the Lambo out of the UNLV campus.

* * *

Butterscotch and Pink Toe were worried because after Twan's Mama got killed, they saw less and less of him. And they knew he picked up a bad habit and resorted to candying his nose. They blamed Pimpin Silky for influencing Twan for playing with his nose.

It seemed like Twan didn't care about his money, as if it was nothing. Sometimes they'd see him every 3-4 days. It was killing both of them! Then every time he had that white bitch around he called Oprah, but she seemed to be green and very naïve. He seemed to be harboring this ho, and his whole attitude changed. He was more cocky and snappy. They didn't know if it was the powder or his Mama's death. But he felt like Tony Montana, like he was on top of the world. And they both were curious if that white showgirl Oprah was really making him that high-end 10-band-a-night money. She had to be hoing, extorting, working them casino clients, too.

Twan could've knocked Britney Spears. She was 33 years old now and performed at the casino every night on the strip. Why not get a million-dollar bitch, than just any ol snowbunny? That's how they felt. They plotted secretly on Oprah behind Twan's back.

Twan woke up next to two beautiful women at the penthouse. He had a beautiful threesome last night and had turned Jazabel out on some white girl, then had her eating his white girl. They were both bumping pussies passionately. The powder and alcohol got the best of them. Twan vic'd both of them and told them let him see them both just kiss each other for starters. Then had them kiss each other's clits. Next thing he knew they both were slurping on his dick and fighting over it. He bent the Arabic ho every which way and penetrated deeply. He had to make sure he put that Southern twang down on her viciously so she would think twice. And so she could forever chase it! The power of the "D"!

He sat up and snorted a good wake-up line off the glass mirror, even though it was already 1 in the afternoon. It was a typical Vegas desert nightlife. He took out his smartphone and streamed the new T.I. and Lil Boosie song. Then he texted a man with a great business plan to help him closer to his multi-million-dollar game plan. It was time to incorporate his hoes to a better scale. They all were about to go in triple overtime for the new season till the holidays. Ho-Ho-Ho!! They just didn't know it yet. It was time to turn up!!

"Bitch—Get ready and tell ya sista I'm on my way to pick all of y'all up ASAP!!" Twan spit quick.

"Okay, but Daddy, where are we going? We been wanting to spend—"

Click! Pink Toe was cut off before she could finish talking to Twan. He clicked her straight off coldly, it wasn't no love or sympathy for no ho, period. She texted him twice and Butterscotch texted him once. He replied to Butterscotch they better have on their schoolgirl uniforms like them Japanese girls with the nylon thigh-high stockings. It was time to perform on a big center stage. He texted #Y'alltimetoshine. They were both ready and anxious.

Twan manipulated his smartphone as he smacked both of the 2 lovebirds cuddled up naked in the face and on the ass to awake them. He told them to get their funky ass in the shower and dress real quick because they all had a big date and couldn't be late! Then he instructed Oprah to give Jazabel one of her showgirl outfits. He wanted her in G-strings and white dangling fluffy feathers, too. His master plan was coming together.

Bingo! He found just the number he was looking for that he stored in his phone the other week. It was the con man he met with J Pimp at the Stop-N-Go that J Pimp almost gave the pissy blues to.

"Aye...What's happenin, my dude?" Twan asked.

"Man—who dis? It better be all money in, no money out, right?" the con man replied in a slicker tone than Twan slick fast-talking ass.

"Man—this pimpin Twan that was in the Bentley. Remember you gave me ya card, talkin bout putting my hoes on the main line the real Vegas way, to get dat real Vegas money? Them cards is what I'm talkin bout—"

"Awwhh...Pimpin, yeah—Pimpin!! What's poppin? Hell yeah, Mr. Big Pimpin poppin all stanking hoes droppin! Man, can you meet me at the McDonald's on Donna Street? I'm in North Vegas right now. How bout you just hit me when you ready and bring all ya best hoes, ya whole stable, pimpin?" the con man said anxiously, cutting Twan off, trying to fast-talk him, knowing he was about to strike pimpin and tax his pockets.

"Bet dat up, ya heard me. I'm out cherr! Deuces!" Twan replied as he clicked.

Twan and the girls jumped into Oprah's silver 325i BMW with her Washington plates. He sat shotgun as Oprah drove to Freemont to pick up his two ratchett redbones. It was showtime primetime.

The girls were all looking stank at each other and Jazabel was really flipping out. She really wasn't going. Twan told her to shut up and lean back. Pink Toe sat in the middle console seat next to Jazabel. She instantly became jealous of her and felt her position was definitely in jeopardy. Twan with her? She was gorgeous. She was the type of exotic female that had girls curious, too. They all exchanged mean stares back and forth, including Oprah ginger head ass. She wasn't slick at all. Twan saw her keep looking back in her rearview mirror, trying to provoke the redbones. He told all them hoes to cut it out and Oprah to pay attention to the road and not the backseat. She sucked her teeth and dropped her Cartier frames over her eyes.

Twan texted the con man that he was there finally after Oprah ass got them lost. They waited for the con man to pull back up again. He got distracted waiting on Pimpin and more money called his phone, too. He felt like 2-Chainz, all 3 of his cellphones were jumping! Soon as he made his run, he pulled up on Twan and jumped out of his red Dodge mini-van. He ran around to Twan's side.

"Pimpin since pimpin since pimpin!! I see you, Pimpin…Damn, how much she charge, the platinum-colored-eye blonde ho?? Man—I got 60 bucks and I'll give you the package deal and throw in all fake ID's for all four of ya hoes right now, Pimpin?" the con man said anxiously, full of excitement. He was turnt up and smelt money and pussy so bad he could taste a teaspoon full of it! Twan just shook his head, then checked his hoes first for reckless eyeballing. They were in violation of ho conduct 101!

"Bitch—y'all 2 hoes is out of pocket! Don't look at him! Unless y'all want to leave with him? Now look down, bitch! Matter fact, make y'all chin touch y'all chest—and reckless eyeball ya lap! Matter of fact, ho, have a convo with y'all lap! Smell ya own pussy. Make sure it don't stank with y'all funky asses!" Twan snapped and turnt up something crucial to his 2 out-of-pocket hoes.

"Oowwee...Damn, Pimpin, you got 'em trained like some thoroughbred horses. Damn...see, I couldn't be a pimp! I love to eat pussy too much and plus I'm a big trick!! I tell them all day—I'll pay to play, straight out!" the con man stated proudly in a lustful manner.

"Okay, now to the bizz...First off, you can't afford my thousand-dollar-an-hour hoes unless you got some bands. This Vegas, baby. Anyhow, I do appreciate you showing a Louisiana pimp some Southern hospitality and putting me up on G! Dis a nice little liq and yes, I do want the fake ID's for all my hoes just in case they get caught up. Especially for my two ratchett redbones in the backseat. So give me a player deal and a pimp package?" Twan said quick and slick.

"Oh...okay, you want the pimp package, huh? Man—so let me think. FYI, I usually charge a band! That a rac for call girl poster card and give you a thousand cards and 500 flyers to post in windshields. Now if you talking bout doin profiles and posting pic and hosting a local call page—wheew, that another rac, pimpin. But I'll throw in the fake ID's for a player's price, 7 hundo," he stated slicker than Twan, trying to fast-talk a pimp. However, Twan wasn't going or about to get Hitachi'd around his hoes or period!

"Man, 7 bills? Please...I'll give you 3 bills, nigga? Shit—"

"Bet! C'mon, Pimpin, you ain't said shit," the con man jumped the gun, cutting Twan off, agreeing to the $300.

Twan and the conman shook up in a deal sealed, then he peeled him off 3 bills real quick. They all got out the car, except Jazabel Arabic ass. She had her arm folded with a pouting puckered bottom lip.

Twan looked back and told her to come on! She shook her head no! Twan ran over and tried to pull her out the back left seat. He yanked her arm swiftly! She couldn't believe how strong he was. He pulled her halfway out of the car. She felt his power and strength.

"S-Stop it, Twan! I'm done, I can't believe you. Okay, first the powder sniffing lines and then the kissing another girl threesome last night. But this, these other girls and you really being a pimp? And trying to pimp me out—No! I'm sorry, I'm not a flunky, Twan. Now drop me back off at the penthouse so I can get my belongings and we depart ways for good. Twan, my parents are rich! My dad is a computer engineer and programmer at the airport with his own companies. My credit cards each got over $10,000 limits. If you need money, all you got to do is ask me. And I'll help you or assist in whatever endeavors you trying to do in life, but selling myself and using my body as a man's convenience store isn't going to happen, period, okay! It's forbidden and against my morals and religion. No-No-No!! Twan, drop me back off now, please..." Jazabel pleaded nervously in a very high-pitched voice.

"Damn, gurrl, why you yelling all out here in this McDonald's parking lot, putting me all on blast in front of my hoes—matter fact y'all bitches go into the McDonald's and sit y'all asses down till he ready and don't be ordering food trying to be funny! We ain't here to eat!" Twan stated coldly, dismissing his hoes being nosy as Jazabel was having an episode. The con man opened up the red minivan and grabbed a few pieces of equipment, moving slowly trying to be nosy, too. He wanted to hear and see what Twan was about to do next. She sat quiet. Twan looked dead into her soft gray-greenish sparkling eyes…

"Jazabel, listen to me and please don't cut me off, okay? Now I need you more than ever right now and more than you ever know! Now you know that your exotic features and the fact that you're foreign imported, that boost your value and feature price, unlike the other girls. So you also boost my own call girl service prices, too. You gonna take me to the top! So I hope you spot so I don't drop, Jaz…Damn, Twan needs you. Just take the flicks and make my call girl service look professional and make them tricks blow up them lines. We can vic the casino hotels. When all the tricks call for you, we'll say you out on a date for the rest of the night and would be gladly able to substitute them with another option of girls from the card at a discounted rate. So that it, that all, I promise. Then I'll drop you off, Jaz, that's my word. Now c'mon, you way too gorgeous to be looking all frowned up like one of those ugly girls now!" Twan said nonchalantly in a convincing tone as he reached out for her hand and she extended it back. They both walked into the McDonald's together as she wiped dry her eyes and fixed her hair. She had to build her confidence up. This wasn't like playing volleyball. This was a whole nother foreign field to her. Twan really lit up inside out and cracked a slight smirk as he knew he had him one and she just got vic'd. She was still going, she just was not knowing.

He opened the door for her. The con man told them all to go into the bathroom. This particular McDonald's had a lock on the bathroom door. You had to pay quarters to use it. Then once they got in it was a personal slot machine in there. Only in Vegas will you see some shit like that, Twan thought.

He stood back and the con man did his thing in the McDonald's bathroom and he was damn sure good at it. Twan could tell he was from Cali and did this special a million times before. He even pulled at a draping studio background from his black duffle bag, along with a printer and scanner. Twan didn't know where he got half them machines or the name of them special machines that worked wonders. Knowing dude, it was probably hot! Stolen right from the MVD. This was Vegas, after all. You could get your hands on or into anything.

The con man set up shop clean and instructed Twan's hoes one by one. But for some reason he took extra long with Jazabel and saved her the best for last, which had Twan curious. She was flat-out annoyed and ready to get the hell out of that crowded little bathroom. She couldn't breathe and had felt the anxiety built up to her neck. It took him all of 20 minutes tops for all four girls and he was already loading and printing out his digital HD 3D camera.

When he was done, he showed Twan the finished product. It was a masterpiece, fabulous! It looked so damn professional. Twan wanted to really consider about registering his own legit escorting service with the State of Nevada, shit.

Got damn it!! First thing he noticed was Jazabel's gorgeous ass and how her sparkling eyes popped out on the card. He had centered her. She stood out from the rest of the girls. He put the 2 ratchett redbones diagonal from each other to make them look more spread out, so you didn't see just 2 duck hoes. He also gave Twan a few different options that he could choose from. Twan tipped him and told him he wanted him to print all 3 options. He told Twan give him a day and he'll have all the copies printed out for him. They agreed, shook up, and parted ways. Twan for once felt like an international pimp, like he was doing super big things. He no longer felt ratchett or like a ratchett pimp so they called him. He and his hoes all headed back to the penthouse, as promised. He felt like a king pimp! It was on and poppin once again. It was pimpin in live effect, full-fledged smashing and dragging a bitch!! He streamed his Lil Boosie from his smartphone and got his swerve on as he hit the blunt of Blue Dream kush, making the car dance like he was from H-Town.

Twan was ecstatic back at the penthouse. He had all his hoes there. It was party-party-party, let's all get wasted like Gucci Mane. His 2 ratchett ho redbones couldn't believe Twan's pimp'd out penthouse. They had a trick take them into one when it was the big Las Vegas convention in town.

Twan texted J Pimp and told his young ass to roll through with his 2 hoes and to do him a big favor and pick up Pimpin Silky, too, and tell him to bring the nose candy. Then he threw a party pack of e-pills at his hoes and cracked open the Diddy Juice Pineapple Cîroc and the Grey Goose fifth. He knew all hoes usually liked the white clear liquor.

"All I got is y'all!! My Mama Lela is dead—BITCH!! Fuck dat. Everybody do a line and celebrate with me, the Louisiana way! When someone pass away, we celebrate! Fuck it. We only live once—BITCH! The pussy cracker killed my Ma. Y'all hoes turn-up and celebrate without fightin. Don't be disrespecting my Mama's celebration and party. Now errbody do a line for my Mama smoking ass. Y'all knew how much she loved this shit! It be like dat sometime, and not just in the boot-shaped State of Louisiana—but nationwide is on ya side!" Twan said turned-up as he popped a triple stack Ecstasy pill and swigged it down with the Cîroc, chasing it hard!

All the girls followed suit except Jazabel, the Arabian ho. She just sat there and stared hard at Twan with her keys in her hands, ready to go and be out of his life for good now. But somehow she couldn't go! She didn't want to leave him at all! It was something she loved about Twan. Maybe the thuggish hood in him. But she hated his pimpin and his using and preying on weak girls ways. He was a master manipulator, too. She didn't want to miss out on the excitement. Plus she didn't want to be the Spongebob Squarepants out the bunch and not celebrate Twan's mother passing with him. She saw Twan turn his head and back to her as his ratchett redbones Pink Toe and Butterscotch catered to him with rolled-up hundred-dollar bills with crispy thick lines of cocaine on the platter. Twan waved her off like fuck her boogie ass.

She jumped up, snatched the hundred-dollar bill from Pink Toe, and sniffed a hefty line, then guzzled some of Twan's Cîroc, trying to impress him. Twan saw he had her and needed all her time and just for her to stay another night so he could put Part 2 of his master pimp plan together.

J Pimp showed up at the penthouse bubbly with his 2 hoes, and Pimpin Silky with a black leather Kangol hat. He was old skool with it. J Pimp's tall, long-legged Chinese ho and his snowbunny started busting out and chopping down lines of that puro from Silky.

Everyone was chilling as the Future streamed through the JBL audio system.

"You ain't even sticking to the code! You ain't even playing it how it goes…Pimps up-Pimps up-Hoes down! A room full of money and I'm bout to drown!" Future's "Honest" iTune could be heard throughout the pimp'd-out penthouse.

All the hoes were jivin, rolling hard and faded from all the pills and potions, which sparked an idea in Twan's head. He ran to the back room and got Jazabel's gym bag, then asked for her car keys. He went out and searched through her car like the LVMPD did for contraband. Bingo! Pimpin-Pimpin!! He found exactly what he was looking for: UNLV apparel.

He had 2 black UNLV t-shirts, a UNLV hat, sweatshirt, hoodie, and her 2 volleyball uniforms, the away and home colors. He told all the bitches to put a piece of the UNLV items on and make it look hot and risky. The hoes had tied knots in shirts, raised the volleyball shorts like they were boy shorts, and some were topless with just a UNLV hat on. Twan grabbed Jazabel's Galaxy Note S4. He began recording video skits, telling the girls to freak each other, flash the camera, bend over, and do erotic sex acts for him. It was a Girls Gone Wild UNLV pimp's edition. Twan got it in for a good 35 minutes before all the hoes were horny and really acting on their excessive impulses. The girls started bumping and licking pussies and trying to suck on all the pimps' dicks, which led to one big fuckfest. It was one big orgy, including Pimpin Silky's old washed-up ass, that lasted into the wee hours of the morning. Twan ran through all J Pimp's hoes, too. On the low he was trying to snatch his tall, long-legged Chinese ho. She was definitely dick dizzy, but she remained loyal and in love with J Pimp young underage ass. The 2 ratchett redbones had young J Pimp occupied doing their same routine they did on Twan to recruit J Pimp, even though he didn't like sistas. It was an investment like an insurance policy. Just in case Twan fired them, J Pimp could hire them gladly. Everyone had their own ulterior motives, with that devil in them recruiting and booting. Even Pimpin Silky with his peeling ain't stealing if she willing motto. He was trying to snatch Twan and J Pimp's snowbunnies. He claimed he was checking to see if their game was tight. Really he was finessing the pussy and the 2 white bitches, hitting them with that old-school sugar pimp game. It definitely wasn't no Bay shit, it was some vic a white bitch and snatch a snowbunny up type shit. Twan heard his slick quick-talking ass. He was short-stopping! Twan wasn't trippin, knowing Silky was high and faded. He also watched how his 2 ratchett redbones kept going in on J Pimp after everyone had crashed out hard. He didn't hate, he just let them hoes do them and freak his young pimp partner, but knowing their intentions.

The next day after J Pimp and his hoes dropped Pimpin Silky off, he sat to gather his thoughts before all his hoes woke up. This was Jazabel's big day and he prayed he could wing it right and hit big like Barry Bonds. This would be the grand slam to take him to the Pimpin World Series! And once he got there he knew he would definitely hit some more big ones right out of the ballpark with the Arabian bitch and run to home plate all the way.

He uploaded the video skits off her Galaxy Note 4, before their big orgy, to Amazon.com. He put them for $12.99 a download. He kept a profit of $8.99 per download from Amazon Percent. The UNLV girls was titled "UNLV Girls Wildin Out!" They were already downloading by the minutes and seconds as Twitter followers tweeted across the nation and overseas. Twan was about to hit a mill ticket overnight or in a couple days tops and he didn't even know it. He was thinking more like 60-100 bands the most and that was after 2-3 months tops!

Twan checked his messages and saw the con man had told him his escorting service card was a finished masterpiece. Twan agreed to meet him at the lounge at Caesar's casino. He knew it was hot exchanging fictitious call girl cards. Twan sat there at the lounge and saw the private section where they were giving celebrities lessons on how to play cards, poker, blackjack, 5card stud, Texas hold 'em style, and Omaha. He looked at the professional-looking cards, both designs. And Jazabel, the Arabian exotic dimepiece, was centerfold on both cards. He knew which card he wanted at what casino hotels. Which one fitted which, including from the most popular, to the most tourist attractions. He texted and phoned all his hoes to meet him at the Trump Plaza. He gave the con man a fist pound dap and thanked him once again as he took the thousand pile service cards and stack of flyers as promised from the con man included in the deal, too.

Oprah pulled up first with Butterscotch and Jazabel pulled up 10 minutes later with Pink Toe. Twan was happy to see all his hoes in full compliance and acting as in accordance to the penal Pimp code. They were acting as a sisterhood with that same bond. Twan would always tell them that they were sisters and were all one big family with the same daddy—Twan! He just couldn't believe how good his hoes' behavior was and most of all how his 2 instigating shit-starting ratchett redbone hoes weren't hating and trying to chase his other new bitches off. He still had to watch them 2 hoes, because he damn sure couldn't trust them. But he had to admit they all looked fly just like a hovering drone! Then he thought back to the wild orgy last night and knew they're all thinking they were all on a short leash because they got loose as a goose and fucked every ho and pimp, including Silky old ass, in the penthouse. He would use this as leverage and a vic trick to his advantage, too. Yeah, buddy—Pimpin-pimpin!! After the long silent stares, Twan had to let all their minds wander a little bit like Plies says.

"Okay...Ladies, can I get y'all undivided attention, please? Welcome to the infamous Trump Plaza! I couldn't think of a more beautiful place to start this mission called Operation 'Mama Lela' where our sole mission is to pass out all of these service cards under as many hotel doors, on all floors, in as many casino hotels as possible! Then we have flyers to pass out at the Crystal Mall and business parking lots. Cipesi! Divide and conquer so y'all hoes all be alert from hotel security and them damn cameras. Be stealth and swift. Move slick and agile. Be safe and careful. No arrests, either. Dem LVMPD be lurking around the casinos and guarding the tellys as well…Now Pink Toe, take ya sista Jazabel with you, and y'all 2 cover the Hard Rock and Planet Hollywood. Also pass out some of the flyers at the Rehab pool party because TGT will be there again with Jamie Foxx.

"Oprah and Butterscotch, y'all 2 hoes cover grounds on the MGM and right here at the Trump Plaza. Now help me split these up. Remember, divide and conquer! And my motto—come back successful or not at all! Hmph!" Twan stated like he was the warrior in 300 leading the Spartan Army and chuckled at the end like Kat Williams, dismissing his hoes, waving them off and shewing them off like flies, saying goodbye!

Two hours later things were going according to plan and all his hoes were sticking to the script and vicing the hotels all up and down the strip. Success is best and a true love story, a pimp story—history, like Drake say!! Twan could sniff, smell, and taste success. He had helluva pep in his step. He was a pimp with a limp and really knew how it felt to be a peppy pimpin! Winning and trending hashtag #RIPMamaLela!

He was helping out his 2 hoes covering the MGM Hotel, sliding fictitious call girl cards under the hotel doors on the 5th floor. When he worked his way down to the 3rd floor, he made it halfway down the hallway from the elevator when he heard the hotel elevator go ding!

He heard some walkie-talkies clicking on and off with a dispatch sound in the background.

"Heyyy—You, come here. Freeze, right there!!" the officer shouted in an intimidating tone.

Twan turned around and saw 2 LVMPD officers in tan-issued uniforms with Tasers in their hand and hotel security next to them.

"Oh...shit! Hands up, don't shoot! Rest in peace, Mike Brown—" Twan yelled as he threw his hands up like an NFL referee signaling a field goal is good. Then he turned back around, tucked his 40 or so fictitious cards in his waist and broke fast!! as he shouted aloud, "Save ur selves!!" He did that to sound and play drunk, knowing he couldn't outrun that radio or cameras on foot. He already had an alibi.

He cut for the stairwell exit at the east end of the hotel floors. They gave in on the foot pursuit.

"Baker 1-4, we got a black male suspect running on foot down MGM Hotel stairwell. Request backup on the northeast exit—10-4!" the LVMPD officer radio request for backup for other officers to assist.

"Okay, roger that, 10-4! Can I have a brief description of black male?" the dispatcher replied.

"Yes, ma'am...ugh, he gots on a LSU purple shirt and a purple hat with a tiger on it, turned backwards. Approximately 5 foot 11 to 6 foot even, around 160 to 165 pounds. 10-4!" the out-of-shape middle-aged officer replied, talking into his radio attached to his shoulder, out of breath. All that could be seen on the LVMPD bodycam was Twan fleeing and clearing steps. All the Baton Rouge came out of Twan. That nigga was gone! All the LVMPD could say was, damn, he is fast!

Twan was a whole flight of steps ahead of them as he jumped down the last flight and smacked dead into the wall, out of breath, wheezing like an asthmatic. He looked like Pookie off of "New Jack City" running from Ice Tea, the narc. He pulled open the bottom floor lobby door. He ran and saw a utility custodian closet and rambled into his waistband real quick, scrambling all the fictitious cards out. He was shaking his pants out, trying to get the rest of the cards out. These goddamn skinny jeans, were all he could think. He kicked all of them and stuffed the rest loose ones under the locked door, then fled just as the LVMPD trailed him through the stairwell door. He headed for the emergency exit on the northeastern side of the MGM. Soon as he headed out the door, he was met by LVMPD 2 cars deep...

"FREEZE! FREEZE—DON'T MOVE!" the 2 officers yelled. Twan threw his hands up and shouted back, "Don't shoot!"

The following officers came running out of the MGM exit and bumrushed Twan, slamming him to the ground hard and putting all knees and elbows into his neck and side as they handcuffed him and read him his rights. They picked him up after they quickly pat-searched him, frisking him for weapons and contraband. They slammed his head back and forth on the hot Vortec hood of the Vegas squad car as they interrogated him viciously, disregarding their body cams.

They asked Twan where was his fictitious illegal escorting service cards at? They told him that it was illegal to be soliciting services in the casino hotels without being registered with the Board of Las Vegas and with the State of Nevada, too. Then they told him he was busted and that way to go because a little 8-year-old girl had picked up the call girl card! Which the parents phoned the lobby for a formal complaint.

Twan denied it and told them he was a college student from LSU here gambling, enjoying his break, and that he was just drunk only. They told him, bullshit! And that he was posing as a pimp running on a scheme and going down to Clark County Jail, then slammed him down on the hood again, roughing Twan up.

They asked him why was he running from them then? He told him he wasn't a pimp and he ran because he was drunk and scared of the police because it was a secret war between Black and Blue out here! Then they asked him, "Just give up the guy who paid you to pass out these cards and we'll let you go free. Just point us in the right direction so we can crack this pimp, and take him off the streets! Obviously he didn't care about you. It's way too hot to do this around these household name legendary casino hotels. How much he paid you? C'mon. Like 50 dollars? Think about it. See, pimps give Las Vegas a bad look and make our streets look filthy with their hookers, usually weak-minded white chicks or crystal meth hookers." They tried to turn, twist, and flip Twan to roll over and snitch. Twan played possum and dumb drunk as they were thumbprinting Twan and giving him an obstruction ticket for fleeing from a peace officer and banning him from the MGM hotel casino for life. He saw Oprah with her YSL pumps and Tom Ford on, watching them from across the street.

He was pissed the hell off and kept looking away from the ho! She had him nervous and paranoid. And her dumb ass still didn't know it and probably had all them flyers and same cards in her tote bag, too. He tried to nod the bitch off with a sideways head nod, just as the cop caught on to his little gestures and looked over into the crowd, staring across the street. Damn it! Twan started flipping out and had to think twice and be quick on his toes. He wasn't going to no damn Las Vegas desert jail or for that long ass ride! He started coughing ill and very frantic like he was about to die. It was dramatic as he collapsed to the ground and acted like he couldn't breathe! They kept saying, knock it off! Like Twan was trying to pull a cold stunt so that they could call the EMT medics. Most people pulled this stunt to avoid arrest and jail time. They'd seen it all but for some reason Twan's really felt urgent. It was disturbing. They already told him it was a ticket since they couldn't find none of the cards on his possession.

They asked Twan again, was he all right and asthmatic? And did he need an EMT? Twan told them he had a high fever and his Mama and sisters just got back from West Africa a week ago in Louisiana. And he thought it could be Ebola because he couldn't stop throwing up and had the runs. Twan hurled chunks of his lunch all over the officer's pant leg.

The officers looked at Twan's black ass and immediately freaked the hell out and stepped back! They radioed in to dispatch a special hazmat team requested and a possible Ebola case! They shut down the whole Las Vegas strip and MGM Hotel. They quarantined his ass under his alias Burdette.

Oprah and Butterscotch shook their heads. He made 5 o'clock local news and CNN breaking news, too. Twan was hot at Oprah dumb green as a thumb ass.

- Chapter 10 -

"Sin City"

All Twan's hoes sat worried for the past couple of days now. Still no sign of Twan. They had been working the clients and doing hotel calls from the cards without no narcs or reverse stings. J Pimp and Silky both wasn't shit, thinking Twan was about to be booked into Clark County Jail right along with Fatz da Mac and all the rest of the fuck-ups and P's that slipped up and fell victim to Vegas penal system. It was a whole different world of tango!

After 72 hours of observing Twan in quarantine, they freed Twan once all his tests came back negative. He hurried and caught a taxi to the penthouse. He surprised all his hoes. Of course the 2 redbones lazy asses was the only ones there chill-laxing! He cursed them out viciously and told them to clean up his penthouse and go out there and work them hotels. They told him Jazabel went back home and they sent Oprah out there to work them hotels. They were too afraid after he got booked to work them casino hotels from them fake escorting services.

Twan flipped out! It was against his pimpin constitution all the way, and clearly a flagrant foul. The hoes only had 3 strikes and struck out. He smacked and choked them hoes both out at the same time, attempting to squeeze the life out of the 2 half-naked hoes! Once he stopped he told them gasping hoes to strip! They got butt-naked and he kicked them out his penthouse without no shoes, phone, or nothing! They were embarrassed and pleading, crying out for him to let them back in. They took turns trying to talk some sense into Twan and talking sweet for the next 20 minutes to Twan, praying that he smoked a blunt and calmed down.

Twan ignored them hoes and told them to go get his doe! 72 hours worth they owed and needed to pay the piper and their ho dues. It's finders fees and pimp taxation! Pimps up, hoes down!

He checked all his messages and his social media contacts. He texted J Pimp and Silky to let them know he was free and all Gucci. J Pimp told him he was on his way.

Pimpin Silky told him he got some new pink powder, it got a strawberry taste called Pink Panther. Twan told him to save him some for later when they hit Freemont.

He phoned Jazabel. She was so damn happy but mad as hell. She told him that video he recorded went viral somehow and they were selling copies on Amazon.com and her parents cut her off, mad at her because it was also a sex video of her on YouTube channel called YouPorn streaming her getting flipped by Pimpin Silky old ass every which way! Also she dropped out of UNLV because of that Girls Gone Wild tape and viral video! Her life was ruined and now she didn't have nobody because her family turned their backs on her. They knew Vegas was a bad idea for going to college out there. They preferred her to stay in Idaho close to them. They couldn't understand how westernized she had become or why would she do this. Her dad would give her any amount of money she wanted, all she had to do was call and ask.

She continued to cry her heart out and blaming Twan, telling him he ruined her life and career!

Twan told her he's her family now and she was in the wrong career anyway, and told her to get all of her shit from that apartment and come home to him, because they were all they got since now they both lost their parents. He promised he'll never turn his back on her, EVER! And he knew she only did all those things because she loved and cared for him. Plus he really wanted to see how far she would go for him.

"Oh... So Twan, I was a test this whole time? Just a damn science biology experiment, and losing my family and disgracing my father and my religion for you! So what now, is you going to try to pimp me out now that I have nothing? I just wanted to stay with you till I find a job and different apartment where they don't know my name or face!" Jazabel said in a whiny tone as she kept wiping her river of tears.

"Hell nawh... Jaz, dis Sin City, gurrl, and you know it! Hell no—it wasn't my intention for none of this ill-intent to happen. We all were just having fun and mourning my Mama the Southern way, partying and shit. Things led up to all them events, it's called drugs and alcohol, or like Nicki Minaj say, pills and potions! Now damn, come over here. Ain't nobody trying to pimp you out! Jaz, I just got out the hospital from being quarantined for 72 hours, the Ebola scare had me isolated from the world in a bubble. Shit, I got embarrassed in front of the whole world, they flashed my picture and name. Now I scare every person I come in contact with! You think you got it bad, at least ya peeps still alive! You can at least text them. So you want to trade and be in my shoes? I never came from money, just them Baton Rouge streets. That swamp, bitch! Bye!" *Click!* Twan stated coldly, then hung up.

He knew how she needed him and he got her ass by a purely fluke! He wasn't trying to hear all her pimpin prisms straight up and down! He plotted strategically on her and his fake escort service. He was now 3 days behind.

He went online to check his PayPal account from the UNLV Girls Wildin Out video. The balance made his heart skip a beat! It was a whopping $671,868. Balling! *Ching-ching!* He hit big in Sin City, *ding-ding!* He was frozen for a minute, staring at the green 6-digit figures on the screen!

"When it's my turn to pay, I'ma bail on a bitch! And if she try to make extra, I'ma telling on a bitch! I pack an eleven, I pack a 11—I'll shot at da revern!" Young Thug sang the hook featured on T.I.'s "Paperwork" iTune he had streaming through his phone.

"Heyyy…Ayeee…Heyyy…Ayeee—A-A-Ayeee…" Twan uttered in a happy tone like he was in a money frenzy while cocking his head from side to side. Suddenly everything changed before his eyes, by his surprise! He felt like he was pimpin dolomite and twisted a victory blunt and had to pop a pill and sniff a phat line of that white girl. He ran over to find his Cîroc bottle to see them 2 heifers drunk all his shit, thinking he was just gone all suddenly. He thanked God and blew a kiss up to his Mama Lela, knowing pimpin hoes was the way to go and at least he didn't end up like his big bro TNut that got killed gang-banging in the early 2000s. He felt like August Alsina. "Mama, I made it and I know I made you proud." Even looking down, he knew he made her smile and that she was rooting for him and up there, cheering hard.

"Mama, don't get you and big bro TNut kicked out of heaven yet! Not before I get there to be in harmony with y'all!" Twan said excitedly, talking aloud to himself, losing his got damn rabid ass mind. That money was already going to his head! And he knew that he really sold a million ticket that almost $700,000 was his cut! So that made him officially a million-dollar pimp! True indeed, now J Pimp or Pimpin Silky couldn't call him ratchett no more! He thought about it real quick. He wouldn't even tell them shit! After all, this was Sin City and he couldn't trust nobody. These streets already claimed his Mama Lela, too.

His ringtone was going off after he ignored a few text messages coming in. He thought it was J Pimp hot boy ass.

"Yeah—Yeah? Pimpin? Talk to me quick—not slick, P! Whatz Gucci, my dude?" Twan said slick and quick as he blew the Blue Dream kush smoke out his nostrils like a Haitian do.

"H-Hello! T-Twan?? Is this you? It's Sandy—Creole, as you call me?? Remember I told you I was moving to Vegas? I hit you up on FB and you said you'd show me around Vegas? I transferred my job. I had to transfer cuz it was too many New Orleans niggas coming out there and people we used to go to school and know popping up dead. Bodies getting found everywhere. In lots, dumpsters, cars, and the swamp! And I'm so sorry about Neese, too. You knew she was my girl and we was play cousins. I didn't want to bother you at the funeral cuz you looked too disturbed. And your son looks just like you too—"

"What—man, STOP jiving me, bitch! What you mean son? I ain't never knotted ya nasty STD-carrying ass up! You burnt me twice, ho! I don't know why I even responded to ya scandalous ass. And you knew Neese couldn't stand you cuz you was her girl that fucked her man and gave us both a STD!" Twan stated coldly after he cut her off mid-sentence.

"Please...pspsh! Twan, I was a lil girl in high school back then. And so what, I didn't know how to take care of myself and fast hot in the ass. It ain't no secret and I wanted a fresh start and we both grown now, and FYI this pussy still gushy and fresh and clean! Disease-free, nigga! So stop fronting, and no, Twan, not me, I'm talking bout ya son by that girl from N.O. with Goldilocks, umh… Diamond, I think? Anyways, I seen her and ya son at the grocery store. She was with Choppa Face. I was buying a dub sack. You know Choppa Face been selling weed since we was in high school. And ya BM was using her EBT card. You know she live in the hood and Choppa Face was giving her a ride right back to the projects," Creole replied in a defensive manner.

"Shit, my fault, gurrl, for coming at ya sideways. It's been a minute and I just lost my Mama. Now I find out I got a son? Whoa! My head is fucked up a little! So Choppa Face still alive?" Twan said in shock.

"Ahh, yeah, you know he got shot up some months ago way back! I got ya BM added on FB if you want her FB info or me to send her a message, let me know and I got you, 'Pimpin'! Ha-ha-ha…" she said in a seductive tone.

"Damn, why you say it like dat!? Now bring ya ass to this pimp penthouse, we need to chop-n-pop. I'll text the addy right now," Twan said quick.

He couldn't believe the change of events. Now he had a son? He thought she lost both of the babies? And what was she still doing in BR? He thought at the hospital when he fought her sister that they were moving back to New Orleans. Damn, how can she deceive him and stoop that damn low? Bitches ain't shit, was all he thought. Even though he vic'd her and smashed hard on her, made her rob her dude, a straight killer from New Orleans 9th Ward that shot her and killed their twin daughter for revenge. His mind rumbled at the thought and he gripped his stomach. He felt the room spinning.

Then a swift knock on the door! Things was moving 100 mph too fast! It was a blast from his past! Like he couldn't shake his Baton Rouge karma despite not responding to none of them back home on the book and social media. It all just added fuel to an eternal fire! Shit got ugly. Here he had all the money he needed to retire and run off with his bottom ho? But on the other hand, how could he stop now when he had a seed out there to feed in need? He really couldn't stop pimpin! And he didn't want to step foot back in BR to face his past. And he knew that them 9th Ward New Orleans boys were seeking vengeance for their homie N.O. that he murdered for killing his bottom ho Neese. He wanted to hit Diamond Cutz up on FB so damn bad and check her ass, then curse her smooth the hell out. He couldn't blame her for hating him, really?

It was another knock at the door. Twan yelled out, "Hold up!" He ran to the door and it was J Pimp standing over his 2 cuddled-up ratchett redbones. He told J Pimp to come in while his 2 hoes sat cold shivering on the ground. As J Pimp laughed and came in, the 2 hoes followed. Twan didn't care or pay them hoes no mind. They ran and locked themselves in the bathroom. They sat there for 10 minutes while J Pimp and Twan chop-it-up clowning, then got dressed and left for work.

Twan seen his 2 hoes Butterscotch and Pink Toe ratchett scandalous ass smash past him with their 6-inch clear stilettos. He couldn't wait to knock some better snowbunnies. He didn't believe in firing a ho, or letting no hoes go. But he'd replace them 2 hoes, not chase or waste them.

Jazabel came storming through the front door of the penthouse with her luggage. She was upset, leaning on one hip with her arms folded, glaring hard at Twan. She couldn't believe he was being an asshole and wouldn't help her with her belongings?? She told him to forget it! and rolled her eyes at J Pimp as she flicked Twan off with 2 birdies on each hand, then stormed off to Twan's back room, switching her ass hard. She had a ho walk naturally. She probably just thought she was fierce with a runway supermodel walk. Twan giggled at the silly ho, knowing she just was hot in the ass and wanted him to come cater to her and punish her pussy. He didn't have time to hold no ho's hand or babysit. He noticed her puffy red eyes and swollen face like she'd been crying for 2 days straight.

Then it was a third straight knock at the door. Twan yelled, "Come in," thinking it was Pimpin Silky with that strawberry Pink Panther powder nose candy. But to his surprise it was an old school blast from the past friend...Sandy!

Creole was her nickname that Twan called her. Damn, she was a true Creole indeed. It looked like she belonged to the Beyoncé tree family because she had them Beyoncé Deron genes in here. She stood 5'5", 130 lbs., hazel-honey-greenish eyes, curly goldish-red hair with a glazing honey-dip skin complexion. She was a 36C cup, thin, 21-inch waist with a round apple bottom. She was in an all soft white cat suit with a gripping p-print. She had a real moose knuckle down there and was killing Nicki Minaj! Even J Pimp's jaw was jacked as he grabbed his aching dick! "Damn, P! Who dat?" J Pimp asked curiously.

She seen Twan stuck and all over her so all her plans and hidden agendas were now into full effect. She'd been planning to pay him a visit in Vegas and to fuck him good again once she seen him trending on Instagram, flexing with a multi-billionaire Money Mayweather.

"So, Twan, you gonna sit there and be rude, huh? I told you I'm not that little young, dumb, and full of cum girl from the hood that you went to high school with. Well, maybe still full of cum but I'm not dumb—I'm all woman. Anyways, I'm Creole from BR, Twan's friend, and ask him whatever next?… He was the one that named me that and it stuck with me," she said in a sexy low tone like she was down to suck and fuck them both, but for free! Not a fee!

She walked over to Twan and gave him a big ol warming hug, stood on her tippy-toes and pecked Twan dead on his lips, then told him sorry for his loss of his Mama Lela.

Twan hugged her back and gripped them phatty bottom ass cheeks. He had to catch himself, but really was stunting and fronting in front of J Pimp young ass, letting him know he was the man and had hoes all over the globe. He knew Creole sackchasin ass seen the Bentley coupe J Pimp had parked downstairs in the parking lot. He told her to slow down, she was moving too fast already.

J Pimp asked did they want to ride out with him to pick this bread up and check bread from his hoes at the same time. Plus he offered to take Twan by Silky's on Freemont! They smashed out, taking Vegas by surprise.

J Pimp kept looking back in the rearview mirror. He seen her looking all around the Bentley, jocking! She didn't even know it was a casino rental right off the strip. She kept glancing at him, smiling. J Pimp didn't want to peel his pimp partner's loose ho reckless checking! But if she kept going she was gone. And she was classified under a duck ho, even though she was a Louisiana Creole. The rules was if the bitch wink, she'd fuck! Let her keep up. She'd get plucked! J Pimp grinned as he passed Twan the kush blunt and held the purple smoke deep in his lungs.

J Pimp checked his iPhone 6, his texts were blowing up. It was his Chinese ho, she needed condoms, KY, and Febreeze. She couldn't go on a store run herself and leave the Planet Hollywood Hotel, it was live with johns needing service and dirty tune-ups.

J Pimp told Twan they got to stop at Wal-mart, the one on Berkley, which was the home of the ratchetts! Twan hated that one. It was full of them North Vegas bitches employees. If you Google it, you would see all ratchett managers with purple weaves and big ol hoop earrings with their names in them. It was ratchelistic!

Twan shook his head. He knew at that Wal-mart you was guaranteed to pimp on or fuck on somebody's baby mama. Somebody's baby mama was going or getting sent, either way, fucking around at that Berkley Wal-mart.

Creole secretly snapped some picks of J Pimp driving the Bentley and Twan riding up front. She already was on IG posting pics and showing off for the caption. It read: *2 pimps and Creole Bentley music.* Twan seen her back there texting and passed her the blunt, telling her don't get 'text neck' from all that hunching forward and secret-squirrel girl texting. Them girls were text masters these days, they could text, touch their toes, and fuck!

She hit the sweet kush blunt twice and passed it back to Twan in the passenger seat. She put it up to his lip! And told him to hit it, Daddy. Then she asked if she could take a selfie with hm. He nodded like he was a celebrity. She leaned forward and wrapped her right arm around the passenger seat and it rested on his shoulder while she snapped herself in the pic with him, making her Betty Boop faces. Then she took one of her holding the blunt up to Twan's chapped lips.

"Thanks—Daddy! Turn around and let me fix them chapped lips real quick. I got you, Daddy. Twan, I can't lie, I do miss you, and you know that you always been having me grinning before you was trending, when you first was pimpin. Remember you tried to sic me on Neese and pimp me out to ya old ass brother when we was in high school just to show off to ya older bro TNut? Ha-ha-ha... Damn, Twan, I almost went too, but I was too afraid of ya older brother, he was too big, shit! Being grown wasn't the problem but I already heard bout him! I regret it tho, and now I'm older I really know how to do it discreet and how to get what I want by giving what they need..." Creole said in a soft tone with a heavy Baton Rouge accent.

Mmwwahh!! She kissed Twan with a phat juicy one that had a lustful hint of horny passionate wild hood sex! Twan's dick jumped, being caught off guard. J Pimp seen her stuck on Twan and busting a smooth move. Twan just wiped his lips and shook his head in disgust. "So what you sayin, Creole?" Twan stated curiously.

"I don't know. What it sounds like? You tell me—you're the pimp! Seriously, Twan, I didn't come out to Sin City to go to church, now. I came out here to work. Yes, I want to sell this Creole pussy for you and us ride and stay fly together. I work by myself I don't need no companion hoes. Just show me the ropes out here!?" she stated like a bottom boss ho!

"Damn, bitch! Slow up now...that's what ya fast ass move to ATL for, huh? Or did the Big Easy turn you out? Probably them Atlanta hoes cuz them slick hoes will send a bitch too! But you been my ho and always compete with Neese. Now dat she out the picture, you finally got a shot! I hope you really got ya shots—bitch?!" Twan snapped and went hard on Creole real quick, putting her in her place. She sucked her teeth as

J Pimp started cracking up out loud. She told J Pimp her pussy smelt like water and tasted like Bubble Yum and tight like his skinnys he had on that gripped his crotch! And it's phat and soft like a peach. J Pimp got quiet real quick as he suffered an uncomfortable agony stiffy in his skinnys from her graphic details. It was too much information, but really it was her Creole ass with that Louisiana Southern drawl. Her accent was driving J Pimp ham! He wanted to tell that bitch to shut up. He tucked his Mac 11 under the driver's seat and ran his tall ass into the ratchett Wal-mart. Soon as he left the Bentley, Creole told Twan don't his dude look just like Young Thug with a blonde Mohawk? Twan just laughed and told her yeah, people say Young Thug and him Rich Homie Quan. She really had jokes and was rolling hard.

Twenty minutes later J Pimp came running out of the Walmart with a small blue plastic bag, all out of breath. "Damn, them ratchett hoes was stalking me and ran me out of there. I was in the self-checkout station. Shit, I dipped out and said fuck it, P! Shit, I did a smash and grab and straight stole this shit... P, spark that other blunt?" J Pimp said as he panted like a pit bull out of breath that only suffered shortness of breath from smoking.

"Shit, P, you taking all day and too long. Don't trip—Creole, twist us up 2 phatty blunts. Here!" Twan replied as he threw the sack and blunts into Creole's lap. She complied gladly.

"Oh...shit! Them hoes must have told on me for not paying? Them damn cashiers, P! I told them ugly desert toads that I only liked light-bright next-to-white, snowbunnies applied only!" J Pimp said frantically as he reversed the Bentley and drove backwards, almost hitting a bitch pushing a cart, trying to get away from security and avoid plate detection. Then he smashed off to drop the stuff off with his Chinese bitch and check his bread from the ho!

They stopped by the drive-thru liquor store on Freemont to get faded. That was the only place 17-year-old J Pimp could cop alcohol from without being carded. He was trying to show off in front of Creole, Twan's new guest or bitch? They got some Diddy Juice that Twan turned J Pimp out on. He said really pimps sip, not chug like a thug, not Tupac juice.

Then they started to argue like brothers all in front of the bitch, because J Pimp called Twan a scary ass nigga! Twan said fuck that, to drop him and Creole back off at his penthouse so he can jump in his rented lime Lambo.

What inspired the argument was J Pimp had to go meet up at the MGM hotel and snatch this bread up. He claimed 10 bands? However, Twan told him he wasn't about to get booked or go to jail for nobody, especially out in this desert. J Pimp knew about the Ebola scare stunt he pulled and they banned him for life out the MGM casino/hotel. Twan finally said fuck it and he'll wait outside in the car, because J Pimp was crying about him sipping the whole bottle of Pineapple Cîroc with him to start their night out before they got back to their pimpin and back in their solo lanes.

Like 30 whole minutes went by and Twan and Creole were getting restless in that stuffy Bentley. Mainly they were bubbly from the Cîroc streaming through their bloodstreams. He texted J Pimp for the last time. Then he and Creole got out the car and took their stuff like fuck it!

J Pimp finally texted Twan back with the 10th floor room number, telling Twan he had a sweet liq and to get up here. It was for 10 bands and involved his Creole bitch with him. Twan couldn't lie, that made him want to bust a move and it was a perfect time to test Creole and see what she was about. He wanted to see how she'd perform now that she was grown? She already was a certified and a bona fide ho from back home and his hood, too.

He put her up on G! She was with the bizz and bout-bout it!! They crept into the MGM hotel undetected without any further incident. Twan played like he was drunk in love like Beyoncé say and was all hugged up with Creole, walking her to the elevator with his arms around her. They made it to the 10th floor and stepped off the elevator, then Twan pushed Creole's hot ass off him. She was bubbly and rubbing all on him, horny and shit. He told her to save all that energy for this trick that was about to tip her 10 bands right now! Her eyes lit up and she got into compliance and put her game face on and went into her best ho character. Twan checked his phone and double-checked the suite number. *Tat-tatt!!* He did the pimp tap light and twice!

J Pimp came to the door smelling like kush and alcohol. He told them to come in and sit down while he went and got the old trick! Soon as Twan stepped in, it smelled raunchy like straight ass. But pure—D SHIT!! He fanned in front of his face and told them to spray Febreeze in this damn room! Creole went over to open up the vanity window with the view over the strip. All she could see is all the night desert bright lights flashing and glittering from the 10 floors above! Twan wondered what this old trick was on? And which one of J Pimp's hoes was in there hidden out with the trick? It didn't matter really, she just needed to wash her funky ass and douche her pussy and her funky asshole too.

An old man appeared out of the suite door. He had on an old velvet robe like Hugh Heff. He had black thick glasses, bifocals, with white balding hair. His whole body was limp like he didn't have a backbone or bones period. Creole instantly wanted to throw up and back out saying Hell No!

"Well, hello there? J Pimp has told me all about you. I've been knowing J Pimp for almost a whole year now. Now, as you know, I'm offering 10 grand. This is Sin City and as you know, what happens in Vegas stays in this room? So everyone has fetishes in one way or another, rather hidden, secret or whatever. And my fetish is for pimps! To actually pay them to watch them fuck their own filthy whores they point around town and run in the ground. It's a weird, sick, dirty, twisted fetish, but I pay well. I don't touch, I just watch. I may tell you I can't see, can you switch angles or flip her around. All I request is that y'all both are totally naked. No heels or ghetto chains. What do you say, pimp? Here is the 10 grand as promised," the flimsy old man stated in a peculiar tone as he handed Twan the 10 bands to check.

J Pimp intervened and told Twan he was about to go and shoot craps downstairs and bet 5 bands all on one roll because it was all out of a ho! He told Twan to text him when they were finished and don't be up there making love to his ho! To do a one-take jake, get his rocks off and snake! J Pimp shook the spot and caught the couple in the elevator to hold the doors!

Twan looked at the trick and couldn't quite put his hands on it. He sighed out heavy, then looked over at Creole ol nasty dirty ass. He had put that on his pimpin twice that he'd never fuck her or put his dick in that disease-carrying bitch because she burnt him twice. The last time she made him sick, throwing up like he had the flu! Her shit was more like that Ebola for real. She had that shit that burnt thru condoms. Even though he hit her back in the day bareback straight-up raw without pulling out or nothing. He still felt like her shit clap thru condoms, melting rubbers. That Ebola! She sat there patting her silky wavy hair and batting her eyes, trying to entice Twan. But really she knew Twan was skeptical and having second thoughts about her and this, thinking she was still dirty and burning.

"Daddy—this pussy is in check, believe dat. Let's get these 10 bands. I'll make you cum fast and hard! You can splash it all over my back or bust a nut in my face or cum in my mouth? Come here and sit down so I can show you how better I got!" Creole said in a very erotic, drunken sexy voice, seducing Twan and provoking him once again!

Twan said fuck it! and told the old man to have a seat while he blow her back out and make a porn star!

Creole got up and turned the suite dim, then went back over to Twan and stood in front of him and kicked his legs open like a stripper do before giving a lap dance. She undid her full-body white cat suit and peeled it off slowly. Her clean-shaved pussy had a heart-shape pattern of silky pubic hair centered and pointing down to her clitoris. Her phat pussy popped out. It was a phat juicy plum. All Twan could do is bite his tongue like Damnnn!!!

She turned around and started slow dancing side to side seductively and winding her body like an Amazon snake! Twan hit the blunt and blew it on her soft ass cheeks as he smacked them both lightly. *Pow-pow!!*

She proceeded to drop down to her knees and unfastened Twan's Gucci belt impatiently. *What's up with these pimps in these skinny jeans, and since when did Twan start wearing skinnys, too?* she thought emotionally, because she struggled and still couldn't get them off. She sucked her teeth and without avoiding eye contact, she freed his little man and it wasn't his son either. It was that hook banana-shaped curved dick she missed and dreamed about. Twan was so, so damn unique in all his own special ways and he was packing. She was about to freak this dick and him to the maximum, was all she thought while inserting the head of his rod in her warm, soppy wet mouth. She worked her tongue ring around the head while giving him head.

Twan leaned far back and put both his hands on top of his head. She was sucking the steam off his dick with a clot of spit and hand action. She jacked his shaft while playing with and caressing his heavy aching nuts. It took him right back to his first ho, Neese. That's how he knew they were acting hoey when he got locked up back home. Her head game should be illegal, especially how she was moaning all on the dick like he was fucking her deep and hard. Then her smacking all hard on the dick like it was a candy strawberry lollipop!

The old man started to complain, talking about he couldn't see and he was already blind as an old bat! So he got up and ran over to the light fixture and turned them back up bright! He didn't want to miss the show. It was intense and something was different about these 2 right here. He knew it. He could just feel it. He ran back over to the side of the bed, looking over Creole's shoulder as her neck rolled in a sideways rhythmical pattern.

"O—my God! You're huge!" the old man said in a shocking tone! Twan looked over at him and waved his ass off and told him to say pause or no homo next time he was pimpin and didn't play all that sex playing gay talk.

Creole felt Twan's dick throbbing and jumping as it gleeked out increments of pre-cum. Then she took it out and smacked it on both of her lips as she played with the sticky stream of pre-cum, twirling it around all on her lip and smacking it on her face a few times before putting it back into her mouth.

Twan heard his dick smacking on her face, making a quick popping noise as he fingered the warm wetness of her womb. He said fuck it and started that bitch off with 2 fingers, then worked 3 fingers and had her really going, pulling them in towards him like he was telling her to come here! Which was striking her G spot and had her hot pussy gushing wett!

She couldn't take it and tried to hump Twan's hand, gyrating her pelvis erotically like she was trying to get off and crème all over his fingers real quick.

"Uhh...O...unt-unh... Daddy, I can't take it no more, I'm sorry! You teasing me too much. I'm ready, c'mon! O-o-oooo... Shit...ooweee...oh," Creole said, full of fire and desire from the ecstasy feeling from her brain stimulating her swelled clit! as she tried to straddle Twan and sit on the dick horny.

"Wait up, oh hell nawh, bitch! Creole, ya ass tripping, you must really be drunk. I told you I really ain't going back down dat road or taking that long free trip to the clinic or hospital knowing ya ass, shit—fuck dat! Excuse me, can you give me and my ho a condom real quick so we can move this along?" Twan said in a stern frustrating tone. The old man replied, saying he didn't have none either. Then Twan told him what bout the ho in the back room? He told Twan it wasn't nobody in the back room. Twan was confused. Then Twan told him he had to do a store run real quick and his ho and the 10 bands could stay there until he made it back with the rubbers.

"No—no—no! That wasn't part of the deal. No leaving and coming back. Matter of fact, I'd put up an extra 5 grand right here, right now! What do you say? That even adds more satisfaction and anticipation to my twisted sick fetish!" the dirty old man stated with the hint of anticipation in his voice.

"Daddy, I swear to you that this pussy in check. I'm grown now…I swear it is! Smell it—no scent! Now stop playing and let's get this now 15 bands. C'mon, Twan!" Creole said as she put his dick in her mouth and engulfed it deep down her throat until it touched the canals of her esophagus, making her gag hard. Twan said fuck it and warned her she was dead if she burnt him a third time. He put that on Mama Lela. He already had blown up his pimp all over the addicting thrill for the love of the money!

She straddled him and bucked like a wild horse until she came back to back. He forgot how easy she came and how good her pussy was too. She had Neese beat and still had a nice sweet shot of tight cot! He beat it up, making her touch her toes bent over standing up on the floor, smacking her ass hard. However, he didn't like how the old man stared at him. He was creepy and Twan kept mean-mugging him. Twan picked Creole up, spread her legs wide open like she was doing the split, showing the old creep twisted man all pussy as he fucked her from the back while holding her in a full nelson with her arms and legs. It was incredible and a sight to see and a helluva position to be in! Twan had so much strength and mobility it was crazy. He was driving her crazy and telling her to crème all over his dick in front of the trick! She couldn't take it and came gushing hard down all over his dick and on his balls. Her juices were flowing all down his legs.

Twan took it out and put it in her ass roughly with no mercy. He punished her until he came all over her face and hair. He looked over at the sick twisted old man trying to kick-start his ancient dinosaur but it didn't want to awake and come back from the dead at all and enjoyed itself in full retirement. It was soft as oatmeal. He didn't even think a blue boy Viagra would spark it to life! He told Crole to get cleaned up and bring him a hot rag and grab the other 5 bands and come on so they could get out of there. She gladly complied and dragged her worn-out ass thru the luxury suite.

Twan texted J Pimp and they met up inside the casino. J Pimp was still shooting craps at the craps table. He was striking the house. He had a hot young hand with them red martels he shook so well with his slick Portland roll. Twan told him to come on, reminding him he was hot and banned from this casino, too. J Pimp gathered all his purple and white thousand-dollar chips to cash in at the casino cashier window. He clearly had over 18 purple stack chips and over a dozen red-and-white $500 chips. He had everything put on his black casino pre-paid credit card. The Vegas style and same way he was allowed to rent the Bentley or Maybach. J Pimp asked did they have fun? Laughed at both of them, then told Twan that old man was rich, a multi-millionaire with just a sick fetish but cash him out every time! He had got that 10 bands from him he went gambling with and really bet 5 bands on the first roll and hit big with a hard 8 and got paid double! Cracking the house slick before they could catch on to his slick hood pad roll. Twan shook his head and shook J Pimp wild ass for the night.

Jazabel was up, still looking lonely in her sports bra and laced boy shorts with her knees curled up to her chest, still red-eyed and puffy face. Oprah came running up, happy to see Daddy, squeezing him like a little girl would her daddy after not seeing him for a couple days. Then she went back to her room and got over 12 bands she had been working up these past 4 days from the fake escort service cards. It still wasn't no sign of the 2 ratchett redbones. He told them to come back successful or not at all. He told them all get some rest because tomorrow was really their biggest day yet! He could feel it and had his hoes excited besides Jazabel's Arabian ass. It was too late to turn back now? He had to finish turning her out. Shit, he didn't care. He did tell her to sleep next to him tonight and ran up in her shallow tight wet pussy. He made her come twice but it took her longer than Creole freak-nasty cumming faster ass. He prayed he didn't wake up and piss broken glass or dick fall off in the toilet from fucking his own ho that got priors with no rubbers.

Twan woke up early, probably because he was paranoid. It was 10 a.m., which was considered early to Twan, especially for the Vegas pimps and desert night life.

He walked around his luxury penthouse. It was half-naked hoes laying all curled up and sprawled out everywhere with all that cash money around the exhausted snoring hoes. Twan gathered all the money and smoked a blunt as he counted it up, twice. Oprah smelt the kush blunt and knew Daddy was up earlier, so she wanted to be the first ho up and to cater to him. She helped him count the money, cooked for and fed him, then washed him up, pampered him like a real pimp! She powdered him down, dabbed on his Versace cologne and got him dressed to start his day.

Twan got all his hoes burn-out Wal-mart pre-paid phones that was listed on the fake escorting cards. He charged them up. Some was already ringing. He knew they were mainly inquiring about the centerfold Jazabel exotic imported ass. He checked the status of his

PayPal account once again. Now it was official, over 700 bands all off his UNLV-inspired posing hoes! He awoke all his hoes!

Twan told his hoes to be agile and watch out for vice stings. If it didn't sound right or look right? It probably wasn't right! So be careful, but he wanted to catch all the tourist partying tricks. It was New Year's Eve Vegas-style, which meant they was hosting New Year's parties for all type of celebrities and locals. This is when Vegas came alive. He had all his hoes passing out the rest of the cards and flyers too. They would work parking lots to big events.

Once again they was back in business and all their burn-out phones was jumping and the most requested was Jazabel, of course, and the rest of the hoes were getting envious and sick of it!

Twan heard Oprah's phone going off and ran to the back room and answered the phone to put his second plan together. He came back in the front room with the phone covered with both of his hands with Oprah behind him and whispered for Jazabel to come here. She looked all scared and pissed off like he just insulted her verbally. He told her to hurry up and this was big money on the phone, stop being timid! She stormed over there, not trusting him at all, with her arms folded, pouting.

"What, Twan? I'll work before I go catch a date, a real job! You really don't care about me or anything and what I lost after you came into my life, Twan!" Jazabel said in a dramatic tone as tears glided down both her cheeks.

"Man—listen, this ain't the time to freeze up on me! I need you, okay? When the time and money calls. You see, they call specifically for you, but I send these other hoes, right? Okay, so now even those I refuse to send you and told this trick on the phone, he made me an offer I couldn't refuse—$5,000 just for you to escort him to the Rio Casino poker tournament! No sex or strings attached. You don't got to do no sexual favor—that's my word. I promise you dat. Haven't I always kept my word solid with you? C'mon, Jaz, I need you right now," Twan said nonchalantly in a convincing tone. Jaz told him okay, she'd go. He told her well, get dressed so Oprah can drop her off!

Twan was happy when Jazabel left. He took a drink for victory and achieving sending her off! Even the rest of the girls knew what he was doing to her schoolgirl religious ass. They could see right thru it.

Creole stood there and gazed at Twan. He knew she really was dick dizzy once again and seen he had her back on stuck mode. She was a bad bitch, no lie, a straight Beyoncé that was double-joint with big thick yellow thighs. He told her it's not going to be no playing around, messing around, it's going to be a whole lot of getting down, staying down right chere!

She sucked her teeth and put her head down, continued to text. She, of course, was checking her likes from her Bentley pics with J Pimp and Twan, all on Instagram and Twitter gossiping like hoes do. She looked back up at Twan and told him to be expecting a private caller and that he was welcome, too.

Twan was texting Marissa the bartender for his next plan, he had a cold vic trick up his sleeve. He told her to find a regular there at the Freemont strip club and to set it up for them to meet and he would make it worth his while. He was about to pay him to take Jazabel on a date tomorrow thru the illegal escorting services he ran. He was going to give the trick a large amount sum to drop on Jazabel to make her jump at an offer she couldn't refuse, after the trick posed as just a casino escort request. Then his phone rang with that August Alsina ringtone, "No Love."

"Who dis?" Twan answered.

"Boy, stop that… Twan, you kow who dis is. Here, speak to your son. He doing fine and breathing on his own and spoiled. All he can say is Da-Da-Da! I told him to start saying Ma-Ma! But hold on real quick, and the only reason I called because Creole asked me to do it for Lil Twan, so here…" Diamond Cutz said in a mothering tone.

"D-D-Da-Da… Ahha…ha… Da-Da!!" Twan Jr. baby-babbled thru the phone, slobbering all on it and pressing buttons on his Daddy. Twan was speechless! It caught him off guard.

"Hey, Lil Twan-Twan! Lil Twan, dis ya Daddy, boy! Tell ya Mama to bring you to come see—"

"Hello? Yeah, Twan, I'll send you some pics to your phone, okay. But I'm Gucci out here by myself. You left and I can't blame you cuz you know how these damn streets talk. I finally got my Section 8 voucher. Ya son is 10 months now and he a Mama's boy. He my lil man and a fat boy too. All he wants to do is drink milk and hold onto me all damn day. That's how he started talking, trying to keep up with me. He so funny and act just like you when he wants something. Twan, he do look just like you too. I shouldn't've hated you so much when I was pregnant. Well, Twan, sorry I lied to you at the hospital. I had just lost my twin daughter and shot mad at you. So my sister told me don't say nothing to you so you can stay out of my life for good. You know she don't like pimps. Anyways, I got to go to work and drop ya son off at the babysitter's next door. And I don't want nothing from you or ya money! We fine and this is my son. I'm his Mama and Daddy! Tell Creole to give you my FB info. Bye, Twan, and take care of yaself and stay out of jail!!" Diamond Cutz said with a thick New Orleans accent as she cut Twan off talking to his son.

"H-hold on, Diamond. How you just gonna? Wait, can you bring him to see me? I'll fly you out to Vega. I got stupid money and will give you access to my PayPal account? It's all legit doe. Let my lil man pay his respects to his Grandma Lela! She never knew about him and always wanted a grandbaby, Diamond," Twan said in an irritated tone.

"Okay, that's fine, and sorry bout cha Mama Lela. Yes, I heard, you know word travels fast in this small town. But I'm good on ya PayPal account or ya money. We fine, but Twan, I gotta go. Just hit me on Facebook. I can't promise you nothing, okay? Be careful out there—BYE!" *Click!* Diamond said in a rushed tone before she terminated the call.

Twan wasn't stupid. It sounded like she had some dude playing daddy and probably coming thru the door or pulling up. Bitches wasn't slick and baby mamas were the worst because they were scorn evil bitches that couldn't let go of the past or move forward without being vindictive.

He threw the phone and punched the wall with a 3-piece combo, sick and tired of all the bullshit. More money, more problems. He kicked all his hoes out and told them to get to work ASAP! And the fuck out of his face! Creole got scared and ran out the room.

Twan sat and looked at the single baby pic of little Twan, his Junior that had his Daddy's features that lay dormant in Louisiana Angola State Penitentiary, but looked just like Twan. His eyes got watery as he shed a real tear, the first tear since his Mama's death. Damn, why everyone that he ever loved always departed out of his life? From his Pops, big bro TNut, Neese, Mama Lela, and now his Junior! He sat and looked at life at a different angle, but it was still at a pimp's perspective—everyone was vics and prey in one way or another. It sounded like a fucked-up way of thinking but it was Twan's analogy. He felt like his now baby mama prayed for his downfalls, when he truly was a victim of his own environment, himself. Twan was born into it. The mix! Even though his Pops wasn't a pimp, but a more gangster at heart and a D boy just like his older brother was, too. But not Twan, he was more like G Pa, his Pop's Dad, that was a straight womanizer and had 3 different wives in 3 different states with 15 kids. He got around town and would go from state to state using and abusing women. He preyed mainly on white women with jungle fever that couldn't resist his tall black ass with his slender 6'4" frame. He had all the latest Cadillacs in the '70s, all the Coupe de Villes convertibles and all with plush leather guts. That's all Twan heard the older heads saying and talking about his G Pa Timothy Jo!

Twan texted his hoes all and told them nobody come back to the penthouse until he was 40 bands richer, that meant 10 bands per ho! Everybody must go! Even Jaz and she was pretty soon about to know. It was New Year's Vegas style! Toast to new beginnings and new bands, new bitches, new whips, new vics!! His only thing was to try to catch him something. No New Year's resolution—just his same motto: Go hard and stay sharp! He had pussy to sell.

Jazabel sent Twan a text message back telling him she was still escorting the middle-aged man around the Rio Casino, and what was all the ranting and raving about? That she was willing to do the real escorting part but not the sexting whole thingy and getting down for her crown with complete total strange men! Twan ignored her and told her get back to work and pay attention to her date. And she better had come back successful with all them bands or not at all. He knew his Mama Lela gave birth to a winner, so he had to win! Then he thought right back to his baby mama Diamond Cutz and wondered why God took his twin baby girl away from him? Was it bad karma? Catching up from all them girls he did wrong or smashed on? Why did it always seem like his past was constantly chasing him around in a circle, like a dog chasing his raggedy ol tail?

He smashed off in the lime Lambo, beating that rich gang lifestyle. He sipped some of his favorite Diddy Juice. He pulled up on Marissa, his Mexican bartender, at the old strip joint on Freemont. She had hooked him up with the mark that agreed to solicit Jazabel, the gray-eyed Arabian college girl, for 5 grand. If she didn't budge, the agreement was 10 grand. He paid the mark 2 bands for his services. The mark was about 6 ft. even, white, and in his late twenties. Twan slid him the cash money and his number after he gave him all the valid instructions, then instructed him not to go past the threshold and advised him how such a sweet shot of pussy the Arabian blonde hair, gray eyes had, as an advertisement and encouragement.

Twan had a few more drinks with the mark and stood at the bar flirting with and tipping Marissa, his Mexican bartender, until Pimpin Silky came to meet him. They sat and drank shot after shot like a sailor and sniffed line after line of that new strawberry nose candy.

Jazabel had finished escorting her date around the Rio as eye candy. She got the whole whopping 5 grand as promised for her services. She couldn't believe it. It was her first date she caught and it wasn't bad for 5 hours worth of work, which averaged out to a thousand dollars an hour. She texted Twan back-to-back! With no reply, she figured he was somewhere getting whiteboy wasted with J Pimp as always, supposedly celebrating his Mama's passing and still mourning her death? Then finally Twan replied, drunk texting, saying, *Who dis?* She giggled and told him she was done and had the 5 grand, where is he at, to meet her back at the penthouse. He texted her back and told her to meet him at the old strip joint on Freemont with Pimpin Silky at the bar!

When she arrived Twan was drunk, tripping, fighting with the bouncers/security. They were throwing him out the joint once again. And Pimpin Silky was still at the bar talking to Marissa, shaking his head side to side, then looking up and down. He knew his young pimp partner Twan was bubbly and that strawberry candy was some fire dope! He was scared of Twan's wild Louisiana ass, especially after how he went ham and ape shit all over and on top of his head over his crackhead ass Mama. Jazabel had to drive Twan back to the penthouse in his lime Lambo and leave her whip because he was too faded-faded!

Soon as she took off on Freemont and stopped at the red light, he called hurled as he quickly raised the Lambo door open, then asked her, "Bitch, what you doing driving my shit?" She laughed and told him he was fucked up drunk and tripping, trying to swing on the DJ and cursing him out for not playing that Southern Baton Rouge shit!! for New Year's. The old strip joint on Freemont was jumping like cell phones. It was like a ratchett old pimp convention!

Twan woke up the next morning pissed because he had missed and slept thru New Year's fucking with Pimpin Silky and that new strawberry nose candy. He was Gucci on that stuff and vowed to quit for the New Year. Vegas was one big ol juicy wet pussy waiting to get fucked. He turned around and looked over at Jazabel's tall, slender, volleyball-playing ass in her white lace skimpy thong that looked moist as it clung to her long camel toe. He smirked, knowing that he was about to break that thang-thang in and send her off for sure today and it wasn't no looking or going back! Not from there!

He received a text surprisingly from his baby mama Diamond Cutz, wishing him a Happy New Year's!! And telling him to call her at this number when he gets up because she knowing him, he went hard and all out last night!

He called her back ASAP! She agreed she would bring his son Twan Jr. out there for the weekend but he had to pay for the ticket and all the expenses, including all his diapers and baby milk, too. Twan agreed and gave her access to his PayPal account, telling her to take what she needed and to order her a plane ticket online herself.

Then he woke up Jazabel, telling her to get dressed to impress once again. It was another trick that was paying on the high end of 5 bands just to escort him to the Las Vegas Attraction for a few hours. She couldn't believe it and was excited. She knew this would give her enough to get her own place and Twan would give her some cash after he took his majority of the cut. So she thought. But now she was so with the bizz. Twan seen that and pecked her on the lips real quick, then smacked her with a stinging open hand on her teardrop ass, encouraging her to go get it! Get that money, it's yours, was all she thought from listening to that August Alsina being around Twan. Plus she loved the fact that all the rest of Twan's hoes was gone and she was the only one there laid up with him. Twan felt the New Year's was starting off so swell! And that this New Year was his! Shit, he wished he could send every girl in the world and pimp on the whole world with his hook dick!

However, 15 minutes after Jazabel's Arabian ass left to go catch the mark, Diamond Cutz texted Twan with bad news, saying something was the matter with the PayPal account, it was currently frozen with a 1-800 number to call. And once she called, they said the account was summons in a lawsuit from UNLV legal associates and Amazon was named in the civil suit. So they had to take it off Amazon.com immediately and the judge is the only one who has the power to release or seize all the funds in the PayPal account that was now currently past the $800,000 mark. Twan went ape shit! He couldn't believe it! He started having anxiety overwhelm him and called her to tell her he would send her a couple bands JPay and still wanted them to come out to Vegas this weekend.

Diamond Cutz's eyes and ears was wide open. She didn't really know what Twan was on or who he vic'd for all that damn money, but her baby daddy was damn near a millionaire! She immediately wanted to put his trifling ass on child support. That was that New Orleans 9th Ward coming out in her ass. She played it cool and switched tunes on Twan quick-fast as hoes do. And Twan felt the change in her tone, but he didn't care or wasn't worried about Diamond Cutz funky raggedy ass. Life is such a bitch and she got a Mama named Karma with her bad ass! And Twan just had to be a pimp in it! Sometimes he wished it was 10 of him! He told Diamond Cutz don't trip, he'd get his legal team on it ASAP and all his funds generated was 100 percent legit like a Kickstarter campaign. She told him alright and they love him in a sweet, soft tome. Twan told her he loves them too in an annoyed tone, then clicked her off his line as he pressed his mobile legal app for Las Vegas's best lawyers to hire for his 800-plus bands. That was more money than he ever seen and didn't even have a chance to touch and smell it, yet alone play with it! That's what pimpin was, a cash-only, put it in his pocket transaction sport.

Jazabel arrived at the Bellagio and caught the elevator up to the suite texted on her iPhone. To her surprise it was a much younger, taller man than her previous date. She thought he was too young to be paying for her company and he was probably just lonely and a workaholic! She was obliged he did request her, that let her confirm she had all the other pretty girls beat and was that fantasy girl every man wanted and dreamed of, young and old! She was slipping into her own ways, knowing how easy this was and that her time was expensive that they paid her for. She was more at ease. He asked her did she want a drink before they ventured off to the infamous Las Vegas Attraction together. She agreed as he snapped a selfie of them and tipped her heavily. She was gladly obliged as she blushed from being pampered and showered with Franklins like a Canadian stripper! She felt spoiled.

She kept telling him how nice and generous he was. After she finished her tall glass of sparkling champagne, they went out on the town, stopping at the casino for a few rounds at the blackjack table and trying her luck at the many craps tables. They headed for the Vegas Attraction, where they took a photo book full of selfies like they really were a long-term couple. They had the tourists fooled. He continued to tip her kindly with Twan's own money. She was flattered and he offered to take her out to the steak buffet. She declined, nicely. Then they headed back to the hotel for him to drop her off and pay her for all her services provided.

Once back at the hotel, he came flat out and asked her if he can pay her 10 grand to get laid and she declined, telling him that was illegal and she didn't provide those type of services, but thanks for his hefty offer and that she better be going now! He told her to wait a minute, how about he eat her out for 10 grand? She shook her head no, saying she was sorry. Then he asked her what about a hand job? Or she getting totally naked and spread her legs on the bed while he sat and masturbated quickly to relieve himself. She still shook her head no! Realizing now why he called the services, poor guy was paid but couldn't get laid and was a horny bastard!

He slow-played her as he counted out the money for her services finally with one last offer with ulterior motives. Jazabel was already by the door with her arms folded and leg shaking impatiently, ready to leave because his persistence was awkward and making her feel uncomfortable. He walked up to her with cash in both hands.

"Okay—listen here, this is my final offer. I'll give you this 10 grand just to sit and drink another glass of champagne with me and then you're free to go, no strings attached, okay? What do you say? Have we got ourselves a drink?" the mark said in a lustful tone, as he handed her both stacks of cash!

Jazabel sighed out heavily, reached out for the cash, and told him okay, she accepts only under the terms for no more than 15 minutes and one more glass only because she already was sleepy somehow anyway. And tucked the 10 bands in her Louis Vuitton clutch bag.

He grinned like the grinch that stole Christmas from the Whos! He had his own ulterior motives already in place from the moment he first met Twan! He hated pimps purely in the worst form. So all this was about to be a joy! Right before he headed back to Vancouver, Canada.

He went to pour her a glass with his back turned and slipped her an MSG-X, an instant date rape drug turned up times 10 from Canada that will sedate anyone and put a 1500lb. horse on his ass. As the white powder substance emptied out the capsule, he dropped it slick onto the suite carpet and stepped on it as he poured her some more bubbly and twirled it around.

He turned around and asked the agitated and impatient Jazabel which one she wanted? trying to be slick. She wasn't dumb, of course. She pointed to the half-filled glass in his left hand and smiled at him.

He told her, "Let's toast the New Year's?" She agreed and they both said, "Salud!" (cheers) simultaneously. Jazabel wasn't trying to be rude and take the money and run, but she gulped half of her drink down. Then 30 seconds later she downed the rest, warning him he only had 10 minutes left of her time before she split, not ever seeing the remaining powder substance dwelling in the pits of her tall glass. She was too impatient to notice or realize he had already drugged her the first time with a sprinkled does.

After a few minutes, Jazabel started yawning and stretching like a little kid. Then her head started spinning out of control. She felt like she wanted to throw up urgently, and as if she was about to faint. She fanned herself, trying to get some air to her face. The mark smiled, realizing the pills worked and did the trick he paid for. She stood up real quick, telling him she couldn't take it no more and she had to leave now as she stumbled back like a staggering drunk bum, but it was more like a sideways gallop like a tranquilized horse. And that's exactly what, her body was tranquilized!

The mark quickly caught her and dragged her dangling body to the bed as she continued to fight the drug that overtook her body. He threw her face down onto the bed, then began to toss her clothes off viciously all over the place!

She didn't realize what was going on or was taking place as she floated in and out of consciousness. She just knew and felt something wasn't right. She blacked out and would come to in spurts before she'd black back out to see a shirtless guy huffing and puffing over her, making all types of strange faces over her. She couldn't feel a thing, her whole body was numb.

The mark has his way with her and he flipped her limp body front to back, side to side. He even dry-humped her mouth with his full erect boy-size penis, abusing her every hole. He came twice after he took a brief pause for a cause, then went another round. His whole brazen assault lasted for an hour. She was kept prisoner, held captive by the drug well after the mark fled the hotel and hopped on his private flight back to Canada. He had checked in to the hotel casino under one of his aliases that wouldn't lead back to nothing but a phantom existing profile and old abandoned warehouse. He wasn't worried about her screaming rape!

By the time Jazabel came to it was around 8:30 at night already. She felt groggy as she shook it off and looked around, lost. She couldn't remember what happened. Then she immediately felt the pressure on her anus, it was sore, and her vagina lips were swollen. Then she immediately tasted the bitterness and sweaty taste from semen and sweaty penis. Her red-flag signs flared up and went off as she knew she just had been raped! She looked around the empty room for her clothes, then ran for her purse. All the money was gone! He had raped and robbed her ass! She was pissed as she began crying harder and ran to the shower. She couldn't even look at herself in the vanity mirror! She let the hot water hit her and run down with her head down while she hugged herself tightly for another 30 minutes. Twan had left her several text messages, flipping out. She didn't even want to show up at the penthouse, especially empty-handed. The guy seemed really nice, but he deceived her something awful. Boy, was she wrong!

She arrived at the penthouse with her head down. All of the girls were there and ready to go out to work for the New Year. Vegas was just coming to life!

Twan flipped out and asked her what's wrong? And where is his money at? She had been MIA for hours. And he could tell she had been fucking because she had them low dreamy sex eyes that hoes get from sexual intercourse. She told Twan he took her out to the Las Vegas Attraction and afterwards didn't pay her. He ran downstairs to get the money off his casino card and never came back, and she didn't want to disrespect and disappoint him so she stayed and waited for hours before she gave up. Twan told her he didn't believe her and that she was holding back, warning her not to steal nothing off his plate, else he would chop her damn head off slowly! She broke down crying, saying she wouldn't steal from him!

Twan went into the back room after snatching her Louis Vuitton clutch bag. He had called and texted the mark's number immediately and knew he had been had! He even called Marissa to tell her that mark she selected got over and ran off with over 12 bands of his money, and his plan to vic Jazabel backfired and blew up in his own face! And advised if she seen that mark show his face up in the place to call him ASAP! They done vic'd—A PIMP!

Damn it—it happens... Players fuck up and pimps turn-up!! was all he thought. Which meant he played his hand way wrong, called the bet and got cracked! Struck on the river card and played by the house. Once again now this round was on the house.

Twan looked at it as a learning experience and the simple fact his mind was clouded and altered his better judgment He needed to think like a pimp at all times, not a lousy player. He was more than just a player in this game of life, he was the grand master dealer that won and vic'd everyone else!

Then he knew at least half of his plan worked—she turned a trick but just got robbed. And he vowed not to just snort another line, but to get all the money lost and invested in Jazabel's ass out of her ass! Shit! Two bad-luck losses back-to-back that was his lawyer retainer fee money to free up his 800 bands got. Damn it! Then his dick began to itch. The tip of his dick head itched and in his pee hole. Damn, he hoped it wasn't from Creole's dirty ass. Ever since he fucked her and blew-up his pimp over the love of lucci, it had been a spiral downhill effect. And he was going to use that money to get another spot for his baby mama Diamond Cutz to make her stay out here with his son Twan Jr. right chere in Vegas, baby!

J Pimp hit Twan and told him that same rich old trick had requested to speak to him with an exclusive offer just to meet up with him and hear his business proposition. Twan told J Pimp hell nawh! And that he was Gucci! J Pimp was persistent, until Twan asked him what was he getting out the deal and how much was the trick paying him? J Pimp said it was a measly band. Twan told him he needed half of that and he wasn't bringing Creole dirty ass this time, either! J Pimp laughed and told him to suit himself and texted him the hotel room number at the Planet Hollywood. Twan looked at all his hoes and picked Pink Toe's ass to come roll with him. Butterscotch was super jealous and Oprah ginger head was mad, while Jazabel appeared to be glad. She was about to go sleep off the dragging effect the date rape drug had on her. Twan told her that she wasn't done or off the hook for letting that trick rob her and run off with his money literally and that she was in debt now and didn't have no other choice but to go and ho for his doe! She didn't really comprehend his language.

Twan had Pink Toe drive the rented lime-green Lambo to the Planet Hollywood casino resort hotel. He told her she smelt extra good. She smiled. Twan had her extra wet and her thong sticky. He just didn't know it yet. They caught the elevator up to the 9th floor and tapped on the door lightly. They entered the dim suite.

First impression of the old trick from Pink Toe was ewwhh…this old white geezer! The old wrinkled body bastard! She knew he was a sicko! And learnt to spot them from being a local girl and from experience so she knew he had a twisted weird fetish, too. The oldest ones were always the kinky with obscene gestures and requests looking for spunk!

The trick threw Twan a band as promised for coming off tops. Then he proceeded to throw his proposition on Twan.

"So I told you about my last fetish about how I loved to watch pimps freak their filthy dirty whores? Well, I lied. And as J Pimp puts it, a pimp will do anything for the doe, even sell his own—"

"Pause! Man—what the fuck?!! What the hell you on? Fuck what you heard, that's an old myth and J Pimp bogus for telling you some ill shit like dat. Matter of fact, let me hit dat lil nigga up—fuck dat!" Twan said hot as he snapped, cutting the rich trick off.

"H-Hello, whatz poppin, P? Y'all Gucci?" J Pimp answered.

"Hell nawh, P! This trick came at me awkwards, trying to be on some gay shit, talking bout he got a thing for pimps and shit!" Twan replied, shaking his head in disgust.

"Man, shit, sometime a pimp got to do what a pimp's got to do! Shit, I wouldn't cross the line but he made me a stupid offer I couldn't refuse, 10 bands to bang his asshole out with a dildo. Shit, I know I ain't gay, but I'm 10 bands richer, tho!" J Pimp said with no shame in his game.

"Ahh, hell nawh, P! J Pimp, you bout to get disbarred from the Pimp Association and going against the Pimpin Constitution, too. Stick to our pimp oath, P! Remember ya 5 P's! Really all P's, shit! I'm gone, P, and I'm disappointed in you highly for that one!"

"So—so what, nigga—" *Click!* J Pimp cut Twan off, not giving 2 fucks, then clicked him off.

"Hey—hey, c'mon, where you going, man? Listen, okay—okay! I'll offer you 20 grand—no, right now, look right here, 50 grand right here, it's all yours, just bang me for 10 whole minutes?" the old rich trick begged.

"Damn, Daddy, you better get that 50 grand and jump on all that sh—" *POW! SMACK!* Pink Toe said out of pocket, overwhelmed before she could finish getting the curse word out of her mouth. Twan smacked her words off her tongue and backhand pimp-smacked her! She dropped to the floor as she let out a muffled cry, saying she was sorry!

"Bitch! Don't you ever disrespect Pimpin like that else I'll set ya ratchett musty ass on fire with this flame and kick you in ya funky butt! And as for you, old man, don't you ever sex-play a pimp like dat again!! Me or no other pimp EVER again else you'll be put out ya old ass misery and sent on the LAX flight to hell! Now get ya ass up, Pink Toe, and let's go!" Twan snapped as he banged his fists together!

They shot out the room. It was something about being on the elevator? That ride down to the lobby main floor struck a match! 50 bands? Damn it! He replayed all the sudden drastic change of events. Then told Pink Toe don't tell none of his hoes or nobody else but they were going back up to room 910! First he needed to go on a store run. They raced the Lambo down the strip to the sex shop off the strip, where

Twan purchased a 12-inch strap-on with a red muffle ball, then raced back down the strip.

He told Pink Toe to hold all the sex items and tapped on the 910 room door as he did earlier. The old rich trick answered the door smiling to an oh-so-familiar light knock.

"Well, hello—bad boy! I figured 50 grand would make you change your little mind. Shew, you'd be surprised on who does what for money in Sin City, where everyone's fantasy becomes a reality! Come on in now..." the old trick said in the most fruitiest tone that irked Twan's nerves hard.

"Now listen, this is only on my terms now, you old dirty fruit bat! So she sucks my dick to get me going long and strong and the lights stay off. Total darkness, period. Agreed? So set ya timer for 10 minutes and assume the position off the corner of the bed. Let's get this going and over with!" Twan said in total disgust. Yuck! Then signaled Pink Toe and for her to remember her instructions he told her in the Lambo.

The trick looked briefly over at the duo as Pink Toe began to give Twan head like he was her husband and she missed him! The old man was excited with anticipation to come as he heard all those slurping and smacking noises from that sloppy blow job she was giving him and he shuffled over to cut the lights all the way off dark! Then smacking noises as a guide to lead him right back into the action as he took his place on the end of the bed as instructed. After another 2 minutes the slurping and smacking noises ceased.

The strap-on was in place. The trick was rammed hard without no Vaseline or lube. He yelped! Twan thought about all the white slave masters and how many black women got raped and black men killed and took it all out on him! He began to punch him in the ribs, kidney-punching him, then began to punch the old man with some hooks to the back of the head! Twan was missing as the old man kept ducking his head low. The old man yelled out, "Okay, okay, that was enough." He was finished and instructed Twan to take the 50 grand large and get out! Twan didn't stop punching him till he felt his ribs crack and his knuckles bloody. Pink Toe pushed Twan back and out the way. The trick been collapsed and finally passed out!

Twan ran to cut the lights on and to retrieve the 50 bands. The poor little flimsy old man was beat purple and blue on his bruised fractured ribs. Twan went berserk on him and lost it as he looked at the old man's lumped-up head and bloody face. Twan really fucked him up and thought he possibly could've killed him.

He couldn't believe it, tho, how Pink Toe was in a trance? She was in a zone, fucking the old trick still with the 12-inch strap-on! It was a bloody mess. Twan told her to come on! She didn't budge and kept on giving it to him raw and uncut! She looked demonic! Twan could tell she hadn't never experienced no shit like this before but it wasn't no fun when the rabbit got the gun, tho, and he knew this for a fact as he watched Pink Toe finally return the favor from all those times. She finally got to give a man and a trick a taste of their own medicine and she loved every bit of it and made sure to give that old bastard every inch! He wasn't so tough now. What a wimpy sissy! She fixed the gag ball around the bit of his mouth. Twan told her he was out and seen Pink Toe ignore him once again, as she snatched her Fendi belt and began beating his ass and whipping him on his back with the belt like she was a damn slave master!

"Bitchhh, don't get caught-up or kill the old white man! You bout to make him have a heart attack—I'm gone, gurrl!" Twan snapped as he regretted buying the strap-on for Pink Toe to fuck the old trick while he stood by her and beat the old man's ass for disrespecting a true pimp and sex-playing him as a man! Pink Toe was blowing up the spot so Twan had to take the 50 bands and go! She was stuck in character trippin. If she kept it up and didn't follow behind him she was about to soon be stuck in the Clark County Detention Center. Twan damn sure wasn't about to pick her dumb extreme ass up. He warned her a few times already, she knew better!

As he hit the elevator button he heard a loud *DOOM!* and a crash sound like she threw a water vase or hotel ice bucket on top of his head. Twan jumped, startled. She scared the shit out of him. He was nervous as hell. They were sure to call hotel security for a disturbance call. It sounded like a royal rumble, like she was trashing the place and throwing the old man all over the room. Twan wanted to take the steps. She turned-up on the old possibly dead man. He prayed on the elevator.

- Chapter 11 -

"Clark County"

Ashley looked into the Clark County Detention Center mirror and patted down her hair. She put it in a single braid, then wrapped it around. It was time for her to go in front of Judge Kathy for her initial court appearance for felony murder of Lela Burdette and 1st degree burglary.

The aluminum stained mirror looked more like an aluminum trash can lid. She stared deep and then faded. She had another flashback that she had been suffering from ever since that evening...

* * *

Soon as she heard the barrage of bullets and the loud thud that smacked on the marble foyer and the crashing sound of stolen goods, then the USC college white trick telling her to freeze, holding her at gunpoint until the LVMPD showed up, she sat nervously, thinking he was about to kill her as she assumed he did to Mama Lela as she remained silent with no sounds of life down on the lower level.

The LVMPD showed up and placed her under arrest for 1st degree burglary and accessory to a felony. As they escorted her downstairs, she walked past Mama Lela's body and fell out in a fit. The simple fact that she had been smoking dope with Mama Lela earlier back at the hotel before they went on this caper and she was going thru a crack withdrawal, very moody and agitated.

She instantly seen a gaping bullet hole thru her cheek, giving her a dimple like she was smiling at her. It was a little oozing stream of blood that led to a bigger, dark stagnated blood pool. Ashley felt her stomach tumbling as it weakened from the sights of death from a close one. She also noticed Mama Lela died with her eyes open like she just wasn't ready to go yet. And also caught the watery eyes and a trace of a single tear that flowed softly down the side of her eye and glided down to her ear. She started resisting, saying no as she planted her feet on the ground before they dragged her on. She kicked, rolled like a Florida gator with the police.

The detective tried to interrogate her for hours and build a case against her by trying to flip her to tell on herself and Mama Lela! She was still so shook-up over the fact that her mentor was now just a body left on a crime scene. She denied even knowing Mama Lela and said she met the USC student on Tinder.com, wanting to hook up, not soliciting sex or tricks for money. Then asked for a lawyer, taking on a code of silence. The detectives didn't like that and once they found Mama Lela's number in Ashley's phone and vice-versa, they asked her about it, and she still didn't acknowledge it. They introduced her to the Nevada felony murder clause and booked her into the Clark County Detention Center for felony murder and 1st degree burglary so she could stand her tough act in front of a jury trial. Maybe, just maybe she would have her act together and get cleaned up and focus.

Ashley stood in front of Judge Kathy for her initial court appearance.

"Umm... EXCUSE ME, there? Ashley, can you please pay attention, these are so serious charges here. That's a capital murder charge!! It's not to be taken lightly—now how do you plead? Guilty or not guilty?" Judge Kathy snapped.

"Not guilty, Your Honor... I didn't... I-I-didn't do—"

"H-Hold on, that's not for me to hear nor decide. You'll have your chance in front of a jury trial, and the State of Nevada will appoint you a public defender. However, the Court enters your 'not guilty' plea and hereby sets your next scheduled court date on February 9th. This Court is adjourned!" *Pat-Pat!* Judge Kathy intervened, cutting Ashley off on the record as she replied like an old hag, banging down her gavel.

Ashley sat there confused. She was new to all this court talk and rules of procedures, too. She couldn't believe how far apart the judge set her next court date. What was she to do? She felt that she was Twan's favorite one! And that somehow he would magically save her and come bail her out. She just knew he'd come for her! So she thought? After all, she was Twan's first bitch and been down since day 1 in Vegas when he first took a step off that Greyhound bus terminal when Mama Lela recruited her and Twan vic'd her. It was on and them ever since. Plus even though she didn't know much or grow up in the hood, she wasn't no damn snitch! And knew she would never tell on Twan or turn him in! Nor would she sell out and tell on her girl Mama Lela. She dragged the heavy cold chains that attached to both of her ankles as she took baby steps out of the judge's presence. Tears arose as she left, thinking about Twan and praying he'd come right now to get her. She needed a 3-way from one of the girls. She recognized a few old hookers off of Freemont that was booked for soliciting for their 5th and 6th times. So they were stuck in there with her, too. Then it was the hoes whose pimps would abandon them, not post their bonds or come pick them up from Clark County once they was O.R. However, Twan was different and he'd come pay her fee and bail her out ASAP. She began to find local bail bondsman memos and ads numbers listed on the walls taped above the phones.

The bondsman told Ashley her bond was too high or the fact it was too risky and not worth their time. Some even promised to call Twan for her. But she knew they didn't once she called back and they pretended to be out in the field or busy. She left message after message and it was day after day that went on. Still no signs of Twan! The tough street lance hoes all kept it real with her and told her to forget about the bailsman and they was playing her, too. She needed to be worried about focusing on her case and getting in contact with her lawyer ASAP.

Also not to worry too much about Twan because he was probably mad and focusing on burying his own mom. The girls had a way of bringing Ashley to her senses and giving her a fond dose of reality. Days went by. She prayed and cried.

* * *

Creole downloaded the Vine video that she loved and couldn't get enough of. It was hilarious and too cute to her. It had 8.1 million views. It read "Drunk in Love in Las Vegas" because the person who recorded it with their phone had that Beyoncé song.

The Vine video consisted of a drunk man in a Rolls Royce Phantom pulled over on the Las Vegas strip doing a field sobriety test. He was trying to walk a straight line and touching his nose bubbly, staggering, telling the officer, "Okay, okay, I got it, I got it!"

The only problem was there wasn't no officers. He was talking to himself and was so damn piss drunk, he subconsciously pulled himself over and started walking a straight line in front of the Rolls. He attempted to. It was too funny. However, that wasn't the only funny part, it was the fact that Creole actually knew him and recognized who it was, too. It was none other than J Pimp young ass. And he was too cute. She noticed he had another luxury expensive whip and automatically assumed J Pimp's young ass had stupid-dumb money somehow. She didn't really care how, she just knew it and could smell it! Maybe it was true what they say about a cheese head hood rat? Either way, he had it made. However, she tricked herself, and wasn't hip to the luxury Vegas rentals. It was all show and a desert mirage! She watched the 30-second skit on Vine once again, giggling at J Pimp dancing bubbly off pills and powder and walked a DUI line without police there, drunk trippin!

Some reason she felt a certain way down there and thought about putting her pretty pink pussy all on J Pimp. And she knew she had a pretty pussy, too. Because all the ballers down South from New Orleans to Atlanta agreed. And Twan knew it too because since they was young fucking he couldn't keep his eyes or hands off of it! She smirked devilishly and went back to J Pimp's selfie that she secretly snapped in the Bentley and then began to slide her fingers in and out of her slippery pussy. She had a thing for young J Pimp! Maybe it was just the money he generated. She fantasized about her freaking J Pimp on a boat. She was being naughty, trying to keep her lusty pussy in check. Right now it was misbehaving, it craved and yearned for penetration. That dick! And that's all she thought about. She was what they called a nymphomaniac, and the true definition of it. Creole could freak a whole football team and wake up the next day and do it again!

"I got these streets in a head lock—I got ya, girl, in da leg lock!" Young Thug and Rich Homie Quan streamed thru Creole's Galaxy Note phone as she sat back and had climax after climax.

* * *

"A drop of honey catches more flies than a gallon of gall!" Twan said to his hoes as he recited Abe Lincoln at his penthouse. That was his speech of the day for his hoes! They all were headed out to work the hotels and twerk the tricks and twirl the vics.

Jazabel had been full-fledge turning tricks, thinking she really was in debt with Twan for letting the trick vic and rob her ass. But somehow that rape triggered something. Like she felt emptiness and darkness cloaked over her. Now she was impure. She didn't feel no different from the rest of the girls. She even had a slutty strut and worked her $2500 red-bottom fancy heels like a vet. She rocked her ho attire like a pro, too. Twan was happy she and all his hoes was going and his head was pumped up! Giving speeches like he was Abe Lincoln and shit!

And where the hell was Creole at? She was late, again? He figured Vegas was too much and getting to her head, knowing she was new to Vegas and trying to take the desert night life in. That's why he didn't like fucking with duck hoes. He had to keep his foot far up their ass and keep checking in their pussy and bras for stashing cash!

He had finally hired a big Vegas law firm to challenge the summons that the UNLV legal team put against him which caused the courts to subpoena the PayPal account and freeze all of its assets with a net gross of over $800,000.

He was also happy that Diamond Cutz and little Twan Jr. was coming out there finally next weekend, so he had a full week to prepare. He rubbed his Mama Lela's purple urn and twinkled his front gold tooth that was her ring that his Pops gave her for her blessings. She was finally a Grandma and he was going to show Little Twan her remains and let him rub on her purple urn.

Pink Toe and Butterscotch was both requested to escort a middle-aged gentleman to the Golden Nugget. He had their escorting service card from a close-knit friend who worked in South Central Vegas. They told Twan that the 2 pretty pussy girls were bout to go get his money and turn a trick inside-out and freak his little lights out! All for him! Twan knew these 2 West Coast hoes got that from nobody but Creole's ass talking all like that. Plus they were both easily influenced, especially by Creole out-of-town steelo! Truth be told, Creole looked better than both of them. She was killing them hoes!

Butterscotch and Pink Toe put on their sexy leopard-print cat suits with a pair of leopard ears around the headband with a matching leopard-print tail and leopard matching heels. Twan nodded his head in acknowledgement, giving his 2 ratchett redbones his approval. Them 2 hoes knew how to steal the ho show and dress to impress a trick's eye! They knew how to fish and catch a big trick regardless if they was some little light-bright duck hoes.

"Okay, y'all 2 hoes better suck and fuck and spread that pussy open like acres round Vegas. Y'all better pull up on all these tricks like Uber! Snatch all the clientele! Locals and tourists! It don't matter, the Central Plaza is hosting the annual Vegas Electronics Convention with all the new latest gadgets... So go fetch some big boy app CEOs, hoes! And lil Pimpin Twan, my son coming into town next weekend, so you hoes all grind and rob them tricks blind so my son can shine! Do whatever y'all got to do! Anything goes when it comes to my hoes! Now who luvs you?" Twan said slick as he turned up choppin and poppin!

"You—you do, DADDY!!" all the girls replied simultaneously in harmony.

"Well, chop-chop—BYE, HO!! Now go!!" *Clap-Clap!* Twan snapped as he clapped his hands twice, extra cocky. He was feeling his nipples in depth. His pimpin was in HD-3D fuck panoramic! Heyyy...He bounced his shoulders and did the Lil Boosie bounce, saying them hoes made me do it and Rest In Peace, Mama Lela, his bro TNut and bottom ho Neese, too! as he pulled on the kush from AZ.

Pink Toe followed Butterscotch into the Golden Nugget casino that night. She just had that sick feeling to her stomach. It wasn't that nervous feeling and she surely didn't have to shit in the least of bit! It was more of her 6th sense...something didn't feel right? They both did their ratchett remedies as always, their ritual of popping e-pills and snorting 2 dumb fat long lines of that white bitch, too. And sometimes they downed a double shot of Patrón in the casino before they went upstairs to the trick's room to perform and stay super wet and freak all night long. That's truly why hookers never kept panties on. Being in the way was never the problem, they hated the fact how uncomfortable them sticky soaked thongs made them feel.

However, something wasn't right or clicking at all? Butterscotch and Pink Toe was so damn close like sisters. They been together every day for the past 7 years now. They were besties so they knew and could tell when something was wrong with each other. Butterscotch instantly noticed Pink Toe's slow motion movement like she was dragging for some strange reason.

"Damn, bitch! WTF? Hello? Come on, bitch, don't do this to me right now! I need cha right now, focus with me. I told you bout going too hard before we go on dates! Don't have another one of ya episodes... please! You know you a lightweight, bitch, with ya fragile ass. Now, bitch, get ya head back into the game. C'mon, girl?" Butterscotch pleaded nervously.

"Hell nawh, bitch. I'm Gucci, Louis, and Prada! And it ain't dat— Bitch, I just got a funny feeling, that's all. Now c'mon, let's meet this trick at the front entrance. How my makeup look, bitch? Check my nose, ain't no powder white cake build-up, right?" Pink Toe replied in a soft tone, reassuring her bestie, knowing that she more than likely about to bump and suck pussies with her bestie once again tonight for their millionth time, and frankly it became part of their routine when they turned tricks together. It was the same routine they performed on Twan trying to vic a pimp. It was mind-blowing but Twan sharp ass wasn't going! He wasn't tender dicking, simping or tricking. Straight heartache and headache, hard dick and hard convo for the ho to swallow!

Butterscotch told her she was all Gucci and to come on as they texted the trick once again. He was now 10 minutes late. Where the hell was he? Now Butterscotch was nervous, thinking it could be the law? And a vice prostitution sting they ran time to time to crack down and clean up the strip, a straight sweep!

All of a sudden they seen a blue-collar working fat man with a pot Buddha belly. He had on a blue plumber khaki one-piece suit. He smiled at the girls and signaled them over. He apologized for being late, explained how he owned his own plumbing company and he had to answer an emergency house call himself because they all bailed on him, playing hooky for the New Year, partying hard, trying to continue to bring the New Year in.

Then he told them sorry once again and tipped them a hundred-dollar bill apiece, and asked if they were ready to blow the joint and celebrate the New Year's together? These Vegas tricks had a lot of game on them and would pull little stunts, too, from time to time. After all, they were gamblers, bosses, execs, and vets, too.

They followed the trick back outside to an older white utility van with his plumbing logo on the side. They both told him, oh hell no! They don't leave the strip and don't go far from their pimp! And that PIMP word was the magic one that he needed to hear. He offered them 5 grand large now up front, then smiled and told them to come on and live a little. And that he wasn't the police or a narc. The girls looked at each other.

Butterscotch told Pink Toe it was all good to come on. Pink Toe stood there with her arms still folded like she was cold, staring at the trick cold. He was suspect in her eyes and she still had that bad hunch and vibe about. She noticed he didn't say nothing about not being the feds, though. She asked Butterscotch is she sure? And they should stay on the strip and stick to the script. Butterscotch tapped on her Prada bag twice, reassuring Pink that they was all Gucci, either way.

Pink Toe threw both her hands up high in a fit and told Butterscotch alright!

"Uugghh... Damn, bitch, Miss Attitude! Is somebody coming on their period right now? STOP being paranoid and let's get this doe for Daddy! STOP being so damn noid, too. Ugh, bitch, you fucking up my vibe! I'm gonna need another line, ho!" Butterscotch replied, annoyed.

They hopped on in the utility van and drove off with the trick. He took them to Freemont, the hotel Pimpin Silky stayed at that they were so familiar with. Their level of security went down, even though Butterscotch had her hand inside her Prada bag the whole time.

Soon as they got out of the van and headed into the hotel room, the trick just cringed and a chill quivered deep up his spine like he cracked his back. Just at the P word alone! He hated pimps with a passion! They were all low-life scums and weak bums that couldn't work to earn their livings in his book. And he disliked the weak-minded peasants that the pimps brainwashed and manipulated into their trifling upside-down worlds. They were like maggots and flies to him, disgusting and poisonous fruits to the tree of life. He didn't mind having a good ol time with a call girl or regular hooker. It was just them damn pimps and their infested ass dirty little whores!

The girls performed their regular routine. It was the same thing. They got naked and sniffed lines off each other and climbing up and down each other bumping, kissing, and sucking on each other's pink pussies. Then they both made the trick sniff a line of coke while the other one played with his dick and started sucking and twirling his small balls.

He stood up, fully aroused, enjoying the show, and requested for Pink Toe to come into the bathroom so he can freak her on the toilet while he was taking a shit. He wanted to get head while taking a shit. It was something he seen trending on social media that he was curious about and developed a secret freaking fetish for. He knew wouldn't no woman his age do something that peculiar to his fat bastard ass and they would more than likely call him a sicko, then tell him how much his fat ass shitty turds stink like hog shit. Some straight farm shit!

He reached over and popped a perc 30 pain pill, then guzzled down some cheap Skol vodka as he snatched Pink Toe's arm and dragged her ass roughly to the bathroom and told Butterscotch to rub her pussy from the back and wait on him, as he slammed the bathroom door!

He immediately pulled out the cuffs and cuffed Pink Toe to the shower curtain rod. Then told her don't worry, to relax as he placed the gag ball over her head and mouth, then adjusted the straps tightly.

POW—POW!! "Mmmmm—hmm...hmm," Pink Toe screamed as he smacked the shit out of her face twice. She immediately knew this was bout to go south and be hell to tell the captain!

He pulled out a pocketknife, then rolled out a little black cloth with all type of sharp utensils. Pink Toe looked over, her eyes got big. She screamed for her bestie and screaming the code word for danger—Titanic!! She back-kicked swiftly and hard for her life, catching the sicko fat bastard. He flinched and all his utensils fell off the toilet. Butterscotch heard the commotion and snapped out of her zone playing with her phat juicy pussy and ran over to the bathroom door. She twisted the knob slowly. It was locked. She listened inside, not wanting to piss nobody off. She was just checking on her bestie. She didn't hear no foul play, just Pink Toe's muffled moans from the fat bastard probably on top squishing her.

He stuck the Swiss Army pocket 2½-inch blade into her side, jolting her a few times slowly, then twisting it menacingly as he cut her open. She screamed an eerie cry of pain and desperation. She was stuck and doomed! She prayed she didn't suffer, but from the looks of it, her prayers wasn't about to get answered, because her life was in the hands of the devil soon as she handed over her soul to him.

His fat ass took the X-acto knife used for autopsies and cutting open human flesh. It was a surgical little sharp instrument.

He cut off her nipples one by one and threw them down in the tub, spitting on them. He kept calling her a filthy creature! Then he gaped open her legs devilishly, kicking both of her feet, and reached between her legs and spread her pussy and snipped her clit right off viciously and flushed it straight down the toilet. She seen her own swollen clit detached. She passed out! He seen her faint, then placed the X-acto knife between her legs and ripped her from her crevices all the way to her rectum. The very excruciating pain shocked her body with jolting pain, causing her to regain consciousness once again.

The fat bastard seen her whole body flinch and her eyes snap right back to life! He seen her leaking blood like a pregnant lady hemorrhaging badly after childbirth all over the toilet. It made him sick! He seen the blood coming out her mouth and leaking out her nostrils. He knew he probably punctured a lung and she was wheezing, struggling to breathe as the blood and body fluids filled the lung and breaching its capacities. He knew she was done and couldn't finish the job or have the strength to. He dropped the knife and figured he could at least make it easy on her and give her less suffering. He told her farewell and that he was sorry as he took the gag ball off her. She spit up blood and coughed hard as she choked on her own blood, struggling.

"T-Titanic... Ti-Titanic... bitch!! Uhh...Unhh..." Pink Toe managed to utter out in a low tone that fell on deaf ears as she gasped for air drastically. Her eyes rolled, her body went into convulsions from all the pain she endured. She was a young tough girl with a lot of fight in her. It was just too bad it took all the life out of her as she bled out and faded to the black dwellings. He seen her whole body go limp and slump hard to the right as she dropped down from the shower pole she was cuffed up to.

Now he had to go kill the other cheap filthy whore that was masturbating backwards on the bed awaiting him. He quickly rinsed all Pink Toe's nasty blood spurts off him. He wasn't worried about the blood mist that got into his balding hair. He would simply handle that once he offed the other trick right now. He tucked the same X-acto knife behind his back to catch his second victim. He unlocked the bathroom door and walked out to see her still naked, manipulating her pussy amusingly from the back, tooted all the way up! Sweet! This was going to be an easy kill! He was going straight for the jugular vein in the neck. She had turned her head over on the pillow, smirking hard at him like she was flattered.

B-Bloch! Bloch! Bloch! Bloch! "Motherfucker—you fat bastard son of a bitch, what you do to my gurrl, huh?" *Bloch! Bloch!!* Butterscotch shouted frantically after she shot the fat trick and stood over him and shot him again, unloading her black .380 Bryco semi-auto pistol with her pink Barbie handle that she clutched with madness soon as he got close enough so she didn't miss his fat ass not once she drew down the pistol from under the pillow, pointing at his center body mass and squeezing each shot. He looked like he seen the Grim Reaper flash right before his eyes. One of the .380 bullets lodged directly in his upper side neck. He placed his left hand on his neck wound, stunned as he fell straight back at the end of the bed. Butterscotch stood on the edge of the bed like a gangster, finishing him off as she put 2 slugs into his forehead, busting his melon open. His body twitched. He shit on himself and pissed on himself as his organs instantly seized. She stood over him and spit on him hard twice as she held the .380 pointed at his body like he was going to come back to life. She watched his pale dick go limp and shrivel up. She quickly snapped out of her murderous trance and thought about her girl and jumped off the bed and ran butt-naked to the bathroom to check on Pink Toe to see how bad she was hurt? She heard her say their secret panic word 'Titanic.'

Butterscotch stepped into the bathroom and lost it! She automatically knew her bestie Pink Toe was gone! It was blood everywhere like Freddie Kruger got to her ass. She hoped that the coke and drugs in her system numbed her girl's suffering, some of it, at least. But Butterscotch knew her girl suffered a horrible, painful death.

She sat down and talked to her bloody corpse like they could talk. She kept saying, "Girl, I am sorry—I'm sorry," and that she killed that motherfucker, too!

She sat there till the LVMPD busted open the hotel door 8 minutes later from all the dispatch calls. They arrested her and took her into custody. Pimpin Silky seen her in the back of a squad car and texted Twan.

* * *

Creole placed the vibrating ring around the condom, then sat on the dick as she mounted herself backwards. She began to ride the dick as he sat up in the hotel chair. She touched her toes and twerked her ass viciously, swinging it side to side on the dick, making her booty roll the New Orleans way, putting on a show, showing off all her hidden talent. She fingered her asshole slowly, then raised off his dick and inserted it in her ass slow, as she sat all the way down on it, moaning wildly from the vibrating ring around his dick driving her crazy! She placed both of her feet on his thighs as she squatted slowly and began to hop up and down like a frog on him with a Caribbean island rhythm to it as she moaned, creaming all on his balls as she freaked them firmly with her woman's touch. It did the trick too. She felt him cumming fast and hard like a freight train. She put her feet down and spun around on him, stood up off the dick and snatched the ring off, then pulled the condom off and dropped down to her knees as she slurped and smacked up all his little babies, making them all disappear down her throat like Vegas musicians to the very last drop. He had to push the cum fiend off him as his dick went sensitive.

"Damn, bitch, hold up—watch out, bitch—Fuck! Move dat, Twan is calling. Probably looking for ya ass. Why don't you tell him you chose up? You ain't gotta say my name, cuz that's my big bro," J Pimp said, out of breath to Creole's horny nympho ass.

"Please, Twan ain't nobody but one of my old fuck buddies. I been chose you. Why do we have to tell him? Why can't I just text him anyways? Fuck all dat, look, just watch me play with pink phat soft pussy as you talk to Twan. He'll figure it out when he hear my loud ass moan! He knows and loves this moan," Creole's scandalous ass said freaky.

"Hello, P, whatz Gucci?" J Pimp answered.

"J Pimp—man, Silky just texted me and told me a trick killed Pink Toe, and Butterscotch killed the trick! I'm fucked up, P! Damn, come pull up on me and let's ride out and sip on a bottle. I need to be around some realness and luv. Bet dat?" Twan said, devastated.

"Damn, P...I'm caught up right now with one of my hoes. But bet dat, give me 20 minutes and I'll pull up to the penthouse, P!" J Pimp replied before clicking off.

Creole sat up and smirked with vindictiveness. She knew she had J Pimp's nose wide open and was about to vic a young pimp by putting that Louisiana Creole pussy on him while doing some of her best stunts. She knew most of all he was a boy, a young lil boy and she treated him as one. Her sole mission was to be his bottom bitch! She knew she could slack off and splurge his and her money, straight up! A pimp with a main bitch? Imagine that shit! She kissed J Pimp on his forehead, then twice on his dick after she cleaned if off with the white hotel complimentary towel.

Meanwhile Twan was going thru the most. He couldn't believe his unfortunate luck in Vegas. It's like he took a roll of dice and kept throwing craps, falling straight off—right off! Now his pretty pussy, pink pussy Pink Toe bitch! Damn it! He wanted to say he quit! and tap out, but after his Mama died, he vowed to pimp on long and strong!

Vegas was vicious like that. Sometimes Sin City got deadly and bit and snagged a pimp like a pit!! Twan popped two Green Goblins triple stack e-pills to the grill and swigged the cognac extra hard to wash them down. He had been waiting over an hour on J Pimp now and been ignoring all the rest of his hoes calls and texts. He sat there stuck and half drunk, red-eyed, blowing blunt after blunt.

He snapped out of his trance and drunken slumber when he heard J Pimp pull up and the foreign horn tapped twice the pimp way. Twan stood, grabbed his yac, and pulled his saggy True Religions up. He really thought about telling J Pimp to drop him off at the Greyhound so he can get the hell out of town. He was Cali bound and heard all the other P's tell him about Sunset Blvd and Stockton. Shit, they even had a hot ho stroll in Victoryville too, all the way up to the Bay and Eugene, OR, as far as Sea-Town.

Them Green Goblin pills had him geeked up and his mouth froze and stuck. He kept grinding back and forth on his teeth with his dry mouth. The pills had him into his feelings, trippin. He was turnt-up and felt like sliding J Pump Young Thug-looking ass all over that damn rented Bentley! Maybe for taking too long when he was serious and things was serious. Another one of his hoes bit the dust while another one of his hoes went to the Clark County Detention Center. He just wanted J Pimp to chop-it-up and vent to. Especially since it couldn't be his Mama no more. He looked in the mirror at his Mama Lela rest in peace hashtag above his eyebrow and kissed his 2 fingers and planted them on his tatt. He shot outside ready to box and call J Pimp out of that Bentley coupe!

J Pimp seen Twan was turnt-up drunk trippin and told him his bad, he got caught up! Twan told him he should've dropped err-thang because it was a ASAP for him and to get out of the car as he took his shirt off and threw it at the Bentley and squared, bouncing around, showing off his footwork drunk!

J Pimp got out the Bentley and said fuck it! Twan rushed him, swinging wild and drunk. J Pimp ducked and dodged each slow haymaker. Twan tried to catch him with a heat missile and punch his tall ass lights out. J Pimp grabbed Twan's country wild ass. He bear-hugged him and kept his arms contained as Twan started trying to head-butt him, but was only ramming his forehead in J Pimp's chest. J Pimp told him to calm his ass down right as Twan said fuck that, wiggled his way out of J Pimp's flimsy grip and dumped him hard on the ground. They started tussling all around the parking lot, getting dirty like a bunch of Louisiana swamp gators!

They got to their feet. Twan was quick on his toes and rushed J Pimp again, throwing him all up against the Bentley and slamming him all up on the hot hood! J Pimp told him, okay, he was done! That they were pimps, not fighters, and pimps didn't fight or get dirty! It was way too many hoes to mack and stack on! And to manage! Twan realized he was trippin and rolling off them Green Goblin smackers. He was having an episode and on a good one! Them motherfuckers made him feel more like a damn goon! He loosened his grip off J Pimp and suddenly that pit bull mixed with Red Bull was out of him and gone! He dusted himself off first, then J Pimp as he apologized to J Pimp and helped dust him off, too.

J Pimp told Twan to get his drunk pill-popping ass off him. He sucked his teeth as he jumped in his Bentley and started it up. He felt some type of way. Twan just little bro'd him! And embarrassed him. He struck his pride and couldn't hide. Twan was just too faded to see it, though. He couldn't believe how strong Twan's thin ass was. Twan knew J Pimp would be alright and get over it.

They smoked and choked together as they passed the blunts back and forth like they was tag-team flipping a bitch! The fight gave them both a sense of love and respect for each other. They say some fights bring folks together. Back home in Twan's hood, they call it Locs and Folks because they wild out fight, then come together.

They sat quiet and listened to the Rich Homie mix tapes. They texted Pimpin Silky and told him to come on. Twan seen the detectives and crime scene techs still there with the hotel room wide open and taped off. Pimpin Silky came out with a red Kangol on with a silk red shirt and red Stacys on. It was too much heat around there. Twan had drugs on him and J Pimp had that Mac under his lap.

"GiVinci—GiVinci—GiVinci... GiVinci, my toes and my bros and my hoes... GiVinci on my toes and my bros and my hoes and that's fo sho—fo sho…" Young Thug sang the hook off the mix tape that streamed loud thru the Bentley Bose system as Pimpin Silky got in the coupe.

They smashed off, leaving the coppers in the desert dust getting little! J Pimp looked thru his rearview until they was out of sight, knowing Vegas crackers hated pimps but loved to arrest them! And all the P's in the coupe was quiet and the Bentley was in silence. Finally Pimpin Silky broke the ice. He told them it smelled like a purple skunk in here and to crack a window! Then he offered them a line. They nonchalantly declined. Pimpin Silky snorted a jig in both nostrils with his pinky nail out of the strawberry powder sack.

He told them some gruesome details about what the hotel old manager Abdul said the homicide detectives told him. Also they took the trick's body and he had been shot several times close range by a small-caliber pistol, which Twan knew exactly what gun that was. It was Butterscotch's favorite cute toy. She always toted it all around Vegas. Pink Toe kept a razor blade box cutter on a keychain of bear mace. She didn't like guns and was always scared of them and told Butterscotch to come get this thing every time she had it locked, loaded, and lying around. Then Silky told them how Pink Toe's dangling body was still handcuffed to the shower pole still and probably will be all night long because it was going to take time to gather and record all the evidence.

Damn—it was all bad and fucked up! They all shook their heads. Twan was sick and mad at these hating tricks killing hoes and taking his bitch from him. Shit was cra-cra! He told J Pimp to stop at the drive-thru liquor store to get another fifth of Yac, and for them to go gamble at Caesars Palace. J Pimp went on to say he told Twan about them ratchett drama duck hoes, they problems! Twan wasn't trying to hear J Pimp's young ass. Even though he was right and Twan was dead wrong once again!

It was daylight by the time they all left the casino struck. They went at it for hours back and forth—poker, blackjack, and craps. Pimpin Silky was playing and pulling the quarter slot machine, trying to get lucky and strike for some dope money. He was ready to go shortly after they got there. Twan and J Pimp knew it was because his broke ass was broke and putting all his washed-up little crack hoes money up his sore burnt-out nostrils! So they was throwing him chips here and there, then blamed it on his janky ass for them getting hit! Really it was the casino who was vicing them and had them drunk, making slow decisions and placing dumb bets. It was sweet to the casino, though. It wasn't a such thing of a dumb bettor or a sucker bet?

When J Pimp finally dropped Twan off back at the penthouse, he let Silky stay over with him. All his hoes were laid out thru the penthouse. And he knew it from the minute he entered the door smelling all that wet pussy and sweet perfume in the air! Except Creole out-of-pocket freelancing ass. He also noticed she had been there and got some more of her shit? He didn't know what she was on and texted her 911 ASAP to report now! He watched the news and saw Pink Toe, the trick and Butterscotch's pictures with Pink Toe's Mama crying outside the hotel, hugging some man as the coroner rolled her wrapped-up body out. Twan seen something sticking up awkward like a knee was stuck up from post-mortem rigor mortis. He shook his head.

Two whole days had passed and somehow Butterscotch was calling pre-paid on Twan's cell from the Clark County Detention Center. He told her he couldn't help her and to keep using her self-defense alibi. She had a million-dollar bond. She was hot and mad as hell at Twan's trifling no-good ass. He told her she was just going to have to wait it out and he'll see her and be there when she got out! That he had to prepare for Lil Twan to come out there and needed all the money he can get. Plus he had to pay for all of Pink Toe's funeral expenses. She knew Twan was lying though, and wasn't about to cover shit with his dog ass. If he didn't believe in spending nothing on a ho while she gone, especially a dead one, he couldn't get no return investment on. She knew Twan wasn't shit and full of shit. She hung up on Twan, hating him from that minute forward. She wished she had some dirty-dirt to tell on his selfish ass with. Like another murder to get herself off for exchange of her testimony to avenge her and her day-1 girl.

Twan laughed at Butterscotch, how cute for hanging up. So what, like he cared! He didn't care how fancy pants she got or hot! He just thought she was cute, but really knew he'd never see her or have to worry about her again! He immediately changed his number to a 702 Vegas area code, swapping them out. He finished picking out matching Polo outfits for him and Lil Twan for the weekend. After he tore down the Polo store by Crystal Mall, he had his Jr. Polo this, Polo that! From the baby hat to the little Polo footsies. Then he headed to the Versace and Gucci stores. They didn't have much for the kids but all the pint-size stuff he bought for his lil man. He even bought his baby mama Diamond Cutz funky butt some Gucci and Versace items, mainly frames and bags to butter her up to entice them to stay.

When Twan got back to the penthouse, Oprah and Jazabel both told him that they had seen Creole driving up and down the strip trying to be seen with J Pimp on a few different occasions. Twan didn't give a fuck and knew he couldn't text J Pimp on some flagrant pimp shit because he would be in straight violation! He did text Creole though to check his punk ass disrespect bitch! He told her it's all Gucci, to come get her raggedy shit before he burn her stanky ass thongs up! She texted him back finally—*FUCK U NIGGA!!* in all caps. He replied and told her no, fuck her disease-carrying flat-backing ass. She texted him back in their texting wars, that's why she chose-up and got her a rich one! Twan texted back in all caps too—*LMAO THOT!!* She replied she was a rich THOT and next time he say that ho over there, make sure he say that rich ho over there!!

Twan was hot! She had his head aching. She was problems! Old bitch really brought old problems fo sho! He kicked himself in his own ass for the last time. He had to finally live and learn. He been up still for 2 whole days straight and felt like he was hallucinating? She had his pimp bones ache! He wasn't really eating or drinking fluids. Just getting his Nicki Minaj on—pills and potions! And they really had him beyond floating! He was hallucinating, seeing shit, then blinking fast like he was fighting sleep, but it really was from him thinking the room was so hot in January that it was melting!

He called out for Oprah to help him! Her white ass was scared, saying, "Oh my God" and panicking, asking Jazabel what to do? Should she call the ambulance? Twan quickly snapped out of it and slapped Oprah.

Pow! "Bitchhh!! What the fuck? We don't call 911 or do police, period! Now go get me a bottle of water and roll me a blunt, that's all. I just ain't been sleep and my body shaking and all-out exhausted, but my mind restless! What pimp you know that rest and sleeps? Huh? Now, ho, chop-chop! And find my e-pills and bring em here... I'm Pimpin Twan from Southside of BR and I'm out chere—bitch!!" Twan said in a low raspy tone, trying to turn up but he was too burnt-out and turnt-down! Oprah's scary ass quickly shuffled around and rounded up all of Twan's requested items while Jazabel stood at the door looking at him, amazed.

Two hours later Twan's body finally relaxed and his nerves settled like some tired, worn-out sleepy toddlers. He scrolled thru his smartphone. He hit his Tinder.com app and fished around for his next potential new ho! After all, the name of the pimp trade was cop and blow, stop and go! It's all on and out of a funky ho!! Pimps up! Hoes down! PIMP—PIMP—Hooray!!

It was a lot of ducks, straight renegades freelancing all out of pocket of the pimp code. They was all out of bounds, getting all on the net for themselves. All hoes had to pay their dues and pimp fees regardless, because all the pimps was been hip to the skip off the rip! And trying to send the next bitch—If?? She hadn't already been before anyways. It was truly the name of the game and an art fashion to this ism that not everybody had or could articulate nor imitate. You can't teach this or preach this, he had to have them pimp bones and pimp juice for it! No textbook schooling nor room for squares, a pimp's worst nightmare.

It was even some snowbunny renegades soliciting johns, too. And he tried to solicit their ass himself. He posed as a trick to catch a vic! Really it was to catch a big fish! He just needed a bit with his little bitty shrimp dip and J hook he had out with his short fishing line. He didn't need a boat, raincoat, or 12-foot rope to fish. He could hook a fish right from there off the net! He didn't have to go babysitting off the shores or at the lake for days just to see if he get a bite. He knew where they was biting at. And them hoes was biting like some hungry hippos. They always loved his bait and loved his new special flavor. Twan just knew which bait to use to catch and snatch them hoes up out the water. Some he may lose and some may slip away. Hell, he might even throw some away, too. Some may even not make it and die or get stolen or eaten and swallowed up whole. Oh well, that was how it went and it be like that sometimes, but however, it was still plenty of fish in the big ol SEA!! Some people got soaked or drowned trying.

Then his jaw jacked wide open in the middle of his mind rekindling, thinking. It was nobody other than Creole wild disrespectful ass. He stumbled across her Tinder profile. She had 2 different profile pictures posted. He knew it wasn't nobody but J Pimp behind his madness because he specifically told all his hoes Tinder is a BIG NO! It was a no go and he deleted all his hoes profiles off there right after his Mama Lela got killed from her and Ashley catching a bad turned deadly date on there once he found out. Then he went on PlentyofFish.com and checked and sure enough, it was Creole's ass with the same profile pics posted that it looked like J Pimp took for her inside the hotel suite. This time she had posted under a different alias, soliciting tricks the cyber way.

He said fuck all the rules, this was personal, and now J Pimp jumped the gun and broke the rules of engagement of the P Constitution. He wasn't even abiding by the laws of the land and sticking to the code. He never called Twan and served him his papers or gave him an option to buy the bitch back. Pimpin Silky laced both of their gators up tight enough for them both to know better. It was different and more personal with J Pimp because he knew J Pimp and he was more like a little bro to Twan! He should've known better, though. Pimps don't bring their hoes around other pimps! He went against the grain right there like a motherfucker!

Then he thought back to how J Pimp would bring his hoes around and know Pimpin Silky 'peeling ain't stealing if she willing' article of faith that he lived by. Pimps can't be trusted around other pimps' hoes.

Shit, really pimps didn't hang out 24/7 like homies anyway, only to meet, greet, and cheat. To chop-n-pop and share some good game every now and then. Even back in BR Twan knew this, that the old pimps met up once a week to sit down and eat and talk big shit, usually with their bottom bitch or solo. You never truly caught them with all their hoes all at once in one spot, especially around other P's. Them hoes were their lifelines! And they usually had a lot of ho business to go attend to. J Pimp didn't text back but he finally picked up.

"Hello—Yeah, whatz Gucci, P," J Pimp uttered, tired.

"Man—Nigga, you know whatz Gucci—NIGGA! Straight up! So you gonna hit me with a lo-low blow below the belt, P? Dat's breaking the rules. You supposed to be like a lil bro to me! J Pimp, you supposed to go down in the hall of game, not the wall of shame, P! And all this shit ya jaw-jack about over a duck ho being drama and dark days and dark clouds shit blah-blah! And look at cha? Mr. Hypocrite! Man, fuck dat stanky rotten pussy hole bitch anyways—"

"What, nigga, fuck you. She my bitch now and already made me 8 bands. She laid up right here. Look, I pay you a couple bands for the bitch, ya dig? But my bitch ain't going nowhere! Believe dat, P!" J Pimp said, cutting Twan off rudely.

"Awwwh...shit! Okay—okay, bet dat up, J Pimp. Congrats! You did that, my dude, no doubt I see how you getting down. I'll holla at cha fo-sho! I know peeling ain't stealin if she willing. It only obvious. I'm gone doe, you did that. I'll see you out chere!" *Click!* Twan replied, defeated as he hung up and took it all out on his 2 hoes!

"Bitch, y'all get the fuck out my face—get her the FUCK out my face—BYE, bitchhh!" Twan shouted in a high-pitched, scratchy tone, mimicking Young Thug as he snapped his 2 fingers twice. They both sucked their teeth and put their heads down, looking at the ground as they vacated the penthouse.

Twan took out his Black Diamond kush he had from the AZ dispensary plug out of the glass jar and rolled a stupid phat blunt to blow to the face and ease his pimp pain. He really felt like he needed a new bitch, especially now that Creole done chose. Damn it!

* * *

Two days was left before Lil Twan and Diamond Cutz was coming to Vegas from Baton Rouge. Twan was anxious. He sat at the MGM Grand casino waiting for Jazabel, who became the highly requested foreign bitch on the strip. She was getting 5 bands per escort, catching big high-end executive dates. She also was now a bona fide ho! Twan had vic'd the poor schoolgirl. However, he knew she wasn't that innocent and was a real low-key freak between the sheets. Oprah was still bringing in that high-end Seattle snowbunny money, too. So Twan was only 20 toes deep but still flowing and still going pimpin on long and strong, still waiting to knock him a new snowbunny.

Twan sat in the rented Lambo. He was texting a mile a minute, choppin and poppin his P's! He was a pop artist, truly. He couldn't understand what was taking Jazabel so damn long? She better had snatched all the money. She claimed to hit a big one for 8 bands cash money, all hundreds. He texted her again, annoyed, telling her she had only 30 seconds until he was dashing out on her ass!

All of a sudden Twan looked up and his eyes sparked a glowing red, as his madness fueled his bloodstream, pumping it to a boiling steaming temperature which shot his pure adrenaline to his heart. Twan felt his heart thumping hard from the sight of the Bentley that pulled up across the street. He could see Creole in the passenger seat glancing over at him, playing it off like she didn't see him, period.

Twan tucked his phone and hit his kush blunt one more time and took a hard swig of his yac. He was about to check the shit out of J Pimp's foul ass for pulling that flagrant foul! He wasn't sticking to the code. He was about to speak his mind the Louisiana Southern way. Then he stepped out the Lambo and left the doors up…

BDDATT—BBDATT—B-BDDATT!! BDDATT—BDDAT—BBDDATT!! The rapid Mac 11 fire erupted and burst like a volcano!

Twan's shirt did the twerk! Which caused him immediately to hiccup blood as his body simultaneously smacked hard on the street! It felt like his limbs just gave out on him? Fuck! he thought as he coughed up blood. He was sprawled out and hit and that Mac kept sparking like a raging lunatic. He just sat and laid there stiff, playing straight possum. He prayed this wasn't the end…

J Pimp seen Twan get out his Lambo and started to come his direction, cutting across the street. He didn't know what Twan was on or how he was feeling. He wasn't trying to figure out or be in another tussling match. He was naturally paranoid and a trigger-happy band-happy type youngin. And he definitely wasn't about to let Twan run up on him and embarrass him in front of his Creole bitch. He let down the passenger window and told Creole to watch out as he extended his arm from the driver's seat, letting Mac 11 9mm rounds spin, emptying the whole 32 in the magazine. He seen Twan get popped and drop! He didn't know where or how many times he hit him. But he knew the Mac had a mind of its own. He peeled out and was about to ditch the

Bentley coupe and lose the now dirty hot Mac that he could possibly have a head on it now?

Jazabel came out the hotel door just in time to catch all the action. She seen both the Lambo doors up at a 90-degree angle and Twan trying to run across the street. All of a sudden gunfire erupted. She ducked down screaming out frantically for Twan. She kept yelling his name, especially when his body dropped like a sack of potatoes and he laid stiff!

Twan heard the Bentley tires screech off as J Pimp darted down the strip. He tried to concentrate to control his breathing, as he panted and huffed like a baby after it got thru crying hard and trying to calm down. He turned around on his back and lifted his head up, looking down at his bloody shirt as he felt his stomach leaking. He looked up at a spooked Jazabel. She seen his blood-stained teeth and dropped to her knees, holding his hand and lifting his head up as she told the nosy crowd of gambling tourists in awe to go get help ASAP and call the ambulance now!!

Twan sat there thinking about how his Mama and big bro got shot, now him. Then not ever seeing or holding his own son, his flesh and blood! He wasn't going and it wasn't his time to go!! Then he couldn't believe he got popped by another pimp? Wow! Only in Las Vegas. This Wild West desert was unpredictable like that and unfortunate, too. The paramedics rushed him to the Clark County Hospital. Twan didn't have no insurance. Jazabel secured his Lambo and all his belongings. Then she rode with him in the ambulance.

The ambulance EMTs stabilized Twan. He had non-life-threatening wounds, he wasn't just in critical condition. They told him he suffered two gunshot wounds to the stomach and for him to breathe thru the oxygen mask and try to relax as they put the IV in his arm and put a tube hose that suctioned all the blood and body fluids out of his stomach, relieving his pressure and pain. Then they injected 3 cc of morphine through his IV to stream thru his body. It was surely some dope because Twan was numb and floating. Jazabel seen his eyes rolling, knowing he was high as a flight to Paris! All of a sudden the EMTs inserted a catheter up his dick to his bladder to drain it and the blood mixture too. Twan's eyes blinked super fast, then he passed out.

* * *

Twan had been in the Vegas Medical Center ICU for the past 3 days now. He had 2 successful surgeries. His stomach was stapled all together in a ratchett J shape. It was ugly and for sure to leave a scar. J Pimp was now an avowed enemy like Satan! But first things first. Creole was going to be the first to go because she was going to be the easiest to catch. He thought of a master plan for both of them as he laid there on his back with his tender aching throbbing sore stomach. He couldn't turn to his left and barely could turn to his right. Plus he kept having stomach spasms, making all the anguished ugly faces. He was sick and miserable. It was pimp down—pimp down, when it was supposed to be hoes down!

Then there was the fact that he missed out on the opportunity to see, meet, and greet his lil man. It was better late than never, though. He had bought them all that shit. And Diamond Cutz was already holding a grudge against a pimp and for getting their daughter shot right out her stomach. He knew his son was a miracle survivor and special like his Pa! 2nd generation pimpin and carrying a pimp vine in his blood and bones.

Soon as they transferred him to the 5th floor, his new room, he seen Oprah and Jazabel, his 2 puffy-eyed, loyal to the soil hoes. It had been days now without him and they both stayed 10 toes down. Most bitches that wanted out of the hooker's lifestyle would've used this time to dart and run off! They had flowers and Get Well Soon cards with red lipstick prints marked all over them. They stayed sleep in both the room chairs right by Twan's bedside for the next 72 hours, watching TV. Twan didn't say much, he just had a look of obscene murder on his pale face. He had lost 2 pints of blood in the process and he waited for another blood donor to match his O positive type blood, then he could get discharged once the transfusion was completed, which took a few hours for the machine to pump into his body slowly. Twan felt like he was dialysis himself.

He told his hoes that pimpin wasn't for everybody and it was in him, that's why it was hard to find his rare blood type and get a match or donor. He tried to lick his ashy dry cracked lips. Jazabel seen him and gave him some water thru the straw to hydrate himself. She hated seeing all them tubes in him! Twan been in the hospital for 3 days now and had been put on bed rest light duty per the doctor orders. However, he was out taking old man steps. Each and every step he felt the pain in his stomach.

He been texting his baby mama Diamond Cutz. She was acting retarded and coming at his throat with all that damn Baton Rouge drama! She was telling him that's what his dumb ass get and how he was a jerk face and need to just give that pimpin lifestyle up before he be dead or in jail, and his Junior be fatherless! Then she told him he was probably going to get killed by one of his own hoes that was sick and tired of him sending her and kill herself too from Twan fucking her life off miserably. Twan got hot and blocked her, then deactivated his Facebook page to cut all ties off with the drama queen wishing death upon him.

He received a text from Pimpin Silky telling him he had got that for him and to come thru ASAP! Twan switched up to an ivory Cadillac Escalade EXT. He knew J Pimp knew the Lambo and would see him coming in that lime-green Lambo a mile away. He couldn't penetrate that way. He wanted to get up close and personal and pop his Bluetooth. He had that same face as his big bro TNut, a straight killer!

He pulled up the big ol Escalade into the hotel on Freemont, holding his stomach with his right hand and turning with his left like it wasn't nothing! Pimpin Silky stood there with his black Kangol hat on in the doorway. He was fidgeting with his nose like he just got thru snorting the Grand Canyon dry. He seen Twan getting out the new Escalade holding his stomach, taking little ol baby steps and holding his stomach like he was sick and about to throw up any second. Pimpin Silky shook his head as he lit up a Kool cigarette, trying to spark his empty lighter. Twan finally made it to the room and stood up, afraid to sit down from all them stomach pains.

He told Pimpin Silky that one bullet they didn't take out and the other one was millimeters from his colon. He was blessed not to be walking around with a shit bag, they told him, until his colon healed itself.

"Twan, damn… Say, youngin, I know you and J Pimp beefing and on the freeze tag game and shit. But Twan, y'all know pimps ain't supposed to be hunting and killing pimps? And it's all over a silly ass ho! I was notorious for that and ain't nobody ever shot me in the Bay to Atlanta, P! And the only reason I'm doing this favor for you is because J Pimp went against the grain and out the bare sole respect for ya Mama, ya dig?" Pimpin Silky said as he handed Twan the 12gauge Moseburg pump.

"Thanks, P! You know I feel you but not trying to hear all that shit, ya heard me. It's a new era out chere... And—and dis not for J Pimp. I got something special for Mr. Mac. I'ma introduce him to my partna Mr. Chop-Choppa. Dat's what we call it nowadays back in Louisiana, ya heard me? And for that maggot-ass bitch, I'ma introduce her to the real crawling nasty maggots that's gonna eat all her filthy rotten flesh! We call this shotgun back home suey!" Twan said in a menacing tone with that killer blank look in his face.

Silky seen that killer's glow in Twan's face that he couldn't read or want to get between, especially with that 12-guage pump in his hands. He watched Twan step slowly like he was walking on eggshells as he held the shotgun down at his right-hand side.

Twan had already set the action play in motion. He had called his favorite con man from Cali and met him at the same McDonald's with Oprah and got her another fake ID. Then he had Oprah wear a blonde wig to cover her red head and put some heavy dark shades on to check out a hotel room.

He created a profile on Tinder.com and posed as a trick, to catch a fish! She finally agreed to meet him at the hotel for $1500. He told her that he wanted her waiting but naked on the bed in the room by the time he left out the casino!

Creole had J Pimp drop her off and bounced. Creole walked around to the hotel off Freemont, room 113, as she double-checked on her iPhone to make sure the number was the same. After she double-checked to verify it, she entered the dark, empty hotel room. It was stuffy in there. She cut the lights on and turned on the air. Then she texted the trick to let him know she was there awaiting naked and to bring some expensive champagne. She tossed her iPhone on the nightstand and began to strip! She laid on the bed and spread her legs and began to rub her clitoris and press her 2 fingers in and out her hole like the true freakazoid she was, trying to warm it up hot!

Two minutes had gone by till she had to pee. Her moans had ceased suddenly and she jumped up to empty her aching bladder. She and J Pimp had been drinking all night. It was close to 1 a.m. She smelt her hand. It had a fishy tuna smell to it. She pulled her head back and her hand away with a 'yuck' look on her face. Then she froze cold...

Click-clack! "Yeah, you punk ass bitch, suck a pink dog dick—" *DOOM!!!* Twan said slick after he cocked the shotgun and pointed at her stomach before blasting her back out of the bathroom.

Creole couldn't believe it? She thought she was seeing a ghost and J Pimp killed her childhood friend from back home. The shotgun blast knocked the breath right up out of her! She shook her head no with her mouth froze before Twan got off. She laid on the ground, gasping for air and wheezing horribly from the double buckshots piercing right thru her left lung. She knew this was it and could feel the warm piss streaming down her legs. Then she felt Twan kick her down there like a punter.

"You punk ass bitch, feel my pain. Except ya going underground to sleep with maggots and dwell in hell, ho! Scandalous bitch!" *Pow! Pow! Phhugh—Phughh!* Twan said, full of vengeance with a devilish look to his face, scaring Creole in her darkest hour. Then he kicked her twice, once in the pussy and the other in the head as he spit twice on her face like a madman.

He grabbed the shotgun and shuffled out the room as Creole gasped and choked. Her life was slowly losing its strength and grip!

Twan made it to the Mustang rental unseen. He heard sirens in the background as he crept out like a thief in the night discreetly, no speeding or driving like the movies.

J Pimp kept texting Creole. He needed that $1500 and it's been some hours now. It was now 3:30 in the morning. She sucked and fucked like a champ! He hated driving down by the strip at the wee hours, because all they did was jack-up pimps and haul them with everybody else out to the Clark County Detention Center. It was called the late night sweep to catch P's on the late night creep.

J Pimp was all gas, no brakes, dodging all coppers. He had a brand new Mac on his lap. Nowadays you needed something with plenty of rounds and super-fast runner. He wouldn't stop for the LVMPD anyways, he would take the jake on a straight chase on the late night and get smooth away. He knew their computerized engines was no match for his foreign horses—*VROOM!!* He smashed hard on the throttle, shifting gears to go get his ho. As he looked on his lap at his screen, it was still blank. No messages. He punched the throttle harder as he slid the shifter into 5th gear.

Soon as J Pimp pulled up off Freemont, he seen the detectives outside the room and the LVMPD behind the yellow tape by the Vegas white coroner's meat van. He just knew it was Creole and all bad. Then it clicked—Twan!!

* * *

Twan popped 2 perc 30 mg and a xanny bar and took 2 hard swigs of the cognac to ease his abdominal pain. He pulled on the Black Diamond kush slowly as he thought about how Tinder got Creole's ass caught-up and killed. He told that dumb ho. She had it coming, that was for all them times her funky ass burnt him with her plagued spread stanking pussy. He seen her smell her fingers, then yanked her head back from her dirty hands. She was the type of bitch to lie and testify in court with her right hand on a stack of Bibles.

Then he planned and plotted on J Pimp's demise, too. It was coming soon, like the next Kevin Hart movie. He was dead already! Twan made a promise that he would get up close and personal and bring it to J Pimp's front door to shut his shit permanently. He'd welcome him to the murder show with that Louisiana Southern hospitality himself. Choppa City in the casino! He smirked as he loaded up the Chopa-47 banana 30-round clip. He sat and waited for his hoes in the dark, drinking hard and looking at his screen on the charger. He was on some other shit paranoid. He was waiting to see if Pimpin Silky said anything to see if he got away with it or if the streets was already talking? He figured he was Gucci, though. He was ready to go to the grave tonight. If someone tipped off the penthouse, he'd shoot it out with them crackers, no doubt. But J Pimp, he wanted some face time with him and Mr. Chop-Choppa!

Twan dozed off. By the time the girls came home, it was dawn and the restless Vegas strip seemed to finally slow down. It looked abandoned. But you could never let that deceive you. By far it was still riff-raff and hanky-panky going on all day and night long. The girl let him sleep and placed his money by his side, then crashed with him after she took a little light ho bath like a bird.

The next week Twan and J Pimp was playing a game of cat and mouse as they hid and hunted for each other, switching different whips like poker chips. Twan was doing a little better and was healing up, too.

His pain wasn't so achy, but he stayed so drugged up like a pill script junky and a synthetic research monkey.

He pulled up at the Trump Plaza awaiting for Oprah. She had just texted him that she had ripped off a big trick for 10 bands, plus she had the $2500 that he displayed. Twan told her to hurry up and come on then.

Oprah came running out of the Trump Plaza with security tailing shortly behind her. Twan quickly put the truck in drive as he thought about fleeing the scene, but he couldn't leave his whopping almost 13 bands right now. Fuck Oprah! He could leave her dumb game goofy square ass. He thought about telling her to just throw the damn money in the seat and tell her let's split up and for her to run that way, ho! Oprah ran and jumped in, all out of breath, before the casino hotel security could reach the truck.

Twan heard sirens wailing and blurting as spotlights hit all in his face and on Oprah. The LVMPD blocked Twan and Oprah in, then drew down with their service .40 cal weapons, screaming, "FREEZE!!! Hands up!!"

They rushed the truck and snatched Twan up, then dumped him on the ground. They ripped open his stomach wound again as they roughed him up like a pit bull in training to fight hard. Twan started tussling with them dirty cops and resisting as he yelled, challenging them all irate and hostile. They put elbows, knees, and boots all on his head and neck. Then they hog-tied him and tossed his skinny fragile ass in the squad car next to a crying Oprah. Of course they didn't even touch the snowbunny. She probably wasn't even handcuffed. Twan seen all the bands in the evidence bags and knew he was booked!

After they took Twan out of medical, they booked him in Clark County Detention Center for robbery, aiding and abetting, with a bond set for $50,000 cash only, no 10 percent. He found out quickly Oprah snitched him out with her loose lips singing like an Adele big ass. This was the only bad part and down side about these snowbunnies. They were funny like that and would turn over like a Slinky. Mama Lela would always say and warn him how they'd be quick to scream rape just because they caught up themselves or to save themselves.

Twan had a 3-way call to his lawyer firm and they told him he needed to appear in person at the firm and at civil court in front of a judge. He couldn't get extradited to a civil court matter, because it wasn't District or Superior Court. It was more personal. Then he asked if he could sign over power of attorney to the law firm or his baby mama to be there in his presence? They told him it didn't work like that and it was no sign of Jazabel either. Just his luck she ran off or J Pimp probably made her disappear. He prayed Oprah didn't tell it all? And they throw a shot-up skinny lightweight pimp under the jail. It was all bad, they was about to send him up the Colorado River! He was facing 2 felonies and up to 7 possible years if he lost in a jury trial. Looks like Twan had to tap out and sign a plea for being just the getaway driver! They was trying to fast-track him thru the system and offer him a plea for 3-4 years. He declined and kindly told them crackers trial, even though they advised him he was certain to lose and get stuck with all that 7 hard years. Twan said fuck! and needed some time to clear his mind and pray to the pimp gods for punishing him.

He found Ashley, Butterscotch, and Oprah snitching ass, all had access to each other and shot a kite, telling Butterscotch he got her for sure to smash Ashley and get Oprah to sign an affidavit to recant her statement. Then smash her, too!

Fuck—pimp felt stuck! He leaned back on his jail bunk. He looked at the ceiling with that sick feeling to his stomach and it wasn't from his wounds. He was so close to the top and conquering Vegas while making himself a household name as an A-list PIMP! And putting his state of Louisiana out there and city Baton Rouge on the map!

It was all shattered pimp dreams and felt like he had taken a turn for the worst and 10 steps back. Now he was stuck out of town in the belly of the beast without no money or no hoes!

How did Vegas boil down to this? He lost his Mama Lela and now his son's next possibly 7 birthdays. He struck out this time and couldn't refill his hole.

He should've jumped on the Greyhound and dipped out of town soon as his Mama got killed in this raggedy ass desert!

He knew he was about to have it hard because nobody liked pimps. Especially in the penitentiary. Everyone hated and tried to Hitachi a pimp every chance they'd get. It was hard on the yard in every state. At least if he was back home he could sign the plea with ease, knowing who his Pops was and how much clout he had alone up out of BR that N.O. niggas respected him, his gangsta and grind.

Twan seen Fatz da Mac kick his cell door and blew him a kiss and played it off like they was cool and shit was all Gucci before the detention officers pushed him on off the door to his cell.

Twan shook his head and got straight off the bunk and started doing slow push-ups back in county mode like before, just in case he had to get some of these clowns up off him and they tried to test a PIMP!

Damn, now orange is the new PIMP! They was about to respect his pimpin or check it, ya heard!!!

THE END

Stay tuned for Part III:

Orange Is Da New PIMP!

About Author

Hitachi Choparazzi is a New York City native, by the way of Omaha, who is currently incarcerated in level 5 solitary confinement in Florence, SMU-Eyman Complex, serving an illegal sentence awaiting on Supreme Court Appeal to correct his sentence with time served. The error forces him to serve 2 years extra.

He is an entrepreneur, tattoo artist turned author. Also the sole owner of Chop-a-Style Publishing and Productions, and the owner of Chatmon Sr. Literary Agency. He has written over 20 books and including scripts to pitch to Netflix. All this while he was incarcerated to start his reform act.

Founder and CEO of Billion-Dollar Blueprint and the BDB movement/ youth movement, an innovator entrepreneurship where he believes everyone has their own blueprint, like everyone has their own unique thumbprint. Based on 3 core principles—Education, Elevation, and

Innovation—which he teaches the youth and people how to format and discovery key. BillionDollarBlueprintmerch.com

The face of lockdown society movement along with the voice of lockdown society movement. IncarceratedLivesMovement.com #ILM #BDB

"I do this for y'all. I love y'all, rep y'all, and believe in y'all! I won't stop giving y'all all the raw stories as God bless them in my head. I have a hundred of them up there. Anybody that has a hot hand, send me samples or any comments, suggestions to my FB, IG Hitachi Choparazzi or email: orders@chopastylepublishingllc.com Chop-A-Style Publishing LLC and Productions. TeflonLuv!"

Hitachi Choparazzi prides himself on having his own signature Chop-a-Style where he freestyles all his books. They all rhyme with innovation and original storylines. He writes prequels, sequels, trilogies, and more. Does it for the people who love to read and for all those incarcerated in state, federal B.O.P., county, and women's facilities. FB,IG,Tiktok, Twitter, YouTube-Hitachi Choparazzi

Emails: Hitachichoparazziauthor@gmail.com
Billiondollarblueprintmerch.com

Other Books and Scripts by the Author

Non-Fiction

- How to Rap; The Elementary Teaching of Hip-Hop

- How To Tattoo & Start-Up Business

- How To Digital Detox

- How To Start-Up a Food Truck Business

- How To Stop School and Mass Shootings: Dear Parents

- Incarcerated Lives Matter: The Hitachi Choparazzi Blueprint

- How to Love

- The Switch: A Social Awareness Self-Help

- Nipsey Hussle Lockdown Society Dedication–Tribute

- If Trayvon Martin Could Talk; Injustice

Fiction

- The Eagle and Weasel (1-5 series kids' book)

- She Go! (urban novel)

- Reality Show 3D-HD (urban novel)

- Hot Thots (urban novel)

- Liqz (urban novel)

- Paranormal Whisper (horror novel)

- Pimp of Da Ratchets (urban novel)

- Pimp of Da Ratchets II Vegas (urban novel)

- Pimp of Da Ratchets 3 Orange is Da New Pimp (urban novel)

- Hitachi (urban novel)

- Penitentiary Pimp (urban novel)

- Weasel Society (urban novel)

- The Big Pep and Plucker Story-She Go! Prequel (urban novel)

Screenplays/Scripts

- Top Notch

- Hot Thots

- Pimp of Da Ratchets

- Weasel Society

- Million Dollar Games—A Secret Society

- The Eagle and Weasel (animation)

Available at Barnes and Noble and Amazon

Welcome to the exclusive lives of 4 extremely hot THOTs. This book will show you how to spot a THOT. From THOT tops to THOT flops, all the way to THOT Snaps and claps.

This book is the first-ever with a double twisted love triangle. Watch as Chicago, LA, ATL, and Seattle THOTs entwine at Coachella.

Some on fleek and some looking cheap, but they all cheat! They all commit aTHOTery with their THOTery acts, shameless.

Raunchy, with steaming hot sex scenes to sex swings. From wild threesome ménages, and twerking, to bare-it-all raw. Too hot! THOT gum pop...

This page-turner is an eye-opener to the very end, with a bombshell-dropping, shocking ending. The secret life of THOTs

Available at Barnes and Noble and Amazon

Billion Dollar Blueprint is a movement we challenge and inspire you to find your individual blueprint. Our mantra is "We believe everyone has their own blueprint like everyone has their own thumbprint". With these three core principles

Education

Elevation

Innovation

Hitachi Choparazzi is the founder and CEO. Orders available to support incarcerated busincsses.

Orders available at: billiondollarblueprintmerch.com

www.ingramcontent.com/pod-product-compliance
Lightning Source LLC
Chambersburg PA
CBHW060310310726
48976CB00007B/2273